POUND OF FLESH

D. ALEXANDER WARD

Let the world know:
#IGotMyCLPBook!

Crystal Lake Publishing
www.CrystalLakePub.com

WELCOME
TO ANOTHER

CRYSTAL LAKE PUBLISHING
CREATION

Join today at www.crystallakepub.com & www.patreon.com/CLP

For Leann, who never let me give up the dream of telling stories—who sometimes nudged and other times dragged me along this path, and who believed in this particular story even when I did not.

I wish you were here to see it, dear friend.
You are a part of these words, as you will be part of all the stories I have yet to tell.

PREFACE

The story of *Pound of Flesh* includes depictions of supernatural horror and violence. And in its telling, it also deals with spousal and child abuse, both psychological and physical. If you are the victim of abuse or someone traumatized by abuse, please be aware that you will come across some of that within these pages.

For me, those scenes of such abhorrent (and downright evil, in my opinion) behavior in the book were the hardest to commit to the page. I endeavored to do so in an effective but measured manner, highlighting not only the abuse but the effect it has on the characters and how they respond to it. The worst horrors of this world are not supernatural—they are the ones we inflict upon each other as human beings. Without question, it is what terrifies me the most.

Having said all this, I want you to know that *Pound of Flesh* also deals with the proven mettle of abuse survivors. It deals with the complicated and often incremental triumphs of their surviving. It also reveals the good in the world that stands against such evil, the sacrifices made, and the lives reclaimed from broken bones and broken psyches. Above all, it trades in the love, commitment, kindness, and friendship we can give to one another. And that, more than anything, is what I hope you take away from the story.

Well . . . that and maybe a couple creepy feelings or troubled dreams. After all, it is a scary story.

D. Alexander Ward,
Hanover, Virginia
January, 2022

PART I:
MANIFESTATION

"In any case life is but a procession of shadows, and God knows why it is that we embrace them so eagerly, and see them depart with such anguish, being shadows."
—Virginia Woolf, *Jacob's Room*

1

October

THE AUTUMN AIR was thick with the decay of flora, the wet leaves silent underfoot as—with weapons in hand—the young boys stalked each other through the woods. After a long week of middle school, Noah Belton and his friend Tommy Wren were playing war games in the forest near Cady's Run, the trailer park where they lived.

Noah was hunkered down in a ditch when he caught a glimpse of the two fair-haired children; young ones whose blond mops went streaking by as flashes of gold between the breaks in the trees. They were running and giggling in the carefree way children do but Noah sensed something odd about them—something out of place. He'd never seen them around here before and certainly didn't recognize them from school or the bus stop. It was clear to him they didn't belong.

And the blond children were running, so Noah gave chase.

As he followed them, Captain Red of the Galactic Marine Corps—Noah's war games moniker—held a rusted and unloaded old BB rifle in the crook of his arm. He had been sneaking down a shallow ditch toward Carl Wright— a boy from school who was only occasionally cordial to Noah and Tommy—when he had spotted the blond children. Taking long strides and hopping over fallen trees and limbs, Noah kept an eye out for Carl since he suspected that this afternoon's cessation of hostilities with the stout boy had more to do with Carl itching to shoot one of them with the paintball gun he had brought to the game. An actual paintball gun, while Noah and Tommy were equipped with lousy BB guns and no ammo, leaving them with only the very best *pew-pew-pew* sound effects that their mouths could produce.

But there was no sign of Carl and the blond boys were outpacing him with every step.

As the dim forest broke open to the sun and the ragged shore of Ashwood Lake, Noah caught sight of Tommy crouching behind a rotting stump along the wooded edge. He barreled past him and then stopped, the heels of his high-top Chucks digging into the soft earth. The two blond boys emerged from the woods and now stood together by a black gum tree at the edge of the forest, their backs to him, not more than twenty feet away. The taller boy's hands were by his side, fingertips just about level with the cuff of his rolled-up shorts. Noah couldn't see the younger one's arms, which were in front of him maybe clutching something close to his chest.

"Hey, Carl!" Noah shouted into the woods. "There's two kids down here. Lost, I think. Don't shoot them."

Noah glanced over at his friend but found Tommy's face screwed up in confusion.

"What kids?"

"The blond kids." Noah pointed.

Tommy's eyes followed Noah's finger, but now there was nothing to see. Noah's mouth fell open in surprise.

"What the—"

A burst of splashing sounds interrupted him. Footfalls running through shallow water. He turned in the direction of the sound, but only ripples on the water remained. The blond children had disappeared from view.

"So, where are these kids?" Tommy asked, tucking the long bangs of his raven-black hair behind his ears.

Noah scanned the edge of the woods. A moment

passed and Carl crept from the forest, plodding toward them, winded from the dash down to the lake. Noah's eyes searched the trees for any sign of the little boys, hopeful that he might catch a quick blur of yellow hair through the branches, but there was nothing.

Tommy looked at Carl and motioned behind him. "Lake's a safe zone."

"Not from me it ain't." Carl brought up the pistol and pulled the trigger, splattering Tommy right in his chest. Then he squeezed off another round that burst dead-center on his forehead.

Noah gasped, both surprised and impressed. That was some pretty good shooting, he had to admit.

"What the hell, Carl?" Tommy said, wiping orange paint away from his eyes and glasses.

Noah looked up at the bully, knowing the next shot would be for him.

Carl raised his gun. "Where you want it, queer?"

Noah scowled and shook his head, closed his eyes and winced in anticipation.

Carl squeezed the trigger but the resulting pop was flat and muted, the pistol having misfired, and orange paint now oozed out of the barrel.

"Shit!"

Carl held the gun with the barrel down, letting it all spill onto the dead leaves. Without another word, he turned and lumbered toward the woods to return home—now that his weapon of intimidation had been rendered useless.

"Hey, Carl, did you see those two little kids?" Noah called after him.

No answer.

"Well, did you?"

Carl didn't even turn to offer his final taunt. "Nope. Just you two lovebirds running through the woods like a couple of tree huggers. Later, dipshits!"

After Carl departed, Tommy knelt down by the water's

edge and scooped some up in his hands, splashing it on his face. The orange thinned and ran down his cheeks and the long slope of his nose.

"Such a dick."

Noah shook his head. "I told you not to invite him."

"Yeah." Tommy dipped his black-framed glasses in the water and wiped them off. "Guess you called that one right."

"Don't worry about Carl, *Sergeant Black*," Noah said. They had come up with their war games monikers—creatively enough—based on the color of each boy's hair; Tommy's a slick, dark flop and Noah's a buzzed flat-top of bright red. "At least he didn't kick us in the nuts this time."

"Yeah, true," Tommy said, and the two boys walked back toward the woods.

"I still don't understand where those kids could have gone, though."

"Again with the kids?"

"Yeah."

"Well, what'd they look like?"

"You really didn't see them?"

Tommy shook his head.

"Brothers, maybe," Noah said. "With blond hair."

"What, like the Von Trapp family?"

Noah laughed loudly. As was the case with most boys his age, he despised *The Sound of Music*, though his mother watched it every year when it came on the television. Still, Noah had to concede it wasn't a bad comparison.

"Yeah, a little like that. Plus . . . " he lingered a moment, turning over a thought.

"Plus what?"

"They just . . . they didn't look like they belonged here."

"What's that mean?"

"Well, for one thing, they were wearing summer clothes."

"Summer clothes? Well, that *is* weird."

Noah nodded. "Hey, maybe you can mention it to your dad?"

Tommy's father was a deputy with the Bedford County Sheriff's Department and part of the Maritime Patrol for Ashwood Lake. Deputy Wren drove a cruiser home most of the time but kept the patrol boat docked at a marina that was within walking distance of the trailer park. Sometimes, when Tommy's dad knew it was going to be a quiet day, he would take the boys out on lake patrols, which they thoroughly enjoyed.

"Sure. I'll tell him to put out an APB on the Von Trapp twins right away."

Noah cracked a smile. "I'm serious, though, Tommy. Those kids have to be lost or something."

His friend nodded. "All right, all right. I'll mention it to him. Right after he grounds me for getting paint on my glasses."

As they entered the woods and began to climb the hill toward home, Noah turned and looked back at the lake and its empty shores. He sure hoped those kids would be okay. These woods were no place for lost children. There were black bears that roamed at dusk, coyotes, wolves, and not to mention the afternoon was dimming toward sunset and the forest would soon be dark and cold.

2

Sunday was church day. This was a fact for most of the country but especially for the South where churches of every denomination would fill with sermons of warning and hymns of praise. Afterward, fathers and sons would loosen their ties and cast off their sport coats to toss around a football or baseball in the backyard. Sunday fried chicken, collard greens, biscuits and the enticing aromas of other Sunday food staples would waft from the kitchens of most homes and after lunch, such a lazy day might even include a nap on the couch as the television or radio droned on in the background. Yes, indeed, Sunday was a day that many looked forward to—even those whose church attendance was in question. For most, it was a day of meditation and rest.

For Noah Belton, however, it was quite the opposite.

Without fail, every Sunday the Belton family piled into Hugh Belton's old Ford truck and rambled along the mountain roads, then parked alongside other vehicles in the crowded, gravel clearing outside of the Pentecostal Church of the Evening Star. It had been called Ashwood Pentecostal Church when Noah was younger and, from what he could recall, not an altogether unpleasant experience back then. At such a young age, he had sat in his mother's lap where she gently bounced him on her knee to keep him calm during the service. Afterward, he would be ushered off into Sunday School groups with other children where they learned about scripture and were allowed some playtime. During this time, the grown-ups would gather to pray, and it was then that the pastor would direct the congregation to surrender to the Holy Spirit and speak in tongues. Once, when Noah had been sent inside to use the bathroom, he had spied on the grown-ups. He had peered through a crack in the door to the sanctuary, where they were all gathered together in a tangled mass. Some convulsing and shaking, eyes rolled back in their heads, while others milled about uttering words that were not really words . . . at least no words Noah could recognize. Although he didn't fully understand what he had seen, he was not troubled by it, and continued about his business.

Noah had thought the pastor a decent and pleasant sort of man who always seemed to have a kind word to spare. But the old pastor had up and died a couple of years back. There one day and gone the next. A new and unfamiliar pastor was brought in and from that day forward the church changed.

Unconcerned with "the trappings of this world," Pastor Gorman allowed the small church building to fall into disrepair and uncleanliness, quickly ending the Sunday School groups for the children and insisting that they join with their families for the entire experience. Noah's father had explained that Pastor Gorman wanted to immerse his flock in the blood of the Lamb and to make Christian soldiers of every man, woman and child. For Noah, though, under this new pastor, the church had grown strange and bent and it was no longer a place of solace. Sunday service had become something to be survived rather than celebrated.

Noah had invited Tommy along to church a while back, hoping it'd be more bearable with his best friend present. It proved to be the one and only time Tommy attended. What he saw there had given him nightmares for days afterwards.

Today, Pastor Gorman was all smiles and handshakes and slaps on the back as the flock entered through the front door. The notion of brotherhood seemed to end there, though, as the rest of the sermon was fueled by rage and accusations against the pastor's flock. Shifting his aching bottom in the unforgiving seat of the metal folding chair, Noah loosened the shirt collar that was so tight around his neck. Up front, the pastor leaped left and right, waving his hands in the air maniacally.

"I ask you, brothers, are you Christian soldiers?"

Various responses from the congregation; spoken affirmatives and nodding heads.

"Are you? Are you *really*?"

Silence from the congregation.

"Because if you are, then our Christian nation, our Christian world is in awful sad shape. I'm not looking to create a lot such as you! Soldiers, you say? Ha! Look more like Girl Scouts to me. You think I'm looking to create a Girl Scout troop full of believers? That what y'all think?"

Shaking heads.

"I ain't interested in my soldiers going out there into this world riddled with evil and selling their little cookies of truth and righteousness to everyone no matter who they are. Damnation, no! I'm trying to muster up a Force Recon, a . . . a Navy Seals of Christendom. I want you all out there armed with swords and rifles of faith, ready and willing to skewer and shred the non-believer, the sinner, the homosexual, the communist, the feminist. Love thy neighbor and thy brother, I say unto you . . . so long as they follow the way of the Lord!"

An eruption of support. "Hallelujah! Preach on! Amen."

"But though you are to be soldiers, you are not, yourselves, pure. It is our worldly burden, ain't it? A sickness visited upon all humanity, springing from that one day in the garden when Eve took a bite from that apple. When she surrendered to temptation. And all the world has been a flood of misery ever since. It was weakness. As black and terminal as a cancer—that is what weakness is. And it lies inside of every one of you."

Acknowledgement. Nodding heads. "Pray for us sinners."

The pastor quietly surveyed the flock, his eyes wide and dark, set deep into his sweating brow.

"But do not give into the weakness. Do not give in, because if you do . . . if you do, brothers, I will take you up to the mountain and let you stare into a deep chasm in the rock where you might see your future! A future at the hands of demons and the minions of Hell who will delight in an eternity of stripping the flesh from your bones, my brothers. Those are the wages of weakness . . . of frailty . . . of sin. When temptation comes calling, are you gonna answer?"

Hands raised and people stood up, shouting, "No!"

"When that devil, Old Scratch, comes a'knockin' on your door, are you gonna say '*Well, sure thing, Brother Scratch! Come on in and make yourself at home?*'"

"No! God save us!"

"That's right you ain't! You're gonna pick up the sword that the Lord has given you, the one that I sharpen like a razor every Sunday, and you're gonna gut Old Scratch like a fish! Lo! You will see spilled from his entrails all the blood and the darkness of humanity from the beginning of the beginning!"

Noah shifted in his seat again. He knew what was coming. Now in a frenzy, they would soon begin the laying of hands on the sick and the cursed. And as far as Pastor Gorman was concerned, they were *all* sick. *All cursed.*

"When the Devil comes calling, what you gonna do? Let me hear you say it!"

"GUT HIM LIKE A FISH!"

"What are you gonna do?"

"GUT HIM LIKE A FISH!"

Noah was mouthing the words. He knew his father might be watching and he didn't want to seem uncommitted.

"GUT HIM LIKE A FISH!"

Somewhere, the music began playing on a stereo, and the people—now worked into a lather—milled about, grabbing hold of one another. The eyes rolled back in the heads of some and their mouths opened, spilling the unintelligible language of tongues and shrieking as if in pain. One young woman collapsed onto the floor and others gathered around her, laid their hands upon her and prayed for the relief of her sickness and the salvation of her soul.

The ocean of people in the grip of the Holy Spirit surrounded Noah. They babbled, some with lidless eyes of white and others with scowls of determination. They touched his brow, bending his head back and exposing his neck.

For Noah, the scene bore a disturbing resemblance to all the zombie movies he had ever snuck a peek at. To him, the moans and screams and shouts filling his ears were not the music of the Holy Spirit. They were sounds of agony and torment. As always, Noah succumbed to the faithful, letting them prod him and pray over him.

As the flock, with its many arms and grasping fingers, lifted him, prone, above their shoulders, through the throngs, Noah glimpsed his father staring over at him, smiling.

After church let out, it was their custom to hop in the truck and head straight home to Cady's Run. Occasionally, Noah would be allowed to go outside and play but more often than not, his father would instruct him to go to his room and read over the Bible passages that may have been touched upon in Pastor Gorman's sermon. Noah would comply without protest or comment and spend the rest of the afternoon daydreaming or reading some comic book contraband if he had any available. Later, he would be permitted to watch one hour of television before supper, though the show and its content was always subject to his father's approval.

Today was different, though. Sitting in the cramped back seat of the pickup, staring out the window, Noah noticed that his father had neglected to make the left turn toward their home. He had done so without saying a word and Noah wondered if he hadn't realized his mistake, but waited, thinking his mother would surely mention something any minute now. The radio was tuned to a talk radio program where a man with a pinched voice pontificated about the state the country would be in under the leadership of the new liberal President. Noah didn't understand much of it and didn't care to. Politics was a thing rife with argument and conflict and Noah had enough of that in his life on any given day of the week.

After a few more minutes passed, Noah decided to speak up.

"Where are we going, Dad?"

Noah saw his father's eyes glance at him in the rear view mirror and Noah could almost feel the words in his mind. *Don't tell me my business, boy. I know where I'm headed.* But his father said nothing and looked over to his mother instead.

His mother turned around, her shoulders raising and dropping as if she was about to perform an act of great effort.

"Well, Noah, you know how Friday was your dad's last day at the mill?"

Noah nodded.

"The good news is that he's found another job."

"Where?"

"Whitetail," she replied.

Noah had heard of Whitetail High School out in Westlake. They were fierce rivals of the Bedford High Cougars football team. Westlake was a good ways away from Cady's Run and Chesterton Junior High, though. A cold feeling began to grow in his belly.

"We have to move, don't we?"

"It's just across the lake."

"But not in Bedford."

"No," she relented, allowing only the slightest frown to form on her face. "not in Bedford."

"It's not even in Whitetail, really," his father added. "It's outside of it. Real country living."

His mother glanced quickly at her husband and then back to Noah, her eyes full of compassion.

"Right. Well, the new job is in Whitetail but the place we're looking at living . . . it's on the lake. But it's a little bit out of the way."

"Out of the way?" Noah asked.

"Not too far from the dam."

"The dam? But there's nothing out by the dam. Everyone knows that!"

Noah could see his mother's eyes pleading for him to

remain calm. She didn't want him to upset his father. But it was too late for that.

"Dammit, boy, don't you make me pull over and straighten you out! The job's in Whitetail and that's where we're going! Understand?"

Noah was afraid to meet his father's eyes in the rear view mirror but he knew that it would only make things worse if he didn't. He looked up and found that stern brow staring at him, eyes trembling with brewing anger.

"Yes, sir," he replied, meek and diminished.

After a moment, he turned back to his mother. "Where am I gonna go to school?"

She didn't even turn to look at him, kept her gaze straight ahead as the road unfolded.

"Not exactly sure about that just yet. We'll figure it out."

"But it won't be Chesterton, will it?" He knew the answer perfectly well but he was a little bent out of shape and still wanted to make his disapproval known.

"No, son," she said, her voice going sweet. "But we might be living in a brand new housing development. In a house all our own. Not a rented trailer for once. We're going to go see it now. That's where we're headed."

"Uh-huh." The dam at Cross Mountain. There was nothing out there but thick woods, campgrounds and logging roads. A housing development? He had never heard of any neighborhoods out there. It all sounded more than a little odd to him.

"Does it have plumbing?" he asked.

His mother turned and fixed him with a glare that told him to shut his mouth.

"Yes, son. It has plumbing."

3

After they turned off the main road, they traveled for some time before Noah's father announced they were getting close.

Noah sat in the back quietly, looking out of the window with a furrowed brow as the old Ford wound down lonely roads dark under the cover of trees. Since turning onto the back roads, Noah hadn't seen a single car pass. As they wound around a sharp curve, blue sky broke the shroud of trees ahead and after a mile they saw the entrance to the neighborhood. It was flanked on either side by tall, black metal fencing made to look like wrought iron. A carved wooden sign was posted to the right of the entrance in a bed of mulch full of bright, freshly planted mums. *Cedar Banks*, it read. The outline of a tree was artfully depicted next to the development's name. Below were a score of wavy lines meant to suggest water.

It looked nice so far, Noah had to admit, and his spirits perked up a little.

As they passed through the entrance and the development came into full view, Noah's skepticism returned. A small group of single-story houses dotted the land that sloped down toward the lake. Not all that much bigger than their trailer home, they looked like the on-base military housing Noah had once seen on a field trip to the Army base at Fort Lee.

Hugh wound around the circular road and Ada sat forward in her seat with anticipation. "Oh, tell me it's one of the baby blue ones, Hugh," she squealed.

"Afraid not, Ada. It's this one coming up right here."

Noah peered over the front seat and saw a green sedan parked in the gravel drive of a home with light brown siding. A man in a suit stepped out of the house and waved at them as his father turned and pulled the truck to a stop behind the car.

After cutting the engine, his father got out of the truck and his mother followed, leaning the front seat forward for Noah to climb out.

"Mr. Belton?" the tall man with the balding head asked, extending his hand.

"You the real estate agent?" his father asked, even as the man aggressively clasped his hand.

"Tom Marley," he said, making eye contact.

"Hugh Belton. Good to meet you, Mr. Marley."

"Please. Call me Tom," the man said and then motioned to Noah and his mother. "This your family?"

Noah's father looked back and nodded. "That's them. My wife, Ada, and my boy, Noah."

"Missus Belton," Tom said, and stretched his hand out to her. She declined the gesture, but bowed just a little and raised her hand in a quick wave. Noah knew that his father was not fond of her touching other men, no matter the circumstances.

The real estate agent smiled and dropped his hand, nodding likewise. "Ma'am," he acknowledged, and then turned to Noah, who stood with his hands in his jacket pockets.

"Noah, go on and greet the man proper," his father barked, and Noah raised his hand.

"Pleased to meet you, Mr. Marley," he said, as the agent took his hand in his own.

"What a fine, young man," Tom said, a grin sweeping over his face. "And so polite!"

Hugh grimaced at his son.

"Indeed, *Tom*," his father said with special emphasis on the man's given name.

The agent stood for a moment, silent and awkward with his practiced salesman's grin frozen on his face.

"Well, Tom, how about we see the house?"

"Of course!" the agent said, jerking as if suddenly woken from a dream. He stretched out his arm toward the stone walkway that led up to the covered front porch of the house. "After y'all."

His father stepped forward and his mother gestured for Tom Marley to go ahead. She glanced back at her son.

"Do I have to go?" he asked, shifting uneasily, his hands now jammed back into the pockets of his jacket.

She got a familiar look on her face and started to insist, but his father interjected.

"Let the boy run, Ada. Been cooped up like a hen for the past couple hours."

Noah looked up at his father who stood with Mr. Marley before the front door. It seemed an unusual allowance from him, but then over the years, Noah had noticed that his father tended to be more permissive when other grown-ups were around.

"Thanks, Dad." He nodded and turned back down the walkway.

"Don't wander far, Noah," she shouted after him. "Stay in the neighborhood."

Noah scoffed at the idea of the few houses being called a neighborhood and walked on.

"Don't you worry, Missus Belton," he heard the agent say. "It's safe as can be around here. Lots of space for a young man to roam."

Noah heard the front door open and close behind him as he rounded the house and headed down toward the banks of the lake.

Here and there around the water's edge, patches of reeds grew with a thick layer of other plants like a wild hedge behind them. In the backyard, a short, wooden dock extended from the grass out above the surface of the water and Noah sought it out immediately. It looked new. The planks were tight and stable and the wood fresh and bright, untouched by algae and the weathering of age. Attached to the outer pylons were metal cleats where a small boat could be tied up.

Standing on the dock, the lake seemed greater in size than it appeared from the narrow cove where Cady's Run was situated. From Cedar Banks, the lake looked almost like a sea; vast and twinkling in the afternoon light with nary another bit of shore to be seen. He could not help but smile as he beheld its majesty. Looking to the west, the view was dominated by the long, hulking shape of Cross

Mountain, which he had been unable to see from the old neighborhood. From here, though, the mountain was a dark and gigantic thing dominating the horizon with its wide, flat ridge that spanned the length of the lake and beyond.

Though the sight of it made him feel small and cold, he could not deny its beauty. It would be a perfect place for his and Tommy's war games.

Noah and Tommy had come up with the premise of their war games when they were both very young, after some birthday sleepover Tommy had gone to where the parents let all the boys watch the movie *Aliens*. Although they were now older—perhaps too old to be running around in the woods playing pretend—they had continued their adventures. Quite simply, there had never been much else in Cady's Run for the boys to do, and nothing else that ever interested them.

The world they had created was inspired by the movie Tommy had seen that night—which Noah had never and *would never* be permitted to watch—and Tommy's *Sgt. Rock* comics, a few of which Noah had read on the sly without his father's knowledge.

Captain Red and Sergeant Black were officers in the Galactic Marine Corps, who defended Earth against threats from outer space. The greatest of these threats was a race of giant, zombie space insects called the Horde, who were nearly un-killable except by the Galactic Marines' special, glowing rounds of ammunition. Nuke bullets, the boys called them, although neither of them had ever given much thought to exactly what that meant. The nuke bullets, when they hit their mark, got stuck in the armored flesh and limbs of the creatures and, in minutes, reduced them to piles of foul-smelling jelly that bore more than a little resemblance to a loogie hocked up and spat upon the ground.

Theirs was a war game born from the imaginations of two boys who had no other close friends and who could not bear the thought of warring against each other. From a young age, Noah and Tommy's enemy had always been a common one, even if only imaginary.

Noah glanced around at the deep woods and the vast lake, the dark mountain dominating the horizon, and it sparked his fantasy. This remote place was just the sort the Horde would choose as ground zero for their invasion of Earth. Yes! In fact, the Horde had already sent a scouting party. They were scrambling down the mountain, the clicking of dozens of monstrous legs like ice pebbles falling through the trees. And now, trapped deep in the forest as he was, and without his brother-in-arms, the fate of Earth rested solely on Captain Red's narrow but capable shoulders.

He cast about the woods for an appropriately sized and shaped stick, found it, and snatched it up. Cradling the stick-as-rifle in his arm, he smirked.

"Brotherhood! To the last man!" he shouted, and let loose a barrage of fire that mowed down the front line of his enemies a hundred yards distant.

But their numbers were many. After all, they were called "the Horde" for good reason.

Within seconds, he would be attacked, so he raced along the edge of the lake in search of some proper cover. Noah found it in the woods, in the hollow of an old tree. He ducked in, pinned himself against the natural alcove, and waited. As the enemy approached, the only sound audible beyond the collective whisper of their stealthy limbs was the sound of his own breath. Shallow and quiet.

A twig cracked somewhere in the distance. Not an imagined twig, nor a sound he had planned. It took him by surprise, certainly, but not as much as the playful laughter that followed—a bout of giggling he recognized.

But how was that possible?

Noah stepped out of the hollow and scanned the woods. He saw nothing, and all was silent for a moment, then he heard the children's laughter again. At the periphery of his vision, he saw fast-moving shapes of ivory skin and yellow hair dash between the trees. He wanted to chase them but something in him, some instinct, grounded his feet to the earth where he stood.

Then came another crack and Noah turned to look up the bank. What he saw, he could hardly believe, and he blinked his eyes a few times to banish the strange sight from his mind. But it remained there still.

A figure slipped through the trees along the crest of the bank above, sending crows scattering from among the branches. A long, graying beard hung from a weathered face, its head crowned by a small, gray pillbox cap that had seen better days. Before Noah even noticed the manner of the figure's dress, he recognized the cap as that of a Confederate soldier from the Civil War. The soldier glided along through the fallen leaves, bending and stooping, holding something close to his chest, clothed in the drab, gray wool coat of a Civil War infantryman.

Noah took a step backwards and then dropped the stick clutched in his hand to the ground where it landed with a rustle. The soldier seemed to hear it and looked up from his wandering, searched the woods until his gaze settled on Noah standing there by the hollowed tree. It was then that Noah realized he could not see the houses, for he had made his way far down and along the banks of the lake. Probably, he was not even in the neighborhood anymore. A feeling of remorse came over him. Without intending it, he had done exactly the opposite of the last thing his mother asked of him. He had wandered too far.

Noah watched as the phantom soldier cocked its head, studying him for a moment. Then it moved through the trees toward him.

4

The inside of the home at Cedar Banks was clean and the beige-toned walls smelled of fresh paint. The hardwood floors were old but had been restored, giving a uniform shine to them and smelling of Murphy's Oil Soap.

Ada looked the living room over, pleased with what she saw. Hugh walked about, though, stone-faced and checking the corners and crevices for details like cracked seams in the plaster and poorly laid trim along the baseboards.

"It's a three-bedroom, just like the others," the agent said. "Obviously, you have the main living room here."

"Look, Hugh," Ada said, "there's a fireplace."

She pointed to a white-painted brick fireplace against the far wall. She loved the idea of a crackling fire on a cold winter night but Hugh glanced at it only a moment before muttering under his breath about the "filthy, troublesome things."

Deflated, Ada walked the kitchen, checking out the cabinet space.

"Mr. Marley, what were all these houses built out here for?"

"Oh, I guess your husband didn't tell you?"

She looked over at Hugh, but he didn't even acknowledge her. He was running his hands over one of the living room walls searching for any unevenness that would indicate repairs.

"Never got 'round to it," Hugh said.

"Ah, well then, Missus Belton, all these homes used to be sleeping quarters for workmen. See, this was a workers camp under the Work Projects Administration during the 1930s and 40s. One of the nicer ones from what I hear. They housed them here, fed and clothed them in exchange for their labor."

"What were they working on?" Ada asked, sensing that since she had lived nearby all her life, she ought to know— but then, history was not something that had ever interested her very much. Besides, she was from Eastlake and unless one got around a lot, that might as well have been a whole different state.

"Cross Mountain Dam," Tom replied and pointed in the general direction of the mountain. "They dammed up the Roanoke River, called the Ash River around these parts. Created all of Ashwood Lake that way. I think they also worked to clear trails and logging roads on the mountain and in some of the nearby National Parks and Forests."

She nodded. "Interesting."

Tom followed them as they walked through the house.

"Yep, these homes here have been rebuilt from the inside out. They kept intact the good parts; the foundations, the stone chimneys, the framework and such. But they re-framed the inside and changed the two-room sleeping quarters into the cozy, three bedroom cottages you see here today. It's secluded and quiet. Only phone is located up at the manor house, though. Unless you folks want to pay to have a line run to the house here."

"Don't care too much for the damned things myself," Hugh said.

"What's the address here?" Ada asked.

"Number 5 Cedar Bay Drive," he said, "on account of the open area of the lake out there that folks call Cedar Bay."

They were in the largest bedroom, presumably the master, and the room included a wide window from which Ada could see Ashwood Lake glittering in the distance. Ada stood before it. She raised her hand and touched the cold glass.

"Well, you know that five is my lucky number, Hugh."

He came to her and stood next to her, gazing out of the window.

"Your people still prepared to let this go as a lease-to-own? Same price we discussed over the phone?" Hugh asked the agent, though he did not turn to meet the man's eyes.

"Yes, sir. Just like all the properties at Cedar Banks. They're not exactly selling like hotcakes, being so out of the way and all. They'd make fine vacation homes for some of the well-off, but with times being as lean as they are right now . . ."

"We'll take it," Hugh said.

Ada turned to face him, even more surprised with the abrupt decision than the agent. After all, Hugh hadn't exactly been singing praises about the house.

"Well, congratulations, then!" Tom Marley smiled and reached out his hand. Hugh Belton took it and gave it a quick, firm shake.

"You all are going to be very happy here, I think," the agent said as they returned to the front door.

"Are there many other families that live here? I didn't notice much traffic on the way in."

"No, ma'am," the agent replied. "You all are the first family in." He opened the door for them as they stepped onto the porch. "In fact, you're the only owners living here at all. Well, besides—"

"Noah?" Ada blurted out. "What in the world?"

Following her eyes, Hugh and Tom saw the boy coming from the woods at the crest of the banks sloping down to the lake. He walked toward them not alone but beside a tall, gangly man dressed from head to toe in the gray uniform of a Confederate soldier.

"Ah! I see your boy's met Mr. Winston. He's the other resident I was about to mention. He's also the property manager here. You get a busted pipe during the winter or your kitchen stove is on the fritz, Mr. Winston here will get you all fixed up."

"What's with the uniform?" Hugh asked, almost chuckling.

The agent nodded and smiled. "It's true Mr. Winston is a bit eccentric. Dresses like that quite often. He's a Civil War reenactor, but he's one heck of a good man to have around. Been here a good while. And he knows this place better than anybody."

"And he's our only neighbor?" Ada asked, still looking

askance at the old man in rebel gray who walked beside her son.

The agent nodded. "Real quiet, too. Except for maybe a musket firing every now and then."

Tom Marley had a good laugh at his own joke and even Hugh joined in the chortling.

"Yes, ma'am, y'all are gonna find it real nice up here," he said, waving the property manager toward them to meet the new residents.

"Nice and quiet."

5

On the ride back to Cady's Run—to his real home—Noah's parents broke the news to their son that they had decided to take Mr. Marley's offer on the house and they would be moving into it as soon as they could get all their things packed at the trailer.

This came as no surprise to Noah. The new place was much nicer than their trailer home and he knew from his father's rants that it was better to own a home than rent one belonging to someone else. It was something his father called equity, although Noah didn't quite understand what that meant. Everything about the house had seemed fresh and bright and clean, which Noah had to admit was pretty nice. The view of the lake was gorgeous and the woods were vast and thick and full of wonder. The house had its very own dock on the lake, where Noah imagined he could sit and fish or maybe even someday get a little john boat that he could take out and explore the many coves and creeks of Ashwood Lake.

The only problem was that Noah had to imagine doing all of this alone.

As he had discovered, there were no other kids, not even any other families that lived at Cedar Banks. No one except for the strange old man, the property manager who the real estate agent called Mr. Winston. When the man had run across Noah playing in the woods, though, he had introduced himself as Clay. Before he spoke, Noah had been convinced he'd stumbled upon a Civil War ghost. And why not? A teacher of Noah's had once said that in the state of Virginia, you could hardly walk a country mile without coming across some old house with important history or a cemetery or a pasture that was once a battlefield.

Upon seeing the old man, Noah had been terrified, unable to move as he came his way. But then the soldier called out to him and asked him if he was lost and from where he had come. Once his breath had returned to him and his thrumming heart calmed in his chest, Noah had explained that his parents were looking at a house close by. It was then that the soldier introduced himself and offered to lead the way back.

Noah had wanted to ask the old man about the uniform he wore but he was shy and also unsure if doing so would be considered rude. His parents later explained that Mr. Winston was a Civil War reenactor.

After they got home, later that night, Noah rested his head on the pillow and went to sleep with a heavy heart. He knew the next day would begin a change that involved him packing all his things into boxes to be transported to the new house. It meant no more Chesterton Junior High and it also meant saying goodbye to Tommy—his only friend in the whole wide world.

Halloween came and went, although the holiday—rooted as it was in paganism—was not observed in the Belton household. Noah had become resigned to this long ago, but not without some amount of bitter longing whenever the time of year came around. No Jack-O-Lanterns adorned the trailer steps, no cut-outs of black cats or whimsical witches were hung on the front door, and absolutely no candy was dispensed to the children of the neighborhood, who knew better than to go knocking on the Beltons' door on All Hallows' Eve.

It took them the better part of a week and a half to round up all of their things. When moving day came, Noah's father borrowed a trailer and hitched it to his truck. A buddy of his from the saw mill also showed up with a box truck. The vehicles were loaded with cardboard containers of every size and shape, furniture, their refrigerator and their washer and dryer.

While his father was packing the last of it into the truck, Noah and his mother said cordial goodbyes to their neighbors and when it came time to say farewell to Tommy, Noah fought hard against the lump in his throat. He couldn't break down. Not where his father could see. He would surely be taunted endlessly for it. Maybe even worse. So, he shook hands with his friend, his comrade, his brother-in-arms, and in their parting, Tommy slipped him a folded scrap of notebook paper on which he had written his phone number and address.

"You know," Tommy said with a smirk, "in case you forget."

They drove away from Cady's Run and the eastern shore of Ashwood Lake, bound for the lonely woods of the west and none of them said a word. The space between them was filled with a reflective silence. For Noah, it was like leaving the freshly covered grave of a loved one behind, faced with the immutable fact that life will go on and do so, unimaginably, without the deceased as part of it.

It was barely November, but there with his parents, in the cab of his father's truck—there in those moments of silence—Noah could feel the warm familiarity of autumn suddenly slip away and the icy claws of winter come scratching at the window.

6

November

Nearly a week had passed and still they were unpacking. Noah didn't remember it taking so long any of the other times they'd moved, but this time the process of settling in had become a grueling exercise in culling and organization. It wasn't that they were being lackadaisical; there was just so much to go through. His mother unpacked things and stowed them away in the new spaces available to her, trying hard to organize the hurricane of clutter that their trailer at Cady's Run had been. It also meant much of the same effort for Noah. When packing to move, he discovered a half dozen sealed boxes of miscellany hiding in his closet, which had been heaved onto the truck along with all the others. Now, having unpacked all of his clothes and books and a few old toys, he was left with a row of boxes from a room cleanup more than two years ago. They should have gone into the throw-away pile back at Cady's Run but had somehow come along in the move.

Noah reached into his pocket and unfolded the small Buck knife. He slit the first box open and peered inside. Books. Thumbing through, he recognized them all as children's books that he'd had from years back. The second box was much the same. He pulled a few items to which he had a sentimental attachment—a few volumes of the Hardy Boys' mysteries, Choose-Your-Own-Adventure and Dr. Seuss—and slid the two boxes into the hallway next to the other boxes that were to be carried off to Goodwill.

Opening the third box, he slumped down and began picking through the intermingled mess of old, half-broken toys and rocks, sticks and various objects picked up during his playing in the woods and saved for some strange but unrealized purpose. Then something bright and shiny at the bottom of the box caught his eye. An old model rocket in the shape of the space shuttle Columbia. A remnant of something he and Tommy had built together. There had been another one—launched down by the lake quite successfully, though it was inevitably lost to a watery fate. The rocket was small but in reasonably good shape for having been at the bottom of the box for so long. He flipped it over; the propellant cartridge was still lodged in the tail of the rocket. A long fuse protruded from it and, as he twirled it around his finger, an idea came to him.

What better way to break from the boredom and tedium of unpacking than to launch that sucker into the sky by the lakeshore? He would dedicate the launch to Tommy.

Of course, there were a few elements missing, most notably the stand that provided a level surface and a guide wire to get the rocket off the ground on a straight path. No matter. He snatched a shirt from his closet and tore it from the hanger. Unwinding the hanger, twisting it until it was mostly straight, he whipped it through the air and smiled. *Problem solved.*

He ran down the hallway into the kitchen, rummaged through one of the drawers and found a pack of strike-anywhere matches. His mother was on a step-stool in the living room, struggling with hanging a picture. Noah kept the rocket hidden behind his back. It wasn't that he cared if she knew what he intended to do but he didn't feel like suffering through her hundred questions about it and likely insistence on watching over him as he did it.

"I unpacked three boxes, Mumma."

"You did, huh?" she said, a nail stuck between her teeth as she attempted to level the painting of a pastoral countryside in winter.

"Can I go outside for a while?"

"Okay, Noah. Don't go too far."

"Mom," he groaned. He was fourteen years old, after all, but she still mothered him like he was ten.

Outside, he surveyed the area for as flat a spot as he

could find and settled on a barren patch of ground about ten feet from the water's edge. There hadn't been much rain, so jamming the straightened clothes hanger into the hard ground was more of a chore than he had reckoned. After some twisting and pressure, he had it down and bent it out toward the lake.

He slid the rocket down the wire through the plastic sleeve glued to the fuselage and stretched out the fuse string as far as it could go. While it was not shaped precisely like the space shuttle, it was certainly reminiscent of it and Noah was excited to see the thing blast off into the air above the lake. Kneeling down at the end of the fuse, he struck a match that flamed to life with a sulfur stench and cupped his hand around it as he lowered it to the fuse. After a second of contact with the fuse, the string began burning and sparking as it quietly hissed and disappeared inches at a time.

Noah stepped back several feet and watched.

After a moment, the fuse reached its end and the propellant cartridge began to smoke at the base of the rocket. For a brief second, Noah thought that it had been sitting too long and had lost its potency but just as he bent down for a better look, white fire spat out of the tail and lifted the shuttle off the ground along the makeshift guide wire. Gray smoke came in a rush along the ground as the rocket was propelled high into the air.

Noah grinned wide as the craft flew high, growing small against the sky. Higher and higher it would climb until the fuel was spent and then its nose cone would pop open and the plastic parachute would guide it down gently to the lake.

But something was wrong.

Maybe it was the wind or maybe it was the rocket's design, but it had flipped over and was now careening back toward the shore, wobbling but still spitting fire as it came. The celebrated toy had become a missile.

Noah ran up the banks toward the house, watching the

craft as it spun out of control in his direction. It passed him so close that he could feel the heat from the propellant.

His heart sank when he saw where it was headed.

"Moving sure is a bitch."

Ada looked around the living room and adjoining kitchen at boxes which still needed unpacking. She grinned a little at her own words, feeling the cheap thrill of uttering foul language. She would never say such a thing in the company of others, though. Let alone Hugh. Her husband did not approve of women using such language.

She had finally gotten the picture hanging straight. It was a Thomas Kincaid original that she picked up at a mall in Roanoke years ago. Her eyes were drawn to its peacefulness and the soft white snow that covered everything. It seemed so real, so very alive on the canvas.

In the kitchen, she poured a fresh cup of black coffee from the pot and sipped it as she walked back into the living room. She stood and stared out of the large bay window that looked out over the backyard and onto the lake. The afternoon sun broke upon the rippling surface and entranced her as she drew the mug of hot brew to her lips.

Their first week at Cedar Banks had been a period of adjustment. Hugh was settling into his new job at Kemp Family Metalworks, a metal fabrication shop near the municipal airport, just outside of Whitetail proper. By his account, the work was very different from what he had been doing at the saw mill. There he had been responsible for maintenance on the enormous, bladed machines that rendered usable lumber from the naked logs of felled trees. At Kemp—as Hugh had told her it was commonly referred to—he was learning to use and repair the many pieces of equipment utilized to sheer and size and trim and finish metal plates and lengths of steel and aluminum of every shape and size. Although, as the saying went, it was hard to teach an old dog new tricks and the learning process often frustrated him. She had seen it in his darkened mood of late. He was not a talkative man under the best of circumstances but this week, after arriving home from work, he had very little to say to her. He had, however, found the time to criticize her slowness in getting all of their things unpacked.

Still, she was glad Hugh had decided on this house. It was such a step up from their rented double-wide that she wondered if it was undeserved in some way. But that was just nonsense, wasn't it? If anybody deserved it, she did.

She and Noah deserved this new start, even though the boy was still in the throes of adjustment. He was creeping into adolescence, which made any kind of change more difficult. It was hard leaving behind Noah's only friend and all that was familiar to him, but Cedar Banks provided an opportunity for them to better their lives. She had always hated having to tell folks they lived in Cady's Run, a well-known trailer park in Bedford. She hated the look that always followed; a mixture of pity and distaste.

Now?

They had a house on the lake. It sounded positively posh, and she wanted to go and holler it to all the world from the top of Cross Mountain.

She glanced around the living room and sighed. She really needed to get this finished. Not only to put an end to Hugh's sniping comments regarding all the boxes, but also because she needed to get started with Noah on his schooling. With no second vehicle to take the boy to school, it had been decided that Ada would home-school her son. This had checked all right with the county and they had provided a list of materials he would need. Some of his existing school books would suffice but there were new ones to be bought and there were forms and workbooks and reports that would need to be filled out and sent in. Having been so consumed with unpacking the new house, she had simply not gotten to it. Besides, she thought, it was probably good for Noah to have a short break before they dove into the home-schooling.

Ada had just set her coffee down and bent to open another box when she heard a noise from outside. A strange but incredibly loud hissing that grew closer by the second. Before she could even turn to peer out of the window, the hissing ended in a crack and a thud that vibrated the walls of the house.

Something had smashed into it from the outside.

She sprinted for the kitchen door. Out of the house and rounding the corner, she saw Noah coming toward her. On the side of the house, there was a smoky, black spot, like an enormous cigarette burn. Shards of siding lay on the ground along with what was left of a white plastic model made to look like the space shuttle. A model rocket.

Noah came to a stop alongside her and together they gawked at the damage. Her eyes widened and she looked over at him, her baby boy every bit as tall as her. His eyes betrayed the sudden shock and guilt of a child who'd done something wrong and stupid and knew it. There was the natural fear of the consequences of his actions, but there was also something more. A deeper dread that dragged his eyes downward and bent his mouth into a grimace of near agony. Ada recognized it, knew it well. She had worn it more than once herself and not only when she was a child.

"Oh, Noah," she muttered, trembling, "your father . . . "

Her voice trailed off as a sickening sensation grew in her stomach.

Noah's eyes welled with tears, his pouting lips quivering as they shared a look, and a familiar and unspoken despair set down upon them both.

7

Noah went into hiding.

After the incident, his mother had questioned him

about what the rocket was and where he had gotten it. He suddenly found himself faced with a very grim possibility. Even though it had been Noah who launched the thing without supervision or permission, the blame for the rocket and the damage done to the new house would spread to Tommy since it was his friend who had given the rocket to him. When they left Cady's Run, there had been talk between his mother and Tommy's father of bringing him to Cedar Banks for the occasional visit so that the boys could see each other. However, Noah's father was not keen on Tommy to begin with, and if he was seen in any way as culpable in this act of destruction, it would most definitely ruin any chances Noah had of seeing his friend again anytime soon. With this alarming possibility playing out in his mind, Noah handled his mother's question just as most young boys would. He looked her straight in the face and lied.

"I got it at school. Missus Shiloh's science class last year. We were learning about the space shuttle and we all had these rockets to build." Noah rarely lied directly to either of his parents and he was a little surprised at himself; how easily twisting the truth came to him and rolled, silvery, off of his tongue. "We launched them all over a couple of days but on the day the last group of us was to shoot ours off, it rained. So, Missus Shiloh told us to keep them and take them home."

It wasn't a perfect lie and it wouldn't stand up very well to intense scrutiny but Noah's mother was too worried about what would happen when her husband got home to pester her son with the details of his explanation. He could only hope the story would pass muster with his father.

Since confining himself to his room, Noah had managed to unpack and put away the remainder of his old things from the closet and ended up with one more box to go to Goodwill. He slid it out into the hall with the others and it was then he noticed that the clock in the kitchen was pushing 5:30 in the afternoon. His father would be home soon.

Noah sat on his bed, awaiting the inevitable. He picked up his Bible and thumbed through it, absently reading here and there from the Book of Ruth. He hoped it would help some when his father came calling to see that his troublesome son, in the hour of his guilt, had turned to the Good Book for wisdom and direction.

He hoped it would look like penance.

Minutes later, he heard the thud of the side door into the kitchen shutting as his father entered the home. Noah could just imagine his confusion when he walked in and hung his coat on the hooks by the door and then noticed the halfway demolished and blackened rocket ship sitting on the kitchen table. Noah's mother would be milling about nervously until the question was asked and then she would smile in an attempt to downplay the situation even as she explained it to her husband.

Noah saw it all unfolding in his mind.

Then there was another creak as the door opened again and was left that way. Noah closed his eyes, knowing his father had stepped out back to see the damage. Then the door shut as his father came back inside. The walls in the new house were not thin like those of the trailer and Noah could hear only the loudest of noises. For a moment, after the back door closed, there was only silence.

Then Noah heard the side door open again and shut. He knew *exactly* what that meant. His father had gone out to the truck to retrieve Black Billy. All hope for leniency or understanding from his father flew away from Noah in that moment. His body trembled as the footsteps came heavily down the hallway to his room.

Black Billy was the name of the leather club that his father used for the purpose of divine punishment. It was also the name Noah used to refer to his father when he would go on one of his disciplinary rampages. In those times, the gruff but soft-spoken person of Hugh Belton disappeared and became one with the weapon he wielded. Slightly shorter than a ruler, it was a length of heavy rubber wrapped thick in densely woven leather strands to form a handle with a wrist strap at one end and a hard leather knob at the other that was thicker and harder than the hilt.

Burned into the handle but barely visible anymore were letters and numbers that read "*Prov. 13:24*", a reference to a passage in the Book of Proverbs; a declaration that whoever spared the rod, hated his son.

When the door to his room swung open, Noah's eyes were trained on the small print of his Bible, the pages of the Book of Ruth, trembling in his timorous grasp.

Noah glanced up at his father. He stood in the doorway, a scowl on his face, his eyes narrow and drilling a hole right through the skull of his son.

"What're you reading?"

"Book of Ruth," Noah replied, but could hardly keep the unwanted, fearful vibrato out of his voice.

"Oh? What's it say?"

Noah stared down at the book and read aloud from the passage.

"*Where thou diest, will I die and there will I be buried. Thus may the Lord do to me, and more also, if ought but death part thee and me.*"

His father nodded. "You understand what that means?"

Noah searched for the words. "Honor thy Mother and thy Father?"

His father snorted. "That's actually the Book of Matthew," he said. "But it seems you get the gist."

Noah tried to hold his father's eyes but his gaze was pulled toward Hugh Belton's thick fingers and the shaft of Black Billy held tightly in his right hand.

Both hard and flexible, the club's appearance was far less wicked than its bite. Noah didn't know how old it was but its ebony leather was worn smooth with age and it was strong and well-made by hand in a time when machines were not employed to create all of mankind's wares by the thousands. Noah suspected that it had been used on his father by his own parents. Once, he had asked where the name came from.

"Wasn't me who named it," his father had replied. "It's always been called that so far as I know."

It was a vicious tool—an apparently ancient weapon—that was as useful against an adult as it was a child, and his father always kept it under the front seat of his truck. When it had been used on Noah—and it had been used more times than he cared to recall—his father always made him care for the damnable thing afterwards. It was in his best interest, his father had explained, since it kept the rubber core soft and flexible. His body aching as welts continued to rise under his skin, Noah would sit on the edge of his bed and massage Black Billy with a soft cloth and a dab or two of neat's-foot oil, silently cursing the thing all the while.

He feared the sight of it just as he feared his father, for Black Billy was simply an extension of his wrath.

"So, you a rocket scientist now?" his father asked.

"No, sir."

"They teaching rocket science at school nowadays?"

Noah reached down inside himself, fumbling for the lie. He almost had it, but then . . .

"No, sir."

Hugh nodded. "But that's what you told your mother, ain't it?"

Noah nodded, his eyes dropping to the floor with shame.

"Where did you get it? Really," he said, stepping in and kneeling down close to the bed.

Noah's compulsion to tell the truth was almost irresistible in the presence of his father, but there came once more the thought of never seeing his best friend again and a more believable fiction came to him; two untruths, one nestled within the other. It's what he should have told his mother to begin with.

"I got it from Carl Wright."

"The big boy who used to whoop up on you and Tommy?"

Noah nodded.

"Now why would he give something like that to *you*?" his father asked, his eyes narrowing with suspicion that was on the cusp of boiling into rage.

"He didn't." Noah swallowed hard. "He left it out, wasn't paying attention. So, I took it from him."

Hugh drew back from his son as if Noah were the carrier of some hideous disease.

"So, you're a liar *and a thief*," he growled, his jaws clenched.

"Yes, sir."

His father laid the leather club on the bedspread near where Noah sat. He stood for a moment in thought and then sat down on the edge of the bed.

"Son," he began, "because you been so honest with me, I'm gonna let this one slide for you."

Noah couldn't believe what he was hearing and his eyes brightened, though he dared not show anything outwardly aside from shame and remorse.

"But there'll be no supper for you tonight. You can go to bed hungry. I suggest you keep your nose in the Good Book and fill up on what you find in there."

"Yes, sir."

"Maybe your momma's right. You were just looking for something to do. Idle hands are the devil's workshop after all. But that ain't your fault, I guess."

A cruel smile spread across his father's face and he snatched up Black Billy and stood.

"It's hers."

His father stepped out of the room and slammed Noah's bedroom door shut behind him so hard that he thought for sure it must have cracked the door frame.

Then, through the thick walls of their new home, he heard the shouting and something—maybe a lamp or a stack of boxes—knocked over as his father went after her. Noah couldn't see, of course, but from the wailing cries and pleas for mercy coming from his mother in the next room and the guttural curses of his father, he could tell that Black Billy was feasting on pain with a special ferocity.

How many times had Noah been here before? Cady's Run and now Cedar Banks—all of those moments spent in his room, lying on the bed with his knees held against his chest while he listened to Black Billy strike flesh and bone. His heart yearned to help his mother but his courage waned at the thought of going up against his father.

Noah switched off the bedside lamp and lay back. There was a pop as the knob turned and the door to his room creaked open. Cowering there in the bed, Noah wondered if perhaps his father had had second thoughts about punishment and who deserved it.

Was he now coming for him?

He stared at the crack in the door. It squeaked again, opening wider, though his father did not step through. Maybe the door had broken when it was slammed. He could still hear them in the other room. His father was lecturing his mother for not having their son's home-schooling materials in order, for not keeping him focused on learning instead of "blowing up fucking rockets." Each statement punctuated by another thrashing with the club.

Noah stared through his half-opened door into the dark space of the hallway. A feeling came over him that he could not name. His skin crawled and his brow was suddenly wet with a slick of cold perspiration. His heart pulsated loudly in his chest and his ears, so loud that it nearly drowned out the din of the violence close by.

That crack in the door and the dark hallway. A sensation he could not shake, like being watched. He was sure of it except that he knew there was no one there.

In the next room, the sounds of another tussle erupted as Noah's mother tried to escape the constant blows.

"Come back here, woman!" his father snarled. "You'll not deny me the last word!"

Then there was a scuffle and something fell to the floor. Definitely a lamp this time—as it fell, it tipped and sent an arc of light down the hallway. The flat beam of light passed over a figure standing in the hallway just outside of Noah's bedroom. The flash was brief but for Noah, it seemed the light moved slow and lingered along the walls.

It was a man, tall and broad shouldered with a long, heavy coat and a wide-brimmed hat that crowned a head of stringy, coarse-looking hair. The figure was turning his head from Noah's bedroom to peer into the living room where Noah's mother screamed as Black Billy assailed her again. The man in the hallway smiled, beaming with delight at the agony and the fury. That's when Noah noticed the long, crumpled cigarillo clenched between rows of jagged, awful teeth. A cloud of tobacco smoke wreathed him and its odor nearly masked the foul reek that suddenly came wafting to Noah's nostrils, along with a distinct sound of buzzing as if from a swarm of flies. As the light fell across the figure's chin and made its way downward, the man turned to leer into the bedroom once again. Where there should have been eyes, the figure had only deep, black pits. Looking upon them filled Noah with absolute despair.

Then something happened that Noah could not understand.

He saw the familiar shape of his father's balding head and heard the footfalls as he went striding down the hallway toward the master bedroom. As he did this, he did not pass by the stinking man but passed through him entirely as if there was nothing at all tangible about him.

It froze Noah's blood and he turned away from the sight just as the lamp in the living room met with the floor, shattered, and the hallway was pitched into blackness again. He lay on his side, facing away from the door, his hands balled into fists and held tightly against his head. A coldness, dry and brittle, crept into the room and Noah's heart drummed in his ears along with a piercing whine that dug into his brain like the fangs of a serpent. His skin crawled and that putrid scent mixed with tobacco grew closer, invading his space and his senses.

He shut his eyes tight and willed it away, this thing that had come to him unbidden.

Through the open door behind him, he heard his father go stomping down the hallway again, keys jingling in his grasp and he knew at once that he meant to leave the house as he often did after meting out such bestial punishments. Though he could not bring himself to cry out or move, Noah actually yearned for his father to stay. He would have welcomed a beating of his own in that moment if it meant that the dark presence would be ejected from the room. The front door slammed and the truck roared to life, then groaned away from the house and into the night.

The presence lingered a moment longer and then the supernatural stench and ringing sound vanished.

He lay there for a while, his body and mind spent, and listened to the unintelligible sobs and whimpers of pain that persisted in the next room. He wanted to go to his mother, to help her, to comfort her, but he could not. His heart and soul were fatigued and a precious sleep was washing over him.

As he faded, Noah wondered if his mother would be able to walk when the morning came.

3

The first time that Hugh had hit Ada was also the first time they made love. She was Ada Donovan then and they were much younger, both of them in their late twenties, having dated for some time. It was the week before Christmas and they were alone in his parents' home. They had met there to exchange gifts before the holiday, but they were in love and in heat, so things got pretty steamy between them pretty quickly. She undid his jeans and was lowering her head down toward his lap when he yanked her up by her hair and smacked her with an open palm. It shocked her so much that she simply sat there on the couch, wordless, rubbing her face while he explained that such an act was not becoming of a Christian woman and certainly not one that he would take for a wife. In her experience—though she had lied and assured Hugh she had no prior experience—putting her mouth on him was an act of affection that pleased most men. But apparently not Hugh.

She had chosen to let it go, though, and confirmed her understanding of his wishes, and a few minutes later she had made love to the man that would become her husband. That night, she realized that Hugh knew even less about sex than she suspected. He made an assumption that she was a virgin and she had done nothing to contradict him. After they lay together that night, he boasted heartily how it had been a satisfying first time for the both of them.

He never bothered to ask her, though, and she dared not contradict him.

The following evening he took her out for a night of roller-skating and ice cream. It had been his way of making amends for slapping her, she supposed.

And so were planted the poisonous roots of their relationship.

Perhaps she should have left him then and there but it wasn't the first time she'd been struck by a man. Her father, God rest his soul, had been hardened by too many years cutting timber in the unforgiving environs of thick Southern forests. He plied his trade surrounded by the roughest and most dangerous of characters, all of whom worked hard and drank even harder. George Donovan hadn't known anything about raising children to begin with. Then, when her mother had passed away from a sudden aneurysm when Ada was barely out of diapers, her father had found himself faced with just that task. He had done the best he could, she knew, but had raised his hand to her quite often in an effort to exact some discipline and control in the only way he knew. Although many of those times, he had been well into a bottle of Johnny Walker.

At least Hugh—she had often reasoned to herself—was not a frequent drinker, and often there was even a sweet side to him that he shared with her and her alone. For the rest of their brief courtship and in the early days of their marriage, Hugh had hardly ever raised a hand to her. When it had happened, it was because she had crossed some new line with him of which she was unaware. Ada quickly learned that it was best to know what her husband expected of her and to comply without comment or complaint. After all, mostly, Hugh was a good man. A God-fearing man of principles. Principles and flaws . . . like anyone else.

The sun was bleeding now into the bedroom of their new house and she could hear Noah rummaging about in the kitchen getting his breakfast ready. Ada rolled onto her back and gritted her teeth against the burning ache that constrained her movements like a vice. She had made it to bed last night and eventually her husband had returned, though she possessed only the faintest memory of it. His side of the bed was disturbed, though, which meant he had come home to sleep beside her and not alone out on the couch.

At least there was that.

And at least he had spared Noah a thrashing after the rocket incident and the lie in which he had been caught. Ada would gladly take the vicious blows of Hugh's discipline rather than have them fall upon her son. She had always been able to forgive Hugh for his brutality against her. The only times she found herself hating him—*truly hating him*—were the times he turned his rage upon their son.

She lay there for a time and prayed that today would be a better day. She rose, draped herself in a fluffy pink robe, and ambled down the hallway.

Noah sat at the kitchen table, his back to her, munching away at a bowl of corn flakes. To her surprise, the smell of freshly brewed coffee hung in the air. She had shown him how to make it last year and ever since, he surprised her every so often in the mornings with a full pot. She placed her hand on his shoulder as she entered the kitchen.

"Thanks for the coffee, son."

"You're welcome, Mumma."

She poured a cup and sipped from it as she stared out the tiny window over the sink that looked out at the driveway. Hugh's truck was still parked there.

"Seen your daddy this morning?"

"No," he replied darkly.

She stared into the black pool of her cup as if she could divine what her husband was getting up to. A moment later, the front door opened and Hugh stepped in. He was dressed for work in his insulated coveralls and the brisk smell of the cold air was upon him. He stepped in just enough that he could see them framed in the pass-through to the kitchen.

"Ada?" he called, his voice gruff and unrepentant.

"Yes?"

"I spoke with the property manager, Mr. Winston."

"Okay," she replied brightly, though the tone came with some effort.

"He's agreed to carry you into town to fetch whatever school supplies you need for Noah."

Her instinct was to protest. She didn't know the odd, grizzled man and she didn't relish the thought of taking the long ride into Whitetail with him, but she knew better than to say anything.

As if sensing her silent reluctance, he said, "It's done. It's been arranged."

Then he opened the door to leave, but stopped and looked back over his shoulder.

"And take the boy with you. Otherwise there might not be a house to come back to."

Ada said nothing else, just sipped her coffee and

watched as her husband climbed into his truck and backed out of the driveway. It wasn't until the old Ford had gone growling into the distance that the tension in her shoulders released.

Noah watched his mother sip her coffee while he poked absently at his soggy cereal. Ever since their first day at Cedar Banks, she had often voiced her wariness of the old property manager, calling him an "odd duck." His antiquated manner of dress was strange enough, but his mother also questioned the mind of anyone who would choose to live all alone out in this remote place. She suspected he was hiding from something or that he had something to hide. Either way, she didn't care for the strange old man, but Noah liked him.

Maybe he liked him *because* he was such an odd duck. Certainly, there were plenty of days when Noah felt like an odd duck, too.

More than anything, though, Noah welcomed the idea of going into town as a chance to get out of the house. The thought of the figure he had seen outside of his room last night had not left him all morning and the feeling of being watched, though dulled, persisted still.

"Well," he offered in an effort to breach the silence, "It's good we'll get my school stuff, right?"

"I suppose it is," she replied, her voice heavy with a sigh.

She turned to look her son in the eye.

"Why'd you lie to me, Noah? About the rocket?"

His eyes dropped down to his bowl of cereal.

"I don't know," he said. It was a lame excuse and he knew it but he didn't have the heart to speak the truth that morning. When he looked up, her eyes were still on him.

"We got to be able to trust each other, baby boy," she said.

"Okay, Mumma. Sorry."

She stared a moment longer, then cut her eyes to the front door.

"We'd best get dressed, I suppose," she said. "I'll try to make myself presentable. We don't want to keep Mr. Winston waiting."

Noah stood, picked up his spoon and bowl and dropped them into the sink. Out of the corner of his eye, he saw his mother rubbing her back with her free hand, the pink robe riding up, and only then did he notice the bruises and welts that had risen on the back of her legs. His heart broke for her and he wished more dearly than anything that he possessed the courage to say something to her about it.

Instead, he turned and left the kitchen. He stopped in front of the closed door to his room.

Had he closed it? He didn't think so, but then he couldn't be certain.

As his hand wrapped around the doorknob, he heard a loud and low-toned drone from within the room. The knob itself vibrated.

He opened the door.

The beige walls of his bedroom had turned gray, every inch of them and the air between was alive with thousands of flies, buzzing and flying and crawling. As if alerted to his presence, their collective pitch ascended to a higher note and he slammed the door shut before any of them could escape.

"Mumma!" he hollered.

His mother set her coffee mug down on the countertop with some force and came toward him with shuffling footsteps and a tight expression that betrayed the pain she endured with every movement.

"What is it?"

He stepped away from the door, his eyes wide.

"Must have left the window open. My room's full of flies."

"Flies?" she asked, disbelief wrinkled into her brow. "This time of year?"

He nodded and his mother grasped the knob, opened the door, and stepped into his room. Instinctively, he pressed his back against the wall, bracing himself for the flood of tiny, dark insects that was sure to come but did not. Following in behind her, he saw nothing that resembled what he had seen only a moment ago. All was as plain as it should be.

"But I—" he began, but his mother turned her head and curtly shushed him.

She stood there in the middle of his room and cocked her head to the side, listening. The low hum of insectile wings was gone and with it the innumerable horde of flies.

What is she listening for?

Then, with slow and deliberate movements, she raised one foot off the floor and snatched her slipper from it. With a deft killing stroke, she slapped the rubber sole against his bedroom window, then stepped back.

A single fly that had been buzzing around his window was now flattened against the glass in a dark swath of blood and tiny, twitching legs no thicker than a human hair.

"Well, that's the end of that," she said, sliding her slipper back on and smiling at her son as she breezed past him.

He stood alone in his room, struggling to reconcile what he had seen with the plain truth before him. He sniffed the air for the unforgettable stench of the stinking man but detected none of it. Noah's gaze fell again on his bedroom window. Thin, honeycombed wings and smashed fly guts adorned the surface for a moment before becoming unstuck and falling, disappearing from view into the grooves of the window sill below.

The glass pane, however, was still smeared with blood.

"I don't think that's the end of it, Mumma," he whispered aloud to no one but himself. "I don't think that's the end of it at all."

9

It was around 8:30 in the morning when Ada and her son strolled down the street to meet the property manager. Mr. Winston's house was one of the two in the center of the development and had a fenced-in backyard. The siding on his home was light gray but the old Chevrolet truck in his driveway was midnight blue and looked as if it had just rolled off the line. It reminded her of the one her father had driven for a time, though his had never looked so pristine.

"Wow," Noah said, nodding appreciatively at the vehicle gleaming in the cold, autumn sun.

The boy was outpacing her as they walked toward the house. With every step she took, there was a stab of pain that shot from her hip to her lower back. She had taken three aspirin before leaving the house and she was hoping they'd work their magic soon. Ada grimaced and tried her best to keep up with her son but she would need to move more carefully around Mr. Winston. It wouldn't do for him to notice her limping or favoring odd positions. People seeing a woman looking lame tended to suspect things about how she might have gotten that way.

And that only ever brought trouble.

Some might even feel compelled to meddle, which would only make things worse in the end. She had long ago given up on the idea of calling the police when her husband flew into his fits of rage. Hugh might spend a night in jail, sure, but he would be home the next day and Lord help them then. Any kind of permanent separation or restraining order would mean court dates and lawyers, none of which she had the money or stamina for. And where was she to stay in the meantime? If she had somewhere else to go—a sibling's house or even a close friend—that would be one thing, but Ada had no one. She couldn't bear the thought of her sleeping on a cot in some battered women's shelter while Noah stayed with a foster family until the conflict between his parents was all worked out. Such people were strangers and she'd heard too many horror stories about the kind of people who *happily volunteered* to take in children. Besides, Noah was her son—*her boy*. She needed him near her like she needed air, like she needed sunshine.

No, she would suffer Hugh until Noah was old enough to leave the nest. Then, if her husband hadn't changed, she just might leave with her son. It wasn't much as far as a plan went, but it was all she had.

They were headed up the driveway toward the front walk when Mr. Winston appeared from around the back of the house.

"Morning," he said, and nodded toward them.

Ada was glad to see that he was not dressed in Confederate gray, but still his clothes were plain and, from what she could spy of them beneath the buttoned-up pea coat, seemed oddly antique and out of place.

"Good morning to you." Ada slid her hands into the pockets of her jacket, fidgeting.

"So, it's into town we go, eh?"

"Mr. Winston, I hope it's not—"

"Please, ma'am, call me Clay."

"All right, then," she nodded, "Clay it is. Anyhow, I hope this ain't too much trouble. We'd hate to put you out."

"Naw, no trouble at all." He waved it off. "I got a hankering to take a drive anyway and this way I won't have to ride alone."

Clay opened the passenger door of his truck and motioned for them to climb in. As they all got situated and buckled in, Clay started up the vehicle and the old truck roared to life and idled loudly with a low rumble that vibrated the entire cab.

Noah, seated between his mother and Clay Winston, smiled wide.

"What kind of truck is this?" he asked.

"1967 Chevy short bed," Clay replied.

Ada draped an arm over her son's shoulders and shook him playfully. "What is it about loud, smoke-belching machines that appeals to you men no matter your age?" she teased.

Noah shrugged. "It's badass."

"Noah!" Ada slapped her son's arm.

Clay laughed and Ada joined in. Maybe the old man wasn't such an odd duck after all. He had a nice laugh.

"That it is." Clay pulled into the street, dropped the gear shift into drive. "Been around to see the rest of the development yet?"

"No," Ada said, "we've been pretty jammed up with unpacking."

The old man nodded and scratched his chin beneath the long flow of his graying beard.

"Well, there are more buildings that were to be renovated as homes. And the old manor house was supposed to be made into a common building with an office."

"Supposed to?" she asked.

"The construction company finished phase one and barely got started on phase two before the investment money dried up. They did manage to put up fencing around it, though. I'll need to get you all a key to the gate in case you need to use the phone."

As they rounded the far end of the development, they saw another seven or eight buildings on a low patch of land that was close to the water. On a nearby rise sat an old Victorian style home that looked to be in fairly good shape. The other buildings by the water were low, brown structures with marred wooden siding, missing shingles and peeling paint that were hideous to behold compared to the renovated structures that had become the homes of phase one. The grounds enclosed behind the tall, weathered chain-link fencing still bore the hapless earthen ruts from backhoes and other vehicles that had once moved around on it.

A moment later, they left Cedar Banks behind and the old '67 was motoring down the winding state route toward the town of Whitetail. They rode for a while in silence, the asphalt ribbon of road uncurling itself before them.

"So, have you lived at Cedar Banks very long?" Ada asked.

"Longer than you might imagine. I was there in the 1960s."

Noah leaned forward. "Why?"

"Well, when the WPA work camp was shut down in '43, the whole place was abandoned for a good long while. Then in the early 1960s, the Park Service decided it would make sense to use it as housing for park rangers as well as a place to provide training. That's where I came in."

"You were a park ranger?" Noah asked.

Clay nodded.

"From 1965 until 1974. Worked all the National Forests here in the Old Dominion. Worked for a long stretch in Shenandoah and then got involved with the National Battlefield Parks."

"Is that how you became a reenactor?" Ada asked.

"Nope. I was raised up in the foothills around Crozet. Near Charlottesville. Lots of history, you know. Thomas Jefferson and all that. So, I suppose I always had a liking for old things and old ways."

"Wow," Noah said. "You've been around for a long time."

Ada sighed and began to apologize for Noah, but Clay just grinned.

"Well, he calls a spade a spade, don't he? That's right, my boy. I been around a good, long while," he said, then sighed. "Longer than I care to think about some days."

After a moment of silence, Clay leaned down and turned on the radio.

"Y'all don't mind a little music, do you?"

Both Ada and her son shook their heads. "Sunshine of Your Love" by Cream poured through the truck's speakers, filling the vehicle with smooth, acid rock guitar fuzz.

After several more songs, the dark canopy of trees overhead disappeared and the sun shone bright upon the polished blue of the truck's hood. They slipped from the dark canopy of the hills into a flatland area of the valley, the road flanked on both sides by farms whose fields were bordered by acres of three-rail fencing blazing white in the sun. In the distance, they could see buildings of red brick and dark-tiled roofs.

"Is that town?" Noah asked.

"Yep. That's Whitetail in all of its glory."

Ada began rummaging through her pocketbook in search of something, mumbling about the address where she could find the school supplies.

"Don't trouble yourself, Missus Belton. You'll be wanting the School Administration Building and I know just where it is."

"Oh? How's that?"

"It's right smack in the middle of downtown. You see, Whitetail itself don't have any primary schools. Just the high school. Kids that live in town have the choice of commuting to the schools in Altavista or being homeschooled. And Altavista is quite a hike so most of the children in town and in the areas around it are homeschooled."

He looked over at Noah and gave him a reassuring nod and wink.

"So, you're in good company."

"Really?" Ada asked. "Altavista won't send buses into town?"

"Nope. You'll find that folks in Whitetail like to keep to their own," he said with a slight grin. "Like to keep it simple."

Noah and Clay sat in the truck parked in front of the School Administration Building listening to the radio. He much preferred the company of the odd old man than being stuck waiting in some office building filled with cubicles and smelling of stale coffee.

Noah had cranked the passenger window down and was taking in the lay of the land as Led Zeppelin droned on about a stairway to Heaven.

Downtown Whitetail was situated around a town square. The buildings were old and modest, mostly brick, some clapboard and Noah figured they probably looked very much the same now as they had a hundred years past. The dormant, yellowed grass of the square was populated with statues; one on each corner and another in the center of it all.

"Lots of statues," Noah said.

"Indeed."

Noah had been to Richmond once and driven down the avenue where all the monuments of the Confederate generals stood. From what he could tell, the ones in the town square were in no way as grand in scale as those but certainly every bit as ornate.

"Who are they?"

"Which ones?" Clay asked.

"Well," Noah said, considering the question, "how about the four on the corners?"

"Those are all statues of the same man."

"The same man?" Noah turned to him. "Must have been important."

Clay smiled and nodded. "Colonel William Fallkirk of the Confederate States Army. One of Whitetail's own. Each statue is a monument to a different aspect of the man he was. He's depicted as a teacher, a father, and a poet. All of which he was before he became a colonel."

"Which one's the Colonel?"

Clay leaned over and pointed.

"The farthest one there. It's hard to see."

Noah grunted a recognition as he leaned toward the windshield and squinted.

"The Colonel's statue faces north, you see. Always keeping a lookout for a Yankee invasion."

Noah turned his gaze to the old man again, his mouth screwed into a mixture of doubt and confusion.

"That's stupid. The Confederates lost the war. Anyway, didn't the North come down here to free the slaves? Like they taught us in history class?"

Clay nodded. "Mostly that's true. And rightfully so. That's the statue they didn't make of Fallkirk."

"What's that?"

"For all those good things he was, he was also a slave owner."

"Well, that don't sound so great."

"Nope," Clay said with a sigh. "History and the people who made it are . . . a bit complicated, I'm afraid. And often disappointing."

Noah considered this and was curious but nodded, satisfied for the moment, as his gaze searched over the square.

"What about the one in the middle?"

"Ah," Clay sighed and grinned, sat back against the seat. "The real hero of the war around here. That's Lizzie Amburg. But being from Eastlake, I don't suppose you know about her."

Noah was about to confess that he knew nothing about this woman or had even heard her name in history class, but then his mother came barreling out of the doors of the School Administration Building, her arms full of books and a gray backpack slung over her shoulder next to her pocketbook. With the widening grin on her face, Noah thought she must have just robbed the place.

She bumped against the passenger door and Noah threw it open wide, scooting over to give her and her treasure trove of textbooks a place to rest.

"Oh, Noah, we got the king's ransom here," she squealed as she climbed into the truck. "And I can't wait until you see these activity books! They are so cool. These beat your old school books by a mile."

She used the word *cool* in a way that was utterly unfamiliar and gratuitous and so *uncool* that it made Noah wince.

Clay grinned at him, seeming to understand.

Ada piled herself and the imposing stack of textbooks into the truck, giving a few to Noah to hold. Clay Winston pulled away from the street. The old Chevy roared to life and very soon they all watched silently as Whitetail disappeared behind them in its mirrors.

10

Saturday morning found Noah sitting in front of the television watching cartoons. The reception was poor, though, and Noah had to get up several times to adjust the rabbit ears attached to the television. It had been a constant battle ever since they moved out to Cedar Banks. Often, he had even gone to the kitchen to retrieve a fresh length of aluminum foil to wrap around the antennae, believing whatever scientific magic had improved the signal on the last go-round was in need of a refresh.

He had just gotten the rabbit ears adjusted to a good position and was no more than ten minutes or so into the new *X-Men* cartoon when the picture on the screen started rolling and fuzzing up, accompanied by bursts of static that punched through the speaker.

Noah jumped up and bent the antennae once again, although there was little improvement this time. Frustrated, he gave the faux wooden side of the television a good slap just as the front door opened and his father appeared in the doorway.

"That your TV?" he said.

Noah's eyes dropped to the floor.

"No, sir."

"So, you didn't pay for it or anything?"

Noah shook his head.

His father bent down and began removing his boots, placing them on the slab of fieldstone set by the door that his father insisted drew out and soaked up the moisture from sodden shoes. *A tidy home is a Godly home*, he always reminded his son. As he did this, the door was still open behind him and the frigid air seeped into the house.

"Well, then you ought not go clobbering it whenever you can't get the picture right."

Noah nodded.

A moment passed and his father seemed satisfied.

As Hugh stood, he turned to close the door and glanced outside into the wide, gray sky.

"It's too cloudy today. That's why the signal ain't coming through."

Noah's shoulders slumped as he released the rabbit ears.

"Why don't you come and help me this morning? We got us a little project."

Noah switched off the television. "What kind of project?"

"Come on in here with me and I'll tell you."

Hugh opened the broom closet in the living room and pulled out the broom and dustpan. He handed them to Noah, who then followed his father down the hallway.

Of the three bedrooms in the house, they had made use of only two. The third had been cluttered with boxes of files and stacks of old mail and bills that had migrated from the old place to this new one. But his mother had sorted through the mess, bagging up most of it for trash and stowing the remainder on the floor of the linen closet in the hallway. The third room was next to the master bedroom and down the hall, cater-corner to Noah's room. It was windowless and dingy, lit by a solitary, naked bulb at the center of the ceiling that Noah's father flicked on with the wall switch.

"The empty room is the project?"

Hugh nodded, surveying the tiny room and thoughtfully stroking the stubble on his chin.

"What are we going to do with it?"

"We're going to turn this into a little sanctuary."

Noah cocked his head, wrinkled his brow in confusion.

"Ain't that what we go to church for, Dad?"

"It is," Hugh said, but grimaced. "Except our Sundays at the Evening Star church are over for now, it looks like."

"How come?"

"Too far to drive every week. Too much money in gas."

Noah found it difficult to contain his excitement at this new development and did his best to feign disappointment. His father seemed to notice and smiled approvingly.

"We can still keep to worship in our own way, though, can't we?"

"Sure. I guess."

In truth, while Noah welcomed the news that they would not be returning to the Church of the Evening Star with its strange flock who were all too eager to lay hands on one another, and its sermons of hellfire and damnation, he also found the idea of his father leading Sunday worship more than a little disturbing. Not because there was anything wrong with honoring the Lord in the privacy of their own home but because he was not entirely comfortable with the way in which his father would demand they worship; this man who often shouted Bible verse at his mother while beating the tar out of her. Faith in God the Father? Noah had that. In *his own* father, not so much.

"Now go on and sweep up in there," Hugh instructed his son. "Sweep the corners and the edges of any cobwebs. I want this worship room immaculate. Understand?"

"Yes, sir."

His father walked away, toward the kitchen, leaving Noah to go about his work.

He started in the nearest corner of the room, using the broom to brush down the edges and along the wainscoting all the way to the floor. As he came to the far corner of the wall adjacent to the bathroom, he stopped and stared curiously at a crack in the wainscoting. Kneeling down, he found the crack extended beyond the ornamental trim and down the wall and through the baseboard about three feet from the corner. The crack seemed to be more or less straight up and down.

"Dad?" he called out.

After a moment, he heard his father's footfalls come down the hallway to the door and he turned.

"You seen this crack in the wall?"

Hugh stepped into the room and knelt beside his son to have a closer look.

"Lights must have been off in here when we looked over the house," he said. "This ain't gonna be cheap to fix." He ran his hand along the crack, then raised his eyebrows as the wall gave just a little.

"What in the world?"

He jammed his fingernails into the crack and pulled. The entire section swung outward on hinges hidden from sight on the other side of the small door. Inside was a dark, cold space.

"Wow," Noah said. "It's like a secret passage or something."

Hugh fixed his son with a look of disdain.

"Boy, you been watching too many of those Scrooby-Doobey cartoons."

"It's *Scooby-Doo*, Dad."

Hugh ducked his head and peered inside.

"Noah, go and fetch the flashlight from the kitchen and let's have a look."

His curiosity piqued, Noah was up and back from the kitchen in a flash, the silver casing of the flashlight clutched in his hand. He knelt and handed it to his father. They leaned lower and peered inside as he shined the light into the dark.

The flashlight illuminated a narrow space not much longer than a man and about three feet high. Its confines were lined with thin and roughly hewn metal stained dark with age and whatever had been kept there. The chamber was cold with the chill of the outside and as they breathed in, both father and son smelled the strange blend of old, charred wood and something sickly sweet that neither could name.

"What is it, Dad?" Noah asked, hearing his voice echo, tinny against the metal walls.

His father flicked the light around a little more and then drew back into the room, the overhead light shrinking his widened pupils. He sighed. "My guess is that it's an old coal storage bin."

"Coal?" Noah looked back through the walls in the direction of the living room and the brick fireplace there. "Seems pretty far away, though."

"Wouldn't have been coal for the fireplace, son," Hugh said. "It would have been for a stove of some kind. Back in the old days of the Depression, they used coal. Sometimes to heat the house but also to cook."

Noah watched his father turn thoughts over in his mind.

"Could be there used to be a stove in here."

Noah nodded, taking in the insight of his father who—every now and then—shared the kind of trivial knowledge that a normal father would.

"How are you gonna fix it?"

"Well," Hugh began, pushing on the hidden doorway and examining the friction catch that held it in place, "I don't reckon I will."

"No?"

"Might put some weather stripping around the door here to help keep the draft out and a lock to keep it closed," he said, stroking his chin in thought. "But it's a handy spot to keep things. A handy spot, indeed."

Noah watched his father as he considered it, his fingers scraping audibly against the rough stubble of his jaw. There was a twinkle in his eye that Noah did not care for.

"Hey, Dad, if this is the sanctuary, where will we sit for church?"

Hugh smiled wide.

"Lucky for us sinners, your old dad thought of everything." He stood, taking in the surroundings of the barren room as if it were a place of indescribable beauty. "I prayed about the same thing, Noah. And the Lord has provided."

It was just after two o'clock in the afternoon when they finished filling the worship room with the contents of Hugh's pickup truck. Once the room was meticulously arranged according to his father's design, there sat before them four weathered benches made of salt treated wood that looked as if they had once been part of someone's backyard picnic tables. A long wooden work bench, spattered with paint and stains and chewed with dents and gouges, became the altar and was vastly improved upon by an old dark red table cloth that Ada produced at the last minute to lay across it.

And then there was the enormous cross that all three of them had been barely able to drag into the house.

Utterly unstable, tenuously balanced upright by wooden shims placed beneath it, the cross was a thing Noah regarded as grotesque. From the expression on his mother's face, it appeared she did as well, although she spoke not a word. It had been pieced together like a quilt, formed from bits of discarded scrap metal large and small. Hugh explained that he had called upon the Christian charity of a co-worker at Kemp to weld the scraps into a solid form. It was huge and heavy and the dark metal bits were crimson with rust here and there. The edges of it were rough and serrated from the cutting torch—like the jagged teeth of some hungry beast.

Upon seeing the thing placed there in the room, Noah's father grinned wide and stretched an affectionate arm around his wife and son. At Hugh's direction, they bowed their heads in silent prayer that God would see fit to anoint this place with His blessing, and when the last Amen had been uttered, Noah was given permission to spend the afternoon however he pleased.

Noah, of course, headed straight outside.

The day was gray and cold, the sun hidden behind the thick gray of afternoon clouds so common in the days of mid-November when autumn began its downward spiral into winter. The few remaining leaves, brittle and brown and robbed of their color, rained down constantly with the chill wind that blew through the towering trees. They came to rest most often on the dry floor of the forest and other times they landed silently on the surface of the lake where Noah's gaze drifted as absently as the leaves in their falling. The many murders of crows called out among the trees, flitting about the limbs and branches.

Noah's thoughts turned to his friend Tommy. It had only been a couple of weeks since he left Cady's Run, but without Tommy at his side for a bit of play and banter, Noah's entire existence in this new place felt lackluster and droll.

He sat on the small dock that stretched out onto the lake and tried to imagine the surrounding woods being full of the monsters of the Horde. And not the normal, bloodthirsty sort, but the *berserkers*. Vile and impossibly swift versions of the Horde against whom there was almost no defense. Together, he and Tommy might be able to give them one hell of a fight, but Noah stood not a chance alone.

Unless, he thought, gripping the stick-as-weapon in his hand, *a man of quality could stand alone and turn the tide.*

But, no . . . without Tommy, Noah's imaginings fell flat, and it was not long before he gave up on them entirely, cast his weapon into the water and meandered into the woods surrounding Cedar Banks.

Careful not to let his tendency for exploration get the better of him, he stuck close to the shore this time, always keeping the lake in sight. In a shaded cove, he found a magnificent old tree that had fallen. Half of it was hidden below the water where it lay but the other half, including the base of the trunk, still clumped with dirt and roots like tentacles, spanned a good twenty feet from the shore into the water. Noah hopped onto it, testing his balance. Satisfied and confident, he walked the length of the tree and then sat down, his legs straddling the width of it and the toes of his shoes barely touching the water below as he swung them idly. He looked down into the dark water and caught flashes of fish swimming beneath the surface.

Noah searched in his jacket pocket for a stone to toss across the water. He was always spotting small rocks and picking them up, dropping them into his jacket or pants pocket where, much to his mother's dismay, they would inevitably come out in the wash. After thoroughly inspecting his jacket pockets and finding nothing, he leaned over and shoved his hand down into the pocket of his jeans. There he found a handful of small pebbles. He pinched one between his fingers and, with one eye closed and his tongue held between his teeth, Noah drew back to throw. As the whooshing sound of his nylon jacket heralded his throw and the tiny pebble went arcing out over the water, he heard an odd sound.

Though it was unclear, it was a high-toned sound that lilted with the familiar ring of one person calling another. Like when his mother would stand at the back door and holler for him to come home for supper.

Noah pitched forward and the muddy water of the cove rushed up to meet him but just before the tipping point, he locked his left arm around the fallen tree and flattened out, swinging his right leg over and to the back to counterbalance him. Now suspended over the chill water in this awkward position, his heart raced in his chest. After a few seconds, he calmed himself and pivoted on the tree to face the shore.

The woods were empty, but he was now convinced that it had been the sound of a voice. Scooting along the tree toward the shore, he considered that the reason it reminded him of his mother calling for him to come home was that it probably *was* his mother calling for him to come home.

I just got out here, he thought with some protest.

As he got closer to the shore, he stood and carefully walked the rest of the tree, then jumped off and onto the solid earth of the forest.

Weeeee, the sound came again.

Noah pricked up his ears and scanned the woods. The sound was not the wind. Nor was it his mother. He was certain of that, but there wasn't another soul around.

Weeeee . . .

He heard it again, but just barely. Was it the call of some bird? The more he considered what it could be, turning it over in his mind, the farther and fainter it sounded. So, he decided to try something different. He closed his eyes and focused on listening. At first there was only the gentle rush of the breeze, the groan of the trees swaying, the rattle and skip of leaves.

"Weeee Will? Where are—"

The moment Noah opened his eyes and began searching for the source of the words, the sound faded away. It was strange and it unnerved him a bit but his curiosity drove him deeper into the woods. Perhaps his imagination was getting the better of him. He pressed his back against a tree, wanting for shelter and hoping it might shore up his courage. He closed his eyes again and listened.

"Come on, Will. Where are you?" the words came again, clear as a bell this time.

The voice was definitely that of a child—a boy, perhaps not much younger than himself. Noah continued to listen, though there was only silence. He was about to open his eyes when he heard the voice again. Its inflection was taunting as it recited a rhyme Noah had never heard before, making a tune of it that was as lonely as a slow, mountain air played on a single fiddle. The low, mournful sound of a funeral dirge.

"Wee Willie Winkie runs through the town,
upstairs and down in his burial gown,
scratching at the window, moaning at the lock,
where are the children?
It's nigh on twelve o'clock!"

The song was familiar. Like a dissonant, twisted version of *The Itsy Bitsy Spider*. Noah found it pretty grim for a nursery rhyme and hearing it in the child's sing-song voice sent a chill through him. Another long moment of silence followed before the voice sounded again. Who was the child and who was this Will person that he was calling out to? As far as Noah knew, there were no neighbors in any direction for miles.

"There you are!"

Startled, Noah's eyes opened reflexively and as the landscape came into focus, he saw the two familiar mops of golden hair go rushing through the forest, though he heard no sound of footfalls. He considered chasing them, but who knew where he might end up if he did so.

"Don't be stupid," Noah scoffed, chastising himself. How could it be the same boys he had seen back at Cady's Run? That was on the other side of the lake. Had to be fifty miles or more. By boat, it wouldn't be such a feat, though, he supposed, and if one of them was old enough to handle a boat, it was possible.

He cast about the shore, looking for the metal hull of a john boat moored somewhere close by. Except there wasn't one.

It just didn't make any sense. Unless he was imagining them. That seemed a crazy idea but then he *was* the only one who had seen them. Noah didn't feel crazy, though. Not in the least. But if the blond boys were a trick of his mind, they weren't the first. He thought of the stinking man and that undeniable presence in his room the night before.

A primal fear stirred in him and he didn't like the explanation to which his mind kept wandering.

No such thing as ghosts, he thought.

After all, Noah had never seen a ghost in his life. The dead were dead and gone to their eternal reward—not walking the world of the living. He was sure of that. But as the wind picked up and rustled the cold trees around Ashwood Lake, Noah was disturbed by the notion that he was being watched. Invisible eyes seemed to peer at him from every shadow, and quite suddenly and in that very moment, Noah no longer felt so certain about what manner of unusual things might walk the world of the living.

11

Sunday morning, Noah joined his mother and father in the worship room and Hugh led them in prayer and a reading from the Gospel of Luke. Afterwards, they sat down to a lunch of bologna and cheese sandwiches, potato chips and soda. His mother mentioned that the cupboard was getting a little bare. They had gone through most of the food they'd brought with them a few weeks back. She also used this opportunity to broach the subject of Thanksgiving, which was just around the corner. Hugh decided there was probably enough money in the budget to allow for a modest turkey and some of the usual fixings. He also told them that his boss, Henry Kemp, had asked him to start going on some of the weekly deliveries and pickups of materials. It would mean overnight stays once a week, maybe more, and the first one would be tomorrow. They decided that would work out just fine since Ada could take the truck and drop Hugh off at work, then use it to go into Whitetail for groceries.

Noah was initially pleased as punch at the idea of his father being gone a night or two every week, but his enthusiasm was quickly darkened by the memory of the stinking man in the hallway and, to a lesser degree, the blond boys in the woods.

No such thing, he reminded himself, though he was not entirely convinced.

Beyond what he had learned in church, Noah had never thought much about ghosts or spirits or what happened after the body gave up the soul to death. He had heard it whispered, though, that ghosts were the leftovers of people who died before their time. Like fingerprints left behind, but only visible to some. He had told himself many times over the last couple of days that what he'd seen was nothing more than what his mother often called his overactive imagination. Still, it all felt real enough, at least to him.

It all left him at a strange crossroads for a young teenager; deciding between what he knew in his head and what he felt in his heart. As he wolfed down the last of his supper, he decided that a little more information might clear things up. If the things he had seen were real, he would do well to know something more about them. If there was nothing to discover, then that would tell him something, too. Either way, it would present to him a path that led out of this never-ending uncertainty.

As he cleaned up the dishes from lunch, he asked his mother if he could go with her into town the next day and visit the Whitetail Public Library while she shopped for groceries. When she asked him why, he mumbled something about looking for a book on the Civil War and the town itself, to which his mother raised a curious eyebrow. But Noah thought it best not to linger in the wake of a white lie and promptly retreated to the quiet of his bedroom.

Once there and quickly bored, Noah considered going out to explore the woods, but the memory of the blond boys and their disembodied voices were still fresh in his mind. The laughter and the sense of being watched. No, he was not yet ready to be out there again—all alone in the gloomy wilds of Cedar Banks.

12

Monday morning, after they returned from dropping off his father at Kemp Family Metalworks, Noah and his mother worked on his studies and covered geometry and history. The geometry, with all of its formulae and math, he could take or leave. He wasn't particularly good at it and never had been. But his studies of the first settlers in the New World, of things like the Magna Carta and East India Trading Company, fascinated him. In earlier grades, he always learned that these people, led by the Italian explorer, Christopher Columbus, were brave and enterprising adventurers, but the new textbook explained that many were quite the opposite. So many of them had been criminals, released from prison and the punishment of their crimes to go on that fateful expedition across the vast sea; almost a death sentence in itself. Certainly there had been bravery among some of the men but Noah now saw the noble motivations of exploration as muddied by cowardice and self-interest. It was so very long ago, though, and he wondered how anyone could claim to understand their motives for undertaking an arduous journey with such grim prospects. He found himself identifying with them in some ways, these men who had left behind all that was familiar not because it had been their preference but because they'd had no choice. Much like his coming to this place, to this house, it had been a voyage into fear, the only true and always undiscovered country.

After gulping down the last of the bologna and bread for lunch, Ada and Noah climbed into the truck to head into town. As they left Cedar Banks, they spied Clay raking dead leaves into small piles throughout the neighborhood and they waved as they passed. Then there was only the throaty growl of the old Ford as it cruised the winding roads into town. The twang of country music sang through the decrepit speakers and his mother hummed along whenever she knew the tune. The weatherman on the radio reported something about snow coming for Thanksgiving and Noah believed it. The sky was bleached bone-white day after day with clouds.

A plump librarian who wore too much makeup and a name tag that read Wynona smiled as Noah approached the resource desk.

"How can I help you, young man?"

"Yes, ma'am," he said, "I need to search for some information in old local newspapers."

"How far back?"

Noah sucked in a long breath. "Ah, um . . . "

She smiled.

"Not sure, huh?"

"No, ma'am."

The Whitetail Public Library was far more modern inside than the old brick exterior of the building suggested. It took up two floors and was packed with shelves of books along each wall and in every available space. Mixed in with the nutty aroma of the many books, the air was pungent with the metallic, burning odor of the building's baseboard heaters.

The librarian pointed to a pentagonal desk of five computer monitors.

"That's our fancy new Dynix catalog system right there. You ever use one of them before?"

Noah's school library back home had used a similar system and plus he'd taken a few Computer Science classes. He was pretty sure he could figure it out.

"Sure have," he said. "Thanks."

Before getting to his research, Noah wandered the library just to look at and touch the books. He plucked some of the ones he knew from the shelves and thumbed through their pages, his eyes flitting over the words he had already read, finding a comfort in their familiarity, like reconnecting with an old friend. How long he was at this, he had no idea, but finally he decided it was time to get back to what he came here for in the first place.

After taking a seat at one of the terminals, Noah clicked through to search the periodicals database.

He typed in *Cedar Banks*, then added others. *children, Ashwood Lake, blond, missing*. After punching the enter key, he waited while the system processed his request. The results screen displayed one digital image. When he clicked and enlarged it, he saw it was a page from the Ashwood Observer, dated July 7th, 1952. Not much of an article, it was barely more than a blurb that reported the disappearance of a family of five who had gone boating out on the lake just before a massive thunderstorm set down upon the region. The writer indicated that while it was an ill-advised time to be playing on the lake, the family had been visitors from Ohio and not at all familiar with the lake or the impact of local weather patterns.

He considered it but it just didn't feel like the right result. Noah typed in the same search string again but he added a couple variations of the name that he had heard the voice calling for in the woods.

Will, Willie, William, he typed.

This time, when the results displayed, the same article from 1952 appeared but another from the Whitetail Sentinel did as well. When he blew it up, he saw it was another similarly short piece, though this one was from August, 23rd, 1973.

A Local Mother's Plea for Information

Rosemary Carney calls upon the Whitetail community for information about her missing sons. Albemarle, aged eight, and his brother, Willie, aged twelve, were last seen just before the massive thunderstorm this past Friday in the Cedar Bay area. The boys had been in the care of their father (Miss Carney's ex-husband) as they camped by the lake in the vicinity of the old Amburg home.

If you have seen or heard from either of these boys, please contact the Sentinel *or the Rockbridge County Sheriff's Department immediately.*

Noah stared at the glowing screen.

This. This felt right . . . felt true.

He read the brief article over and over again and wondered how it was that two able-bodied boys had simply vanished.

Had they been out on the lake? That would make sense, sure, but the article hadn't mentioned anything about the boys boating on the water.

Exploring the woods, maybe? Goofing about in the thick woods in much the same way that Noah himself had been lately. But wouldn't the older of the two boys have insisted that they hunker down and wait out the weather? Storms—even the bad ones—didn't last forever, after all. Unless they'd become lost in the forest, of course.

Or perhaps something else.

Where was the ex-husband—*their father*—when the boys went missing? According to the article, the boys had been in his care when they disappeared. Beyond that, the article had made no further mention of him. What if he had taken the boys—kidnapped them—as part of some custody feud and had fled?

But what if he didn't? Noah thought. *What if his crime was even worse than stealing his own children? What if he . . .*

He didn't complete the question but, all the same, Noah's thoughts then tilted toward the worst. He imagined the murdered bodies of the boys, forgotten and lying in some remote ravine. A place nearly invisible among the many hills and hollers of this land. There they would have lain, nothing more than two dead things among many, picked at by buzzards and the occasional passing animal. Baking in the heat, soaking in the rains, only to be finally swallowed by the earth itself as the seasons and years wore on. It chilled him to think that a father could do such a thing to his own flesh and blood—but then, how many times might Noah's own father have killed him during one of his fits of rage if his mother had not been there to intervene or to take the brunt of the punishment? If killed, having been gotten rid of like a nuisance, like a pest, Noah had to wonder what dark and unknowable place might be his final resting place.

"Find anything interesting?"

He started at the sound of his mother's voice. Noah turned to see her standing next to him, arms folded, alongside Wynona the librarian.

"Sorry, Mumma," Noah said, his shoulders dropping as he fixed her with a long-practiced look of apology meant to solicit her immediate forgiveness.

"You were supposed to wait for me out front, Noah," she reminded him.

"I know, I know," he groaned. "I just lost track of time, I guess. You all done at the store then?"

"Yep. Now let's get on home before the cold things spoil."

"Thanks," Noah said to the librarian as he pushed in the chair and walked through the library beside his mother.

As Noah climbed into the truck, he glimpsed a dozen or so paper bags filled with groceries standing upright in the truck bed. It was a far more generous haul than he had imagined possible.

He and his mother motored through the quiet streets of Whitetail and then onto the roads beyond. The thin, brown bags flapped against each other, beating a rhythmic tattoo. His mother talked of the Harris Teeter and how nice it was, of the things she bought and the good deal she had gotten on the Thanksgiving Day turkey.

Noah nodded and smiled dutifully, though he was only half-listening. His thoughts dwelled on the article he'd read and the two fair-haired boys long since disappeared from Ashwood Lake.

Boys who—he was now convinced—still roamed its shores.

Once home, they brought the groceries into the house and Noah's mother cooked them the first hot, fresh meal they'd eaten since their move to Cedar Banks. Chicken and dumplings, as only Noah's mother could make them.

After he had helped with the clean-up and been excused to his room, Noah put pen to paper and began writing a letter to Tommy. The other day, Noah had heard his mother ask his father when they were going to get a phone hooked up and Hugh had replied flatly that it wouldn't be any time soon.

"What do we need one for, anyhow?" his father had asked further.

It was hard to disagree. Hugh Belton had no friends to speak of and no one to contact outside of work, so the addition of a phone bill was a needless strain on what was an already tight family budget.

With no hope of a phone call anywhere in the near future, a written letter was Noah's only hope for contact with the outside world. In the letter, Noah briefly detailed for Tommy the lonely and boring nature of the new place but also made a point to tell him that he had again seen *the Von Trapp twins*, as Tommy had named them. He deliberately left out any mention of his research and the revelation that there was no possibility the blond boys he had first seen weeks ago could be alive. Nor did he include any account of the stinking man he had seen outside of his room. Talk of phantom children and filthy ghosts would only make Tommy wonder if his best friend had flipped his lid.

After he closed the letter and addressed it, sealed it in an envelope and laid it on his dresser, he slid under the bed covers and lay there listening to the fuzzy, muted sounds of the TV in the living room until he fell asleep.

13

Having finished the dishes, Ada changed into her nightgown and shuffled over to the couch, where she put her feet up, just as fat and happy as could be. Hugh wouldn't be home tonight and she couldn't imagine a better way to treat herself after that meal than to lazily hold down the couch and watch trashy prime time melodramas.

Halfway into an episode of Knot's Landing, though, she was drifting off, her eyelids impossibly heavy. It wasn't long before she was asleep and dreaming.

Reclined in awkward repose on the couch, Ada's snoring roared to a crescendo and she woke suddenly with a loud and final snort. She sat upright and massaged her eyes, crusted with sleep. The television was still on, filling the room with its pale, blue light while a man on the screen wearing a headset and a polo shirt blathered on about the must-have nature of a futuristic new cleaning product. Her mouth was dry and her belly tight and rumbly, a touch upset from the gluttonous supper they'd consumed.

She rose and went to the kitchen, fetched a glass from the cabinet and opened the refrigerator. She poured a glass of cold milk to help settle her stomach. It seemed suddenly chilly in the kitchen and she wondered for a moment if the heat had gone out. But her thoughts were slow and murky.

Had she been dreaming? Yes. Dreaming about the old place at Cady's Run. She was navigating through the narrow lanes between the trailer homes on a bicycle—a ten-speed like the one she'd had as a teenager—when she glimpsed Nick Wren, Tommy's dad, out back of his trailer, splitting wood. At second glance, though, Ada realized it was not his trailer but hers. Sweaty and shirtless in the summer heat, he raised the axe and brought it down over and over again as lengths of wood cracked and fell away. She knew she shouldn't be staring but when his eyes met hers, she found it impossible to look away. Butterflies and an old familiar feeling filled her belly but all she could think was, *What if Hugh comes home?* Then she had woke.

Ada took another sip of milk, the cold thickness of it running down her throat and into her insides, already beginning to soothe the dull ache. She heard a footfall behind her and pulled the glass from her lips. In an instant, Hugh's tall, solid frame snuggled up against her from behind, resting his hands on her hips.

"Hey, honey," she whispered into the darkness, "got home early from your run up north, I see. Didn't even hear you come in."

The only response was his deep, lingering breath that tossed about the finest of her hairs and tickled the back of her neck.

She placed her right hand on his and as she did, it meandered down her leg to the lace hem of her nightgown and pulled it upward toward her waist. The unusually tender touch of his fingers and the cotton cloth raised gooseflesh on her skin. She grew warm between her thighs and smiled, resting her head against his chest. He pressed tighter against her where, through the thin fabric of her nightgown, he grew stiff and ready against her backside.

His hand slipped down between her legs and hers followed, lying atop his strong, bony and calloused fingers as they nestled into the thick patch of hair and roused waves of pleasure that cascaded up her body.

"Mmmm," she moaned, then inquired playfully, "what's gotten into you tonight, husband?"

When was the last time he had touched her in this way, if ever? In the beginning, there had been some meager amount of passion but as the years of their marriage wore on, their couplings became less and less frequent—and became uninspired and cold. Practically rote. Mechanical and predictable.

Nothing like this.

Her loins trembled with a mounting sensation that had been long absent.

Behind her, the pace of his breaths quickened in her ear and she pressed back against him even as a waft of something unpleasant drifted into her nose.

"What've they had you doing up there, Hugh?" she teased. "You smell like a grave."

A mischievous and guttural chuckle was his only reply as their conjoined fingers played inside of her. It was all so unlike him; the urgency of his touch, the willingness to let her fingers accompany and guide his own. Strange, yes, but an opportunity she would not waste.

She tipped her drinking glass back to finish it, meaning to turn and kiss him, then draw him down the hallway into the bedroom to see what other surprises he might have in store. But as she gulped the last of the milk, there was the faint buzzing sound of a single housefly that landed on her finger and as the cool liquid met with her tongue, it was suddenly bitter and sour and unwelcome.

Instinctively, she lurched forward and spat the rancid milk out onto the floor.

She heard another low snigger from behind her as she summoned the balance of saliva in her mouth and spat onto the floor again. The stench of it, coupled with Hugh's body odor was bad enough, but then she detected another aroma she hadn't noticed before; the sweet but acrid smell of tobacco.

"Damn, Hugh, ain't nothing funny about that. I just bought this milk!" She slammed the glass down on the nearby countertop.

Now fully awake and lucid, she became aware of two things. The first was that she had just cursed in his presence—a thing that was not looked kindly upon—and the second was the puddle of regurgitated milk on the floor, spatters of it gleaming on the surface of the lower cabinets in the cold light of the open refrigerator. A mess the likes of which would surely bring swift and brutal retribution from her husband.

Ada winced in anticipation of the coming blow, grabbed a dish towel from the countertop, bent low, and began swiping at the milk on the floor. Squatting, she sopped and wiped and heard not a word out of his mouth. She turned her head to see what sort of condemning expression he wore on his face, but Hugh was not there.

She was alone in the kitchen.

Ada looked back down at the mess she had been cleaning and found the remaining puddle and the entire kitchen floor speckled with plump, black flies that buzzed and moved erratically.

So many of them. They covered not only the floor, but the cabinets as well. She fought back a rising urge to be sick, then spun around, searching for someone there, something to make sense of this strangeness—but there was no one. When she looked again at the floor and the cabinets, the flies were gone and their buzzing had been replaced by the gentle hum of the refrigerator's compressor cycling on.

Ada stood absolutely still and scanned the kitchen, illuminated by bright flashes from the television. Apart from the mess on the floor, nothing seemed amiss or out of place. Yet she could not shake a lurking sensation that pricked up the hairs on the back of her neck and made her feel ill at ease.

Peering out of the kitchen window at the driveway, the floodlights illuminated only the stippled surface of the gravel and Hugh's truck that she had driven into town earlier. She tiptoed throughout the house, checking the doors, and found them locked just as she had left them. Further exploration revealed her son sleeping peacefully and alone and the queen mattress in the master bedroom empty and undisturbed by anyone. Her husband's boots were not standing by the front entrance and the coat rack was empty.

She looked back to the kitchen. Perhaps it had been a waking dream. Perhaps she had imagined it all.

She returned to deal with the spilled milk, flicking on the overhead light. As she squatted to clean up, she winced at a twinge of pain between her legs; long hairs that had stuck to her thighs.

That part had certainly been real, she realized, though it came as no comfort. Maybe she'd just been sleepwalking. A deep, abiding sleep filled with a sexual dream which she had unknowingly acted out. After all, it had all started with her dream about Nick Wren and had escalated from there. Unusual, maybe, but not impossible.

It might have been enough to explain it and convince her were it not for the stench of an odorous man mixed with tobacco smoke that lingered heavy in the air and tickled her nose.

Flicking off the kitchen light and then the television, she checked on Noah once more and padded down the hallway to her bedroom. The alarm clock by the bed indicated it was just after three in the morning. She crawled beneath the covers, though she kept the bedside table lamp on.

For the rest of that night, Ada lay in bed but she barely slept.

14

Hugh returned from his run up north in a particularly foul disposition. He walked through the front door, shaking off the late November chill as he stepped out of his work boots. He muttered a terse greeting under his breath and took immediately to the couch, turned on the evening news and grumbled about every story that came across the screen.

Ada had actually been looking forward to his return,

hoping his presence would tether her mind to normal, everyday things and that the strange events of the previous night would recede into the background.

When suppertime came, he complained that the London broil she made was tough and barely edible, even though he stuffed heaping forkfuls of the meat into his greedy mouth. She simply apologized and shared a few cautionary looks with her son over their plates as they ate in silence.

As they dressed for bed, she asked him what was the matter. He offered that his foul mood was a result of the stupidity of certain people at work as well as their supplier in Pennsylvania. Because they didn't have all the materials on-hand as promised, he would need to make another trip later in the week.

"Not on Thanksgiving, I hope?"

"I suppose not but probably right after."

As she slipped beneath the covers, exhausted, Hugh sat on his side of the bed and stared wordlessly down at the floor for a few moments before declaring that it was wrong for him to be so glum and that he would make an effort to be more cheerful in the coming days before the holiday.

Ada wondered how he could be so caustic and cruel most of the time and, at other rarer times, so sweet and broken. He was a complicated man, her Hugh. Taking heart in this rare display of frailty from him, she welcomed him into bed with open arms and snuggled against him until she fell into a deep sleep.

Ada was snoring softly but Hugh's mind would not settle. The things that troubled him swirled about, accosting him like a swarm of gnats. The move to Whitetail had been a good decision. There was no denying that. But settling into his new job was taking more time and effort than he had hoped and it seemed that every day brought with it a new responsibility he hadn't signed on for. How many different hats could one man wear? Technician, supply clerk, truck driver. And Wally Jackson—that uppity bastard foreman— was always on Hugh about something or other.

Adding to that was the trouble with Noah. His teenaged son seemed to be listing off-course since coming to this place—becoming more contrary, more obstinate. Both work and home were spinning out of Hugh's control and he seemed powerless to right these things. He wasn't even sure he knew how.

His own mother and father would never have let it get to this point. No, indeed. Mason and Lucinda Belton had run a tight ship when Hugh was a boy. It stood to reason, too, with Hugh and his three brothers in the house—boys as wild as the devil urged them to be. Whenever one of the boys stepped out of line, there were consequences. Hugh had never been grounded. Not unless being grounded was the same as being unable to leave his own bed for a day because he was waiting for the bruises on his swollen legs to mellow.

Good ol' Black Billy.

Hugh had received the business end of that thing far more often than he'd given it. Hell, his mother and father used to take turns with it while whooping their boys. They passed it back and forth like it was a game, hollering and cracking wise. The club was a lot harder in those days, too, which is why Hugh took to oiling it. He remembered the feeling of that leather club, still hot in his young hands from being thrust against his flesh. Hot as the throbbing welts across his back and legs.

With his father, discipline and respect had not been commanded only in the home, though. Mason Belton would not be taking it on the chin at work the way Hugh was. Whether it was a foreman like Wally Jackson or another man on the floor working beside him, it wouldn't have mattered. Had he been disrespected, his father would have smiled through it and said not a cross word to anyone.

But when the whistle blew at the end of the day, he would have gone to see that man with Black Billy strapped to his ankle beneath his dungarees. And he would have made an example of him. One for everyone to see the next day.

That's why no one ever played his old man for a fool. Maybe Hugh hadn't learned that lesson well enough. Maybe, after all these years and the old man now nothing but bones in his grave, Hugh still had something to learn. He'd been too loose, too unsure of himself lately. In all areas of his life. It was never too late to do better, though— wasn't that true?

The next man at the shop to cause him hardship better be made of damned stern stuff.

Hugh peered over his shoulder at Ada sleeping on the other side of the bed and sneered.

Yep, he thought. *Time to tighten up on a few things.*

15

The following Wednesday evening, to Ada's disappointment, Hugh's demeanor was even worse than before and that black mood stretched all the way to the morning of Thanksgiving Day, when he rose early from bed and announced over breakfast that he had to go into the shop for half a day.

"The press brake quit on 'em at quitting time yesterday and Mr. Kemp's got it in his head that I'm his *boy*, I reckon," he spat between swallows of scrambled eggs. "Especially since that damn Wally was supposed to be on the schedule for today. Scratched me in there as soon as something went wrong yesterday."

"That don't seem fair," Ada offered. "Can he do that?"

Hugh scoffed.

"Wally's the foreman. He can schedule whoever he wants *whenever* he wants. Or that's what the sonofabitch thinks anyway."

Hugh pushed back from the table and went into the living room where he laced on his boots and buttoned his denim coat.

"I'm off," he barked and stepped into the cold, clear day, slamming the door behind him.

Ada jumped at the sound.

They watched the truck disappear down the road, then Ada ushered her son into the kitchen to get started.

She was on a mission today.

While Hugh was at work, they were going to create the most perfect Thanksgiving supper there ever was.

Noah, who was not so handy in the kitchen as he supposed his mother would like, was charged with peeling the spuds for the mashed potatoes. He did so with no small amount of protest, for he was eager to go tramping about the woods around the lake. At first, he carved the brown skin from the vegetables quickly and carelessly but he was not skilled with the peeler and when his mother saw him once nearly take off the tip of his thumb, she scolded him, telling him that if he lopped off a finger today, it would be lost forever because there was no doctor quickly available out in these parts.

"Your father needs a good Thanksgiving supper to come home to," she explained as she mixed the creamed corn pudding together. "He needs something to raise his spirits."

Noah nodded and grudgingly continued peeling the spuds.

A few minutes later, he noted the rhythmic thwack of the wooden spoon against the plastic mixing bowl his mother was working in had ceased. He looked up from his own doings and found her fixing him with a deadly earnest look.

"We *need* your father's spirits raised. Understand?"

In his simple and selfish desire to not be here—not for any of this—he had forgotten that the man's slightest displeasure with the meal would likely spoil the holiday for them all.

"Yes, ma'am." He nodded and returned to the task at hand. "I understand."

The meal was finished—completed to perfection—an hour before Hugh came rumbling down the driveway at half past six. With the help of her son, Ada scrambled to remove the dishes keeping warm in the oven and place them onto the kitchen table.

At the last minute, as Hugh trudged up the steps toward the front door, Noah produced the pack of strike-anywhere matches from the kitchen and lit the two tall, white candles in their pewter holders. With everything set, Ada summoned Noah to stand by her side. Together, they waited, their heads held high.

Hugh sauntered in and removed his boots. He didn't even turn to look into the room but slammed something metallic down on the table by the door. Peeking over the pass-through, Ada could see it was a six-pack of beer, now reduced to three cans still strung together by their plastic loops.

She exchanged a nervous look with her son and swallowed hard. Drinking, for Hugh, was unusual, but drinking before coming home was unheard of.

Hugh kicked off a boot and tossed it haphazardly to the side. "What's for supper?"

"Turkey and all the fixings," she replied, forcing a smile.

He stepped clumsily out of his left boot, almost tripping over it, and staggered toward them.

God Almighty, Ada thought, *he drove home like this?*

"Happy Thanksgiving, honey!" Ada stepped aside,

arms outstretched to reveal the Rockwellian feast on the table.

A heaping bowl of mashed potatoes was flanked by a casserole dish full of corn pudding. Close by, an even sheen of butter shimmered atop a pile of cornbread stuffing and lingering at the edge was a bowl of cranberry sauce. It wasn't homemade as Ada would have done it but from the can and dressed up just as Hugh preferred, the way his mother had done it. In the center of the table was a perfect, golden-brown turkey from which steam still rose and a boat of brown gravy sat beside it.

"Well!" Hugh bellowed, sudden and loud. "Happy Thanksgiving indeed!"

He tore a can of beer from the six-pack and shuffled over to the table.

"Though," he began as he pulled his chair, "someone ought to remind old Mister Kemp of that fact."

Ada and her son pulled out their chairs and sat down with him, exchanging concerned looks that escaped Hugh's notice.

Her husband was reaching across the table to the bowl of dressing when they instinctively clasped their hands and bowed their heads for prayer.

Hugh ran his tongue over his lips to wet them and did likewise.

"Son, you say the blessing," he slurred.

Noah looked up in surprise. He had never been asked to say the blessing. Never.

"Me?"

For a moment, his father seemed not to notice the question. Hugh fingered the can of beer until it opened with a pop and hiss and then lifted it to his lips, taking a long pull.

"Well, Noah," he said, cocking his head at the boy, "it is said that a little child shall lead them."

Noah sat still, hands clasped.

"So, then lead us."

Ada cut her eyes at her husband. He was badgering the boy to say grace because otherwise Hugh would just slur his way through it to his own embarrassment.

Noah spoke an awkward grace, aped as best he could manage from the nightly utterings of his father, and then they passed bowls and plates between them to pile them high with the side dishes. Meanwhile, taking up the task of carving the turkey as was tradition, Hugh leaned over the table and hacked and sawed at the bird as if it had personally offended him and owed him a blood debt. The portions came to their plates ragged and poorly butchered, but neither Ada nor Noah uttered a word of criticism or complaint. They simply ate and made small, insignificant conversation.

"Maybe next year we could fry a turkey, Dad," Noah said.

His father nodded but said nothing.

"Tommy and his dad fried one. Year before last. For Christmas, I think it was. They said it was awesome."

The turkey leg that Hugh had been gnawing on hit the plate with an audible clank and both Noah and his mother looked up.

"There it is." Hugh spat the words, his eyes downcast and staring absently at the mutilated bird at the center of the table. "Perfect Nick Wren and his perfect fucking life."

Despite the fact that Hugh had never been one to run afoul of the law, he had no great affection for Deputy Wren. His being a police officer was the only thing that had kept Hugh from openly displaying his contempt for the man.

"Perfect Nick's got himself a perfect turkey. You hear that, Ada?" Hugh said, his glassy eyes cutting over at her.

She looked down at her food, scraping bits of stuffing around on her plate. Her face reddened and out of the side of her eye, she gave Noah a look that was meant to keep him in check.

"No," Noah said, "I didn't mean—"

"There something wrong with the turkey your mother's done spent all day cooking?"

Noah trembled at Hugh's booming voice. He looked across the table and managed a slow shake of his head.

"Hugh," Ada said, a soothing and almost musical tone to her voice. "He's just saying—"

"Shut your face, woman," Hugh screamed, leaning into the table toward her so much that it seemed he might come across it. "Sounds to me like our boy here is ashamed of where he comes from."

"Where I come from," Noah muttered, tilting his head back and running his eyes across the ceiling as if searching for an answer from above. He trembled, though Ada had the sense that it was no longer with fear. Her son's paralyzing dread of his father was now being outmatched by frustration and anger. Hot tears of rage welled in his eyes and Ada watched in horror as the boy's temperance was drowned in them.

"Jesus Christ, Dad!" Noah shouted, rising to his feet at the supper table. "Tommy and his dad are from the same shitty trailer park we lived in. They ain't no more or less perfect than we are. But you know what? I bet at least they're happy!"

There was a brief and baleful moment where all of them suddenly understood the gravity of the words exchanged between Noah and his father, and in that heavy and breathless silence, their eyes met. Ada hung her head.

And then there was only the violence.

In a lightning second, Hugh overturned the supper table and Noah stumbled backward. He fell to the floor, the weight of the wooden table pressing against him. Warm gravy dripped down his face and he spat away a smattering of mashed potatoes. Hugh was standing when Noah tried to push against the table to get from underneath of it but his hand slipped on a thick smear of cranberry jelly. The hysterical cries of his mother filled the room, pleading with his father. She threw herself between them. Noah lay there flat on his back and staring up at the warring gods that were his parents, grappling with one another in a storm of growls and curses.

Hugh got an arm underneath his wife, and tossed her over the upturned table. She landed hard on the kitchen floor and smacked her head against the cabinets. The floor was a minefield of broken dishes and spilled, smeared food. The Thanksgiving turkey was the only thing still somewhat intact where it had landed near the base of the fridge.

A hope that his father would slip on something and fall entered Noah's mind but that was instantly extinguished as Hugh reached down to his ankle. He drew Black Billy from its sheath and glared at his son.

"Blaspheme and raise your voice to me? In my fucking *house?* You ungrateful, heathen cur."

His father came striding toward him and the blows fell immediately, Hugh's eyes red with unchained fury.

Again and again, Noah's flesh and bones seared with pain under Black Billy's sting. He crossed his hands against his face, curled into a ball and hoped for an end that would not come. Somewhere behind him, his mother screamed and pleaded for mercy.

"Thou shalt chasten thy son with the rod," Noah's father roared as he raised the club high in the air and brought it down. "And deliver his soul from Hell."

Ceaselessly, his father throttled him, repeating the phrase over and over again. His mother's cries went unheeded for many minutes until his father eventually stopped, owing more to fatigue than any sense of restraint.

Noah's arms went limp on the floor and he watched his father walk away. He heard the jingle of keys as he plucked them from the table by the door and he thought then that perhaps the punishment was at an end and that his father would climb into the truck and go tearing down the road, leaving them alone at last. He struggled to raise his head, but his muscles were too sore. Sharp pains racked his body whenever he moved. Then his vision went quickly gray, then black and the world disappeared.

When his eyes fluttered open, the first thing he heard was his mother's voice, though it was shrill and still full of anguish. As his sight cleared, Noah saw his father grasping his right leg by the ankle with one hand and dragging him down the hallway toward the worship room.

"What are you doing?" his mother sobbed, following them at a distance. "Please, Hugh! Please stop this right now."

"Don't question me, Ada. This is for the boy's own good."

Noah could see the twisted, pock-marked metal of the cross lingering at the edge of his vision. They'd made it into the worship room. His father let go of his leg and it dropped to the floor with a thud.

His father knelt by the wall, fumbling with something. Noah was too overcome with pain to see exactly what, though, and the world was going gray again. He fought to hold on. Then he was being dragged again. Dragged and then shoved. Not into another room but into a cold, dark space that instantly closed in around him.

"Please, no," his mother whimpered in the background.

With the heel of his boot, his father gave Noah one last nudge and then the square of light spilling in from the worship room was gone and he was plunged into blackness.

His father had locked him in that odd little space in the worship room. This awareness came rushing to him on waves of primal, choking fear. The crawlspace. The secret place.

16

Ada stood by and wept into her hands as Hugh clicked the padlock closed on the crawlspace door. He brushed bits of food from his clothes and looked long at the metal cross against the far wall of the room.

"I'm sorry, Dad," Noah uttered, his voice quaking.

Hugh barked his reply. "What are you sorry for, son?"

"I . . . I'm . . . scared, Dad. What is it? Please just tell me and I'll apologize for it, whatever it is."

Her husband hung his head and shook it slowly. "It pains me to do this, Noah. It truly does. But if you have to ask, then it's not yet time for forgiveness."

"Don't . . . don't leave me in here, Dad. I'm sorry . . . so sorry . . ."

Ada buried her face in her hands again and tears streamed down her cheeks.

The mania in Hugh's eyes had begun to subside and was slowly replaced by a haunted look. He strode out of the room and down the hallway. Ada turned, watched him go.

"What's he supposed to do in there, Hugh?"

Her husband paused a moment, his tall form framed by the hallway darkening in the gray afternoon light. He turned his head, but did not look her in the eyes.

"Pray."

Then he was off, tramping through the house. His keys rattled in his hand and she heard him pulling on his boots just before he opened and then slammed the front door behind him.

From inside the crawlspace, she heard Noah's voice call out, timid and tiny and shrunken with sobs of fear.

"Sorry . . . I'm sorry . . . I . . ." she heard him say, and then nothing, only a shuffling of movement inside the wall.

Then her son screamed.

Her eyes widened and the tears halted their falling as she stared at the crawlspace door.

"Noah?" she called to him. "Noah, are you all right?"

But there came no coherent reply, no words formed on trembling lips. Only unhinged cries of absolute and all-consuming terror.

Something was *wrong*—something even more terrible than Hugh's cruel punishment.

Without regard to her husband or what he might do about her interference, she tore out of the room and searched for something she could use to open the lock. Hugh had the key, of course, and she had no earthly idea how to pick a lock. She needed something to break it. Ada scanned the room and her gaze landed on the stone slab by the door that they placed their shoes on. With some effort, she lifted it and held it against her chest as she shuffled down the hallway to the worship room, the horror of her child's screams urging her on.

Standing in front of the small door, she tightened her grip on the slab and then pushed outward and down. It completely missed the lock but opened a gash in the wood as it fell against it. Kneeling down, she took it up and tried again, more careful and deliberate in her movements this time. It struck the padlock and came to rest on the floor. The lock was still intact. The slab had connected with it but had done nothing other than pull the latch away from the wood of the door. She could see the threads of screws and splinters of mangled plywood poking out.

Inside, Noah was flailing, his arms and legs striking against the chamber as if he were being eaten alive.

To hell with this, she thought. The weight of the slab had dislodged the latch. What she needed now was something to pry the entire latch from the door.

Snapping upright, she raced into the kitchen to search for something that would be up to the task. She pulled open drawer after drawer and considered the contents. Flimsy kitchen knives that would break at their handles, plastic spoons that would bend and snap. Nothing. Nothing at all.

Then her eyes fell on the long-handled, cast iron ladle

that'd been her grandmother's. The one she had held onto for sentimental reasons but never used because it was so heavy and unwieldy. Snatching it from the drawer, she ran back into the worship room where her son's anguished wailing still rang from inside the wall.

She jammed the handle of the ladle between the arm of the latch and the wooden door and pulled down. The latch came forward and more threads of the screws edged out of the wood. So, she repeated this action again and again.

On the fifth pull, the wood cracked, the screws ripped free, and the latch and padlock came away, swinging limply against the wall. She pulled the door open and saw Noah's body. He writhed and hollered, hands and legs thrusting about in the darkness. She reached in and dragged him out of the dark cavity and into the light.

Mixed with the strong smell of urine, there was a lingering odor of sulfur and she noticed a blackened twig clutched in the red and swollen fingers of his right hand, the remains of a match that had burned to the quick and seared his skin. The moment she touched him, his head lolled to the side, limp, as she pulled him toward her. She had never seen such a horribly vacant look in her son's eyes before.

"Noah?" she said, her voice shaking. "Son?"

The boy's eyes fluttered a moment and then closed.

Scooping him up into her arms—no easy task for a boy his age and size—she fled the room and the dark, yawning chamber in the wall. Ada skittered into her bedroom. Once there, she shut and locked the door behind her and sat on the bed, holding her son in her arms.

What a Godawful mess her husband had made of him.

As beaten and bruised as he was, though, his chest still rose and fell with steady breaths and his eyes rolled back and forth beneath their lids, dreaming. She sat there on the edge of the bed, cradling her fourteen-year-old son just as she had when he was a babe.

The tears came again but she did not sob. Anger was growing inside of her and she whispered to the empty room.

"Oh, Noah. Noah, I'm so sorry. I should have stopped this a long time ago, I know I should have."

Ada wiped the sweat and grime from her boy's face and ran her fingers over his scalp and through the fiery red hair that crowned it.

In the quiet of the house, she heard the creak of the floorboards in the hallway outside of the room and the single footfall of a heavy, booted foot. She looked up at the door and burned a hole through it with her eyes.

"You stay the hell away from us, Hugh," she seethed. "You hear me, you sonofabitch? You stay the hell away from me and my son!"

But there came no retort, nor apology from the other side of the door and she was beginning to wonder what he was playing at when a familiar and revolting stench drifted into the room, like smoke, from beneath the door.

Whatever had happened in the kitchen the other night, it hadn't been a dream. The thing that had touched her, that had soured the milk with its foul presence—it was back.

It was here.

Her eyes widened as a new and separate terror closed its black fingers around her heart. She held Noah tighter to her and buried her face in his chest. Would it come for them—that thing out in the hallway? Would it open the door and finish what Hugh had begun?

Considering how she might escape, Ada turned to the window. Outside, the sun had disappeared and night was on the world. An escape into darkness was no escape at all. They had nowhere to go, nowhere to run and no one to whom they could turn. She had never felt so woefully alone as she did in that moment, she and her only child beset on all sides by monsters.

There was another movement in the hall and the sickly

sweet tobacco aroma seeped in further beneath the threshold. She looked up and watched the doorknob rattle back and forth as something on the other side tried to turn it.

Shaking uncontrollably, she screamed, "Leave us alone!"

The walls of the house seemed to swell inward, encroaching upon them as if to remind her that within its confines there was no safe harbor. From the other side of the door, there came a low and malevolent sniggering.

PART II:
TORMENT

"We think cag'd birds sing, when indeed they cry."
– John Webster, *The White Devil*

17

IT WAS STILL dark when Ada woke with chalky lines of dried tears like the threads of a spider's web stretched across her face. Exhausted from the fracas with Hugh and then the terrible presence that followed it, she had cried herself into a brief and restless sleep. By the clock, three hours had passed as she and Noah dozed on the bed alongside one another.

Ada rose and approached her bedroom door with slow, careful steps, reaching out a shaking hand. The fear from before was still with her, still lingering. She recalled the doorknob turning back and forth, the very walls looming larger and darker.

Rushing forward, she unlocked the door and swung it open. The house beyond was quiet, peaceful even. Closing the door, she stumbled back, sat on the edge of the bed and studied Noah.

He was soaked in his own urine, the acrid and septic aroma stinging the edges of her eyes. In the tub, she drew a hot bath and removed his clothes, lowered him into the water, and washed him gently. She spoke to him, hoping for a response but Noah's eyes stared blankly forward whenever they fluttered open. She knew that her son was not fond of tight, cramped spaces, but she had to wonder what could have gone on inside his mind that had impacted him so.

Then again, Hugh's tirade would have been more than enough for most any child. But something had finally snapped in her son, causing him to withdraw deep into the recesses of his mind. Her thoughts turned to fears of a grim future for her child as an unresponsive, barely functional patient in a mental ward where he would live out the rest of his life trapped inside himself. But she told herself she was just being silly, that he would snap out of it, that he was just retreating to a safe place after all that had happened.

He'll be fine. He just needs time.

She had to focus on things she could control and things she could understand and right now that meant getting her boy out of the tub and into some dry clothes.

What if Hugh comes back? she thought. Then, even worse, *What if he's already here?*

Leaving Noah in the tub for a moment, she stepped into the hallway. She was confident that the entity . . . the stinking man . . . was gone, but what did she know of such things? It could be lying in wait, invisible and intangible, part of a shadow on the wall. She stepped quickly into Noah's room and retrieved some sweat pants and a t-shirt from his closet. Her eye caught a glint of moonlight on an aluminum baseball bat that leaned against one of his bookshelves. She grabbed it and scurried off.

After drying and dressing her son, she settled him into her bed and pulled the covers around him. Leaning down, she brushed the damp hair from his forehead and kissed it, whispering good night to him. To God above she offered an unspoken prayer that Noah would be more himself come the morning and also asked the Lord to see them through these evil times.

With the lamp on, she sat up in bed and listened to the gentle rhythm of her son's slumberous breath. The baseball bat lay across her lap and her hands were clenched tight on it, her eyes glued to the locked door. She managed a wry scoff. It was ridiculous—her sitting here in bed, holding onto a fourteen-year-old's toy for a weapon against something which she had no idea how to defend herself.

Surely the presence, the phantom, the odorous thing—whatever it was—would not be the least bit intimidated by the Louisville Slugger.

But it might make Hugh think twice, and that was the threat that truly concerned her. He had done far more harm to her and her child than some haint in the night. In her mind, she saw Hugh stumbling his way toward the room after a long night at the bar, ready for round two. If that happened, she would give him the fight he was looking for and with that baseball bat she would split his head wide open. The specter of Hugh Belton, more than anything, was what kept her awake and vigilant all through the remainder of that night.

As soon as the sun rose enough to fill the house with its dim, amber light, Ada slipped down the hallway to survey the wreckage from the melee the night before.

Still a little rattled, she half-expected to find Hugh on the couch, sleeping it off. What would she do then? Retrieve the aluminum bat and end it right then and there without a fight and without having to watch the light go out of his eyes? Something primal in her demanded it, but what good would she be to her son locked up in the state penitentiary for murder?

Besides, the couch was empty and Hugh was nowhere in sight.

The kitchen was a disaster. There was the overturned table with its legs in the air, the broken plates scattered around it, food cast about on the floor and spattered on cabinets. The air still smelled of the classic Thanksgiving feast it had begun as and this made her stomach growl, though the thought of eating in the midst of such a mess made her feel nauseated. She had to get it cleaned up and the house back in order. She had to focus on things she could control.

She checked on Noah and found him resting easy. As she stepped away, the floor creaking and popping beneath her foot, Noah stirred.

"Mumma?"

She closed her eyes, awash in relief and nearly brought to tears.

"Just me, baby," she said. "Get some rest. You want anything?"

He shook his head and closed his eyes, drifting off again. Ada was encouraged to see Noah had come out of his stupor, though she knew she would need to watch him closely.

She spent most of the morning on her hands and knees, sopping up spilled gravy and scooping the remains of supper onto broken plates bound for the trash. She mopped the floor and wiped down the counters, the walls and even some of the ceiling where food had been launched high into the air when Hugh flipped the table over on them. She opened the washing machine set into the alcove in the hallway and tossed in a handful of wet and soiled kitchen towels.

Out of the corner of her eye, the worship room lingered, silent. A gust of cold wind rushed out of the room and across her legs. Closing the washer, she went to the threshold and saw the crawlspace door still ajar, an open mouth into the bowels of the house from which the chill air came. She would need to close it back up somehow, but Ada could not bring herself to approach it. She looked long at the squat, black space and a nameless shiver of dread washed over her. After a moment, she mustered some courage, grabbed hold of one of the benches and slid it over next to the door. She knelt down and stared into it. There was nothing inside but freezing winter air and the remaining smell of the matches that Noah had lit, a few of which lay scattered and burnt on the metal floor of the space. Slamming the small door shut, she dragged the bench over and pushed it tight against the door. She stood and wiped her hands down her jeans. That would do for now.

Ada closed the worship room door and headed back toward the kitchen.

"Mumma, are you all right?" she heard her son ask.

She turned to find him standing at her bedroom door and warm tears of relief came to the edges of her eyes.

They sat across from each other at the table. Ada drank sparsely from her cup of coffee while Noah picked at his bowl of soggy cereal.

"You're not hungry?" she asked.

He shrugged and glanced out the kitchen window to the vacant space in the driveway where Hugh's truck would be.

"Do you remember me taking you to my room last night, son?"

He shook his head. "Not until I woke up this morning," he said.

It didn't surprise her. Noah had been catatonic when she delivered him from the crawlspace and had remained so, even after the bath. At the time, it had frightened her to the marrow to see him like that but she was grateful he didn't remember being there when the weird thing had come calling at the bedroom door. With everything else, he didn't need the added burden of that memory—whatever the thing was.

"Do you remember your father putting you—"

"I remember that," he said.

She looked down into the black depths of her coffee. When she looked up again, she searched his eyes, searched for some way to connect, but Noah was looking out the window again. She couldn't see them but she knew that beneath his clothes, her son's bruises must be throbbing.

"I'll get you some Tylenol," she said, pushing the chair back.

"No," he replied.

When she looked at his eyes, she saw something there, a deep and abiding pain that no mother should ever have to see in her child. A pain that belonged to someone far older.

"What's it gonna take, Mumma?"

She pretended to be baffled but she knew exactly what he meant.

"To call someone . . . for help," he continued. "Or maybe we could just leave."

"Noah, I . . ." she tried but couldn't find the words. She stared at him, stymied for a moment.

"It's not easy, Noah. It's not easy to leave someone," she finally said.

He looked askance at her, grimacing and doubtful.

Over the years, Ada had imagined this conversation. It was coming to her too soon, though. Now was not the time. She could lie and deflect as she often did. She was practiced at it by now, after all.

Or she could be honest with him for once.

"I can't leave your father," she said. "Not for a while anyway."

"Why not?"

She took a deep breath.

"He'll say one thing and you and me will say another," she explained. "And the judge won't know what to make of it so he'll do what he thinks is in your best interest and send you to a foster family, Noah. A *foster family* . . . while they work out who's good and who's not, who's lying and who's . . . just a liar.

"And things in court take a long, long time. You could be with that family for months. Maybe even a year or more. And in the end, who knows what the court would decide."

She shook her head, tears coming to her eyes at the very thought of it.

"I don't want that," she said. "Do you?"

Noah's eyes dropped to the table.

"No."

"Your father . . . he doesn't mean to be so awful," she said. "He's a good man, you know. Deep down inside."

"He sure ain't acting like it."

"No," Ada conceded. "Not lately he ain't. That's why it's best if we stay together. Where I can protect—"

Abruptly, Noah pushed away from the table and stood. "I don't need protecting, Mumma."

Ada sat there with her mouth hanging open as he stormed off to his room and shut the door. She wiped at her eyes.

Noah was a teenager now and therefore, she knew, immortal. Or so he thought. Her son did need protecting even if he wouldn't admit it but that wasn't the thrust of what she had intended to say to him.

We gotta look out for each other, son.

That's what she had wanted to tell him.

Outside, the winter wind was kicking up and it moaned a ghostly song as it rounded the corners of the house. The lake beyond was a sea of gray water, stippled with rough waves that crested white and then vanished, one after another.

She had never felt so alone as she did in that moment.

13

Her son stayed in his room for the afternoon and into the night, sleeping. Normally, Ada would have said something about it but she thought it best to leave him be. To let him heal.

When morning came, she woke and went to his room. She found the door open and no sign of Noah inside apart from the unmade bed. She checked the living room and the kitchen, too, but there was nothing. A panic leaped into her heart then and she called out for him.

Trembling, she dashed down the hall toward her bedroom, but stopped when she saw light spilling out of the worship room.

She quietly approached the door and leaned in.

Noah sat on one of the wooden benches closest to the door. He was not crouched with hands clasped in prayer but sat still, staring at the crawlspace door and the bench holding it closed, his hands balled into fists at his sides.

"Noah?" she called out to him.

He gave no response.

She stepped into the room to get a good look at him.

Her son glowered at the tiny door in the opposite wall. Had he even noticed her come in?

"Son?"

Finally, he broke from his trance and looked over to her. The scowl on his face relaxed a little.

"Are you okay, son?"

He nodded.

"What are you doing in here, honey?"

"I was just . . . " he began, but diminished, turned his gaze away from her to the metal cross that stood at the front of the room.

Ada sat down on the bench next to her son. He was angry with her, she knew that. She couldn't blame him. The other night and all the times before, she'd done nothing to protect him. Not *really* protect him. It wasn't within her power to do so and she hated it.

"Did you come in here to pray?"

Noah looked at her, curious.

"What should I pray for, Mumma?"

A few suggestions came to mind but she knew they would seem trite and pointless in light of what had happened. Instead, she stood and sighed, placing a gentle hand on her son's shoulder.

"Why don't you get dressed and I'll make you something to eat. Then you can go outside if you want."

He glanced at her, his face long.

"I'm not hungry," he said.

"Well, then go outside. It'll be good for you to get some fresh air."

He nodded and retreated down the hallway to his bedroom.

Ada sat quietly for a moment in the worship room. Before leaving, she closed her eyes and said a motherly prayer.

19

Slipping on his hoodie, Noah told his mother that he was going out. She asked if he wanted some company but he declined.

"Well, check in with me before too long, okay?"

"Sure."

With that, he stepped out of the house and into the cold, misty day. The sky above was a blanket of endless gray and the moisture in the air was so thick that his every breath came roaring out of his mouth and nostrils in a plume of dragon-like smoke. He ambled down the driveway into the street, gazing out at the empty expanse of the neighborhood as if looking for something, though he knew not what.

From across the street, he heard the clanking of metal and a spate of muffled cursing. Clay Winston's blue pickup was parked in his driveway with two booted feet sticking out from underneath of it. He headed in that direction, walking briskly. When he was close enough that he thought the man would hear, he called out to him.

"Mister Winston, you all right?"

The commotion from underneath the Chevy ceased.

"That you, Noah?"

Who else would it be? No one else lives here.

"Yes, sir, it's me."

"Out for a walk?"

Noah looked around absently.

"I don't really know. Just out, I guess."

"Uh-huh."

"You need some help?" Noah asked, now standing next to the truck and speaking to the scuffed leather boots protruding from beneath the chrome front bumper.

"Well," the old man said, "I suppose. If you have a minute."

"I do."

Noah went and kneeled in front of the truck. The old man was fighting with something there in the maze of metal and tubes and hoses that was the engine but Noah couldn't see what exactly.

"Hand me that pair of channel locks up there, will you?"

On a dirty rag laid across the radiator, the old man had several hand tools lined up. But Noah wasn't exactly well versed when it came to tools.

"Uh . . . which ones are those, Mister Winston?"

"They look like a big pair of pliers with one bent elbow and blue handles. And dammit, Noah, didn't I tell you the other day to drop the 'Mister Winston' shit?"

"Yes, sir. You did," Noah replied, smiling as he reached under and handed the old man the tool.

"So, what exactly are you doing, Clay?" he asked.

"That's more like it," Clay said. "Just regular maintenance. This damn oil filter's giving me hell coming off, though."

A couple of grunts later and the old man was scooting out from under the vehicle with the grimy round cylinder in hand. Noah reached down to give Clay a hand up, a gesture the old man seemed to appreciate.

"Thank you, young man," he said as he got to his feet and gave him a pat on his upper arm. "You're a damn sight stronger than you look."

Noah smiled. His mother would call that a backhanded compliment. Still, he knew that he didn't look like much. He was still wiry and slim, having not quite grown into the fullness of his teenage years.

"They say we're supposed to get snow tonight." Clay

said, wiping down the tool with a rag from his pocket. "About damn time. Usually get our first snow up here after Halloween and before Thanksgiving."

Noah nodded.

"But you're from Eastlake, so you know that, I guess."

"Yes, sir."

"So that's it?" Noah asked, peering down at the engine block.

Clay smiled.

"Lord, no. This old beast requires a slow and steady touch to keep her going. I got a few more things to do. But I reckon you're anxious to get on to bigger and better things."

Noah shrugged. "I don't really have anything to do. Besides, this is kind of cool."

Clay slapped him on the shoulder.

"All right, then," he said. "Lay those tools out on the driveway where we can reach them and you can crawl under there and get your hands dirty."

Noah complied, enthusiastically shifting the array of hand tools down below the front bumper. And the two of them got to work.

When the work wore on past lunchtime into the early afternoon, Noah ran across the street to let his mother know he was helping Clay Winston with his truck. Cautiously pleased and surprised, she gave him her blessing and reminded him to be home before dark; his father was due to be home that night, provided he kept to his schedule.

When the truck maintenance was done, Clay twisted the handle of the floor jack and let the vehicle down from its incline. He plopped a wad of goop he called GoJo into his palms and explained it would cut the grease and clean his hands. Noah wiped them mostly clean with a rag, feeling oddly satisfied with himself.

"Job well done," Clay said. "It's Miller time. What's your poison, boy?"

"My poison?"

Clay slammed the hood of the truck closed.

"What do you like to drink, son?"

"Well, I don't . . . " he began, then stopped and smiled. He liked that expression. *Your poison*, he mused, rubbing his cold, bone-white hands together.

"I like hot chocolate. Or maybe a Coke."

The old man's brow wrinkled in thought.

"Not sure if I got those, but let's go on in the house and see what I can offer you."

The layout of Clay's house was identical to Noah's, though it was more cluttered than his home. For one man living alone, Clay sure had a lot of stuff. The walls of the living room were lined with mismatching bookshelves of varying sizes. Upon their sagging shelves sat what must have been hundreds of books.

Scattered about the shelves here and there sat small wooden carvings. They were crude creations, hewn by Clay's practiced hand, into many shapes—some simply geometric, some long and serpentine, and some which were broad and sharp, models of the mountain itself. Still, others were rendered in finer detail. Faces with deep eyes and crooked noses that jutted out from the original piece of wood.

There was an old couch against the far wall and an easy chair with a reading lamp next to it. Despite the clutter, the place actually seemed pretty clean. There was no layer of dust, no cobwebs loitering in the corners. Noah had heard the term "organized chaos" before and now he thought he finally understood what that meant.

There was something about the chaos that actually seemed cozy and inviting.

As the old man went about pouring an iced tea for Noah and opening a beer for himself, Noah strolled and studied the room around him. The walls were adorned with maps and prints of paintings depicting an assortment of battlefields, some with British redcoats battling

Continental Army men and some with Billy Yanks in blue against the Johnny Rebs in gray. In each one, the dead lay strewn about the open spaces against brown and green earth or snow-covered landscapes, all stained crimson.

Apart from this, the strangest thing that he noticed was the lack of a television. There was a small, cheaply made entertainment center meant to house one but it, too, was filled with books and atop it sat an old, garish silver boombox whose speakers quietly transmitted old time fiddling music. Mountain music.

"So, young man," Clay said as he handed Noah the glass of iced tea and sat on his couch, sipping his beer, "how are you liking your new place?"

Noah turned. "It's nice, I guess."

"Your daddy like it well enough?"

Noah considered the question, still taking in the room. In the corner of the living room, against a tall floor lamp there leaned a rifle. It looked older than anything he had ever seen. On the wall behind it, dangling from a hook, was a wide-brimmed hat bearing a silver shield of some kind on its front, a thick layer of dust on it.

"I guess. We aren't real close."

The old man sipped his beer and Noah his tea during a moment of awkward silence.

"Your folks fight a lot, do they?"

Noah turned to the old man, his eyes wide and his mouth gone suddenly dry.

With a wry smile, Clay said, "Your daddy hollers pretty loud."

Noah relaxed a little. "He can holler, that's for sure."

"Well, new place, new job—new life, really. It takes a toll on a man."

Noah sat down on a small, leather ottoman near the radio and gulped his tea.

"You might be lucky just to have your father around, though," Clay said. "My old man was gone by the time I was thirteen years old."

Noah turned his head and regarded the old man with genuine pity.

"Where'd he go?"

"Who knows," Clay said. "Just up and left one day."

Another uncomfortable silence followed. Noah rose and walked over to one of the bookshelves.

"So, the real estate man said you're a reenactor."

Clay nodded.

"Why?" he asked as he perused the books on a shelf, his fingers plucking over the spines.

"Time travel."

Noah turned toward his host with a dubious look.

"*Time* travel?"

"In a manner of speaking."

The old man stole across the room to a doorless broom closet between the living room and the kitchen. In it hung various military uniforms of antiquity; coats of Yankee blue, Rebel gray, and the buff and blue of a Continental Army officer. He reached in and removed from it the plain blue uniform of a Federal infantryman. The fabric was well-worn and weathered, bearing stains of earth and grass. It smelled of campfires and gunpowder.

"This here is my time machine."

Noah looked askance at the old man, doubting him.

"Well, not literally," the old man said sheepishly, placing it back onto the rack in the closet. "But when I'm out on the field and the cannons are sounding and the rifles are cracking and it's hotter than hades in the summertime and this uniform's scratching the bejesus outta me . . . in those moments, I forget that it ain't real."

He sat down across from Noah, leaned in, his eyes intense, his voice low.

"I'm lying in the trench, wondering if my gun will fire—because quite often they don't—and I can hear the enemy boots moving across the field in my direction, the hooves of mounted cavalry. The air's filled with the smell of black powder and sweat, filled with men screaming in agony, hollering. I bring my Enfield rifle up and before I can help myself . . . before I remember that it's all for show, I start to panic and shake. *That's time travel, boy.*"

Noah narrowed his eyes, skeptical.

"Yeah, but you know it ain't real, right?"

The old man nodded. "Sure I do. But for a few moments here and there, it's as real as anything you've ever known your whole life. I promise you that."

Noah gulped and nodded, wanting to break the old man's stare but unable to do so. It was strange hearing the old man talk about re-enacting because it sounded so much like the way he felt when playing war games with Tommy. He cleared his throat and decided to try and steer the conversation toward something else.

"You've read all these books?" he asked.

Clay nodded. "Some of them I've read two or three times."

"Wow."

Clay rose, leaned past him to the shelf beneath the radio and plucked a book from it, placing the volume into Noah's hand. It was a hardbound book with gilded letters on the spine that read, *Collected Stories* by Edgar Allan Poe.

"You ever read that one in school?" Clay asked.

Noah shook his head.

"It's got all kinds of tall tales in it. Some of them frightful, some mysterious, some romantic poems, and some that are just plain odd."

"Sounds cool."

The old man snorted. "I reckon it *is* cool."

"Well," Noah said, looking around at all the books and the prints and the maps, "you sure do like history."

Who was he kidding? *Liked history?* The old man was a walking, talking anachronism. Apart from the electric lights and the boom box radio, refrigerator and a stove, there wasn't a single item of modern convenience in his house. No phone, no TV, no VCR, no computer. The countertops in the kitchen were barren of so much as a toaster or a coffee maker or microwave. A cast iron tea kettle sat lonely on one burner of the range and that was it. Time was always moving forward but Clay's life seemed to be more about going backward.

"Aw, yeah," the old man said. "Always had a love for history. Especially local."

"Yeah?"

"Absolutely." He dashed to one of the bookshelves and searched for some book or another. "I know you're from Eastlake, but do you know how Cross Mountain got its name?"

Clay turned and gazed through the wall as if he could see the mountain looming in the distance.

Noah turned his head, following the old man's stare into nothing.

"I guess I don't."

"Come on outside and I'll tell you."

Outside, in Clay's backyard, they sat in rusty metal chairs around a campfire from the morning that was now nothing but cold ash and blackened embers. Clay set to work right away, carefully placing kindling wood and then a few small, split logs, until the fire was alive once more and reaching up to the sky. The mountain loomed in the distance as Clay sat back down, fishing a pack of cigarettes from his jacket, and lighting one.

"See, back in those days," Clay began, smoke drifting from his nostrils, "this whole area was called Green Valley." He flashed Noah a disapproving expression. "Even though this ain't really a valley. But the old-timers didn't think about the land the same as we do today."

With the warmth of the old man's house left behind and the bitter cold starting to seep in through his jacket, Noah thrust his hands into his pockets.

"Anyway, back then the mountain was much the same as it is now. A barren thing, with nary a soul living on it."

"How come?"

"Well, it's been that way ever since way, way back. Further back than anybody even knows, I reckon. Long before the first white man ever set eyes on it and even longer if you believe the elders of the Monacan and Mannahoac people.

"The Monacan had an ancient name for the mountain that was passed down through the generations in their native tongue but that name was lost . . . forgotten long ago. The Scots and Irish who settled here had their own name for it, though. They called it the Old Green Man."

Noah wrinkled his nose and Clay saw it.

"Not the greatest name, huh?"

He shook his head and sipped his tea.

"Anyway," Clay continued, "Just like the Indians before them, they had a lot of superstitions about the mountain. They regarded it with the same amount of fear and respect that you and me might feel about a nuclear power plant."

"That sounds weird," Noah said.

Clay smiled.

"I suppose," he said. "Anyway, during the time of the Civil War, two ragged, wayward armies on opposite sides of the conflict ran into each other on the mountainside. And what happened because of that battle is how Cross Mountain got its modern name."

Noah listened with rapt attention.

"It was the summer of 1864," Clay declared. "A group of Confederate soldiers who had gotten separated from the 64th Virginia got word that a rag-tag group of Federals, some not even regular Army, were camped on the mountain at a place called Bishop's Gap."

"The rebels," Clay explained, "were led by a man named Fallkirk."

Noah remembered this was the man who was depicted among the statues he'd seen on their first trip into Whitetail.

"The soldier had recently found himself in the leadership position after their commander, Lucius Booker put a gun to his head in the aftermath of their crippling loss at Spotsylvania.

"Fallkirk decided they would sneak up the mountain under the cover of darkness and surprise the Yankees camped there but a turncoat Cherokee scout sent word to the Federals at Bishop's Gap and when Fallkirk and his men arrived, they walked right into an ambush.

"The fighting lasted through the night and into the next day. It was so vicious and wanton that when the men ran out of ammunition, they took to having at each other with their bayonets, their bare hands, rocks, sticks—anything they could use.

"Word of the never-ending slaughter spread to Whitetail, and a nurse there, Lizzie Amburg, pulled together a team of nurses and a doctor or two and decided to march on the mountain herself. She did so, carrying a white flag with a cross emblazoned on it.

"When Lizzie Amburg and her band of unarmed women took the mountain, they took down the rebel and union flags and planted that cross flag. It was this woman of medicine, this woman of healing and care, who did what no soldier could have. She ended the savage conflict between the two weary factions of soldiers and saved a handful of lives on both sides that day.

"She won the mountain," Clay concluded. "In her words: *'Not for the south, not for the north, but for human decency'*."

"So, what happened to the nurse? And the men she saved?"

Clay took one last drag of his cigarette and tossed it into the fire.

"Well, Lizzie Amburg and her nurses did the best they could, saved a few. Most of them boys were buried, though. Right up there on the mountain. Together. Yankees and Rebels laid to rest side by side. No one was sure for a long time if the War Department ever knew. The people in Whitetail took it upon themselves eventually, though, and placed headstones for the soldiers, most of them without names. And it stayed that way for many years. Later, when Miss Lizzie herself died, she left instructions to be buried up there along with those men. And so she was.

"The Amburg family had a stone cross erected where the cemetery was. But eventually, the mountain took that, too."

"It wasn't made a park?" Noah asked. "Don't they make parks out of battlefields?"

Clay shook his head.

"In the scope of the War, it was just a skirmish. Carries most of its weight just in this little area here. The Parks Department never saw fit to honor it as a memorial site. So, the cemetery and the cross . . . all of it succumbed to time and the elements. Only thing that was done was to rename it Cross Mountain after Miss Lizzie passed on. In honor of her as much as the fallen soldiers."

Noah drained the last of his tea from the glass.

"Could you take me up there someday?"

Clay considered it.

"I suppose, maybe. Someday. Nobody goes up there anymore. That mountain ain't much of a tourist destination and folk around here tend to avoid it altogether."

"Why's that?"

Clay stood and poured his chilled coffee onto the leaping flames of the fire.

"Restless spirits, they say," he said, then gazed again toward the mountain with a respectful silence.

Noah, who had been listening with rapt attention to the old man's tale, looked back toward the lake and toward his home.

"Uh-oh."

Clay stopped. "What is it?"

Noah saw his father's Ford pickup in the driveway at his house.

He's home.

Noah cleared his throat and did his best to conceal his uneasiness.

"Looks like my dad's home."

Clay seemed to sense the trouble. "Want me to go over with you and explain where you been all day?"

Noah choked up, an almost-tearful gratitude rising in his throat.

"Thanks. No. It's okay."

Clay studied Noah as he lingered there a moment.

"Guess you better get on then."

"Yeah," he said. "Thanks for the tea and the story."

"No, thank you for the help, young fella."

Noah took slow, reluctant strides across the street, pausing a moment at the front door before stepping inside.

He closed the front door behind him and knelt to remove his boots. Realizing that he still held the Poe book from the old man, he reached behind him and shoved it into the waistband of his jeans, pulling his shirt down over it. The unyielding hardback of the book was cold against his flesh. As he unlaced his boots, he stared down at them intently, silently, as if the process could last forever and might keep at bay whatever awaited him. Once done, he set them aside of the door and stood with all the last-ditch confidence of a convict approaching the gallows.

His mother and father were seated at the kitchen table, elbows on its surface, leaned into each other and suddenly silent.

"Hello, son."

The words, like his father's voice, were as deep and dark as a treacherous cavern. They had all the charm of a hissing snake. But to anyone else who might have been there to hear, his father's voice was tranquil, almost sweet-sounding. To anyone else, there would be no reason to fear a man who could sound that way.

The quivering of his own knees took Noah by surprise but he endeavored to maintain a façade of calm.

"Hey, Dad," he muttered, his voice trembling and weak.

"Where you been?"

Before Noah could answer, his mother chimed in.

"I told you, Hugh. He's been across the street helping Mister Winston work on his truck."

His mother fixed him with a look that urged him to be calm, though it wasn't necessary. Despite the outrage Noah had exhibited the other night, with the return of his father, his fear of the man had come along for the ride.

"Ain't that right, baby?" his mother asked.

"Yes, ma'am."

"Good," his father said, "I reckon that's a better use of time than playing make-believe out in the woods. Come here, son, and let me see your hands."

Noah skulked across the room and into the kitchen, his hands held out palms up the way they did in church.

When his father took his hands, Noah fought a sense of revulsion. A snake running its cold, pitiless flesh over his own.

"That's real good." His father nodded approvingly as he glimpsed the black dirt and grease still lingering in the fine threads of his fingerprints and at the edge of his nails. "Those're a working man's hands."

Releasing his fingers, his father's arm rose and the man gave him a good-natured slap on the shoulder, accompanied by a smile. It was as close to an expression of pride as Noah had seen from the man in all his life.

Instinctively, Noah grinned wide, for no matter how much he loathed this man, his approval still meant a great deal. Hot tears borne of complex emotions he could not name rose to the edges of his eyes and Noah blinked them back.

"We're gonna have supper here soon," his mother said.

Noah glanced away from his father.

"I ain't feeling so good, Mumma," he said, placing a hand over his stomach. "I think I'll just go to bed."

Ada looked to Hugh, who said nothing, only stared out of the kitchen window.

Noah stopped off at the hallway toilet and then hurried into his bedroom. After removing the Poe book and changing into sweatpants, he pulled back the bedcovers and slid beneath them. He left the table lamp on the other side of the room burning and settled into bed, the old man's book turned upside down as he lay on his back and read, beginning in the middle of the book with a story called "Morella."

He was anxious to fall headlong and carefree into the book and the dark fantasy of its stories.

20

Noah awoke with the sensation of a thousand pounds of doom sitting atop him, the pressure bearing down from all sides as if the breathable air in the room had been stolen and in its place was a vacuum of dire and utter hopelessness.

He was not alone. That much he knew in an instant.

He opened his eyes and sat up. As he peered into the gloom, he remained still and waited for his eyes to adjust. Bluish starlight seeped in from the window behind him and cast a cold sheen over the room. But it wasn't just that. Everything seemed different somehow. Not completely, but shifted.

He smelled him before he saw him.

Noah squinted his eyes. The wall opposite his bed was populated with a couple of low bookshelves and a wooden rack with plastic bins overflowing with old toys and all manner of stray objects he had collected during his time in the woods. Leaned against it was his aluminum baseball bat, a discarded leather glove and a Spider-Man night light his mother had plugged into the wall even though it hadn't worked for years. All these things were still there but they were sharing the same space as something else. A long wooden table of rough edges and marred with dark splotches stood against the wall, though the wall seemed much farther away and was colored differently.

Was that a curl of wallpaper peeling away from the far edge? He didn't have wallpaper in his room, did he? It was hard to tell, for the coloring of the world had gone strange; gray seemed washed over everything but especially at the edges of his vision and while some objects he recognized appeared in normal hues, others did not. The world was rendered in some manner that was not entirely colorful, nor entirely black and white—like the old movies his parents sometimes watched on TV that had been colorized.

At the table stood the stinking man with his back to Noah, his arms moving in front of him. Crisscrossing over and over again. Accompanying the motion was a sound of chopping, of metal scraping and every so often there was a dim but perceptible flash.

Noah sat there, frozen. The man hadn't noticed he was there and Noah told himself that if didn't move, didn't make a sound, didn't even dare to—

Before he could stop himself, he breathed. It was a short-drawn inhalation of air that barely whispered as it filled his lungs but it was audible and that seemed to be enough because the scraping noise ceased and the stinking man cocked his head to the right, his left ear listening. Then he tossed whatever he had been handling onto the table and turned. As he dropped his arms to his sides, Noah could see the knife gripped in his hand.

A large, rectangular blade. The kind used to butcher meat.

The stinking man's black gaze searched all over the room. It was as if the man could not see him, and the look of confusion on the long, angular face of the specter seemed to confirm it. Then, as if a curtain was pulled back, the narrow eyes of the man widened with surprise and his mouth, surrounded by many days of rough, dark stubble, pinched into a sneer. His coal-pit eyes studied Noah and he shrank away from that menacing look.

The stinking man moved toward him, his arm outstretched. Despite how far away he seemed, the tall and hulking form of the man crossed the distance quicker than he should have been able to and his fingers grasped at Noah's throat and squeezed.

It was suddenly hard to breathe and there was a sensation about his neck, but not quite what Noah might have expected. It was not as if the palms of the man's hands were pressed against his skin, for there was no warmth, no sensation of physical touch. It was more like his throat was closing up from the inside. The only sensation Noah felt on his skin was bitter cold as the reek of the man filled his nose.

The massive right hand of the stinking man rose high and back, angled the cleaver a little. To connect with Noah's head, he assumed. Probably somewhere near his eyes. He imagined an enormous gash opening up, spanning the distance from his temple down to the opposite cheekbone. Would the blade dig into his brain and black him out instantly and forever or would he live through it and see the final raising of that cleaver? A half-blind moment of pain and utter and absolute horror to be his last? Noah whimpered.

The man growled as Noah struggled against him.

Just as the stinking man meant to bring the blade

down, his gaze drifted to the side, something behind Noah catching his attention. As he stopped, the tight feeling in Noah's throat subsided and sweet air came rushing into his lungs. The man's cleaver arm relaxed and lowered slowly to his side. Noah watched as the stinking man took a step back, his eyes locked on something that Noah could not see. There was a reaction in those cold, black eyes that Noah could not quite account for. Was it recognition? Fear?

It was as if the ghost had seen a ghost himself.

Feeling his limbs come back to life, Noah turned to look behind him and then he saw it, too.

A face at the window.

He skittered out of bed and stood, bare feet on the cold floor, his breath smoky in the impossibly chill air of the room. The face hovered there—the face of a woman. Soft, porcelain skin stretched over the gentle roll of cheekbones, lips heart-shaped and plush. Her eyes were empty and dead but were somehow kindly. Beholding her face and the long, auburn hair flowing from its edges did not fill him with terror like the sight of the stinking man.

He realized he'd turned his back on the loathsome thing that meant to do him in and quickly spun back around, but found no one there. The room appeared normal again, the grayness receding. The table and the strange far-away wall were gone. There was no lingering odor, no malicious, loitering presence, not a single trace of the stinking man.

Turning again to the window, Noah watched as the woman walked away. It was snowing, he now noticed, and had been for some time. The ground and the thrusts of tree branches were covered in a layer of white that mingled with what paltry starlight seeped through the clouds and gave to the world a lunar glow. As she strolled easily away from the house, Noah noticed she left no tracks behind. Her long, elaborate and formal gown glowed a brilliant azure blue. She moved quickly across the snow, across the road and the open ground at the center of the neighborhood, passing between and through trees that stood in her path. When he could no longer see from his window, Noah dashed into the hallway and went to the picture window in the living room. He could just barely make her out, but she was there. It was hard to be certain but if Noah had to guess, it looked like she was headed for the old manor house.

A voice from behind Noah startled him and he turned on his heel, ready to move with speed if he had to. His mother stood at the threshold of the hallway and living room, bleary-eyed.

"Jesus," Noah gasped, half whispered. "What?"

"I asked you 'What is it?'" Ada whispered back.

In the background, from his parents' bedroom, Noah could hear the sawing drone of his father's snoring.

He shook his head.

"I thought someone was outside the house."

His mother's hands clasped together and went to her chest and her brow furrowed with concern.

"Wasn't, though," Noah lied, turning to glance out of the window. "Must have been a deer."

She relaxed, her shoulders dropping and her hands going back down to her sides.

"Go on back to bed. It's okay," Noah said as he walked with her down the hallway.

He broke off into his room, said goodnight and closed the door.

It would be long before he found sleep that night. He lay there in the dark, reflecting on the strangeness of his experience with the stinking man, trying to shrug off the terror that reverberated through him. He thought of the two blond boys in the woods and now this other phantom; this blue lady.

And he wondered how these fantastic things were connected.

If only he could be back in the trailer at Cady's Run. In

simpler times, when haints were the stuff of unfounded tall tales and not curious bits of the landscape or tormentors against which there seemed no defense.

21

Noah and Ada passed the next few days in a white haze that was both magical and confining. The first day, he and his mother went outside and lay down, making snow angels as the puffy flakes lit upon their faces and melted. Using vanilla flavoring and sugar from the pantry, they made bowls of snow cream and ate them outside as more and more of the flakes fell all around them. Snowball fights commenced, accompanied by the building of a snowman fashioned to stand watch in the front yard.

Noah spent some time in the woods, too, wandering and playing at solitary winter warfare. When he was idle or resting, he dusted off a fallen tree or log and sat listening to the gentle whisper of the forest, but never once did he hear the young voices of the blond children. Perhaps, he mused, it was simply that summer phantoms forsook winter weather. He decided it was more likely that his mind was not fully invested in perceiving them, for his thoughts turned constantly to the chilling visit from the stinking man a few nights before.

He had thought of that night often and had come to the tenuous conclusion that it was not so much a visit *from* the reeking ghost as something *else*. An intrusive collision. Like two places, for a moment, had overlapped. After all, the man seemed as surprised to see Noah as Noah was to find the man in his room. Then, of course, there was the blue lady who had peered into his bedroom window and had so captured the attention of the burly, violent phantom. Noah was beginning to suspect that Cedar Banks was a place that harbored not only many spirits, but countless secrets along with them.

22

One evening, Noah was sitting cross-legged on his bed, his math book open before him as he worked his way laboriously through some algebra problems, when his father came in late from work. After a moment, he closed his book and went to his bedroom door, cracked it opened and listened.

His parents were engaged in quiet conversation in the kitchen. While Noah could hear the sound of their voices, he could not discern the words. The tone was reserved, though, even somber. This went on for a few minutes and then he heard the groan of one of the kitchen chairs scraping across the floor and he eased his door shut and retreated to his bed, opened the book again and pretended to resume his homework.

Noah listened to his father's heavy footfalls coming down the hallway and past his room. The sounds of rummaging from his parents' bedroom, the sound of drawers opening and closing, the squeal of the guides on the sliding closet doors. Noah wondered what his father could be doing and then realized he must be packing his things. At this, a light of hope sprang up in him. Was he leaving them at last, going away forever? Would they now be able to leave this strange place behind, maybe go back to Cady's Run? His mother could get a job and maybe he could, too. They could rent one of the small trailers there and without Black Billy in their lives, they could be happy and at peace for once.

The footfalls came back down the hallway and paused briefly at his door. Noah held his breath as he listened, expecting the door to creak open any second and the cold blue of his father's eyes to take his measure. But that did not come and, after a moment, his father went sauntering down the hallway.

Noah rose and cracked the door again—wider this time—and peeked out from around the doorjamb.

His mother and father stood in the kitchen, facing each other. On the floor at his father's feet was a suitcase. A vehicle, its engine loud and ticking, pulled into the driveway, its headlights blazing through the kitchen window and silhouetting them.

Gone for good, Noah prayed anxiously. *Oh please oh please oh please.*

His father handed his mother a wad of cash and she stuffed it into her pocket. He wrapped his thick arms around her shoulders and she reached hers up around the back of his neck and leaned in, returning the embrace.

Noah's hope went cold and a pang of bitterness accompanied his disappointment.

Then his father was out the door and his mother stood alone in the kitchen. As the vehicle backed out of the driveway and turned, the bright headlights swung across the house and penetrated the windows. In the light that swept over her face, Noah detected the glint of tears rolling down his mother's cheeks. How could she be so sad at his leaving? After all that he had put them through, how could she?

How could she?

Unless, of course, he was not well and truly gone.

Noah stepped into the hallway.

"He's not leaving, is he?"

Ada looked up at her son, surprised to see him there. She nodded.

"He just left."

"But not for good."

She reached up and wiped the tears from her cheeks. "No. Not for good."

He hung his head and swallowed hard.

"Noah, do you hate your daddy?"

He shrugged.

"I don't know," he said coldly. "Maybe."

Noah turned to enter his room again but stopped.

"Why don't you, Mumma? Why don't you hate him?"

A sob caught in her throat and he had the sense that he'd wounded her with that question. He didn't mean to, but with that touching embrace he had just witnessed, she had wounded him, too.

"Son," she said, "what happened in the worship room that night? When he locked you in that hole?"

Noah cocked his head to the side.

"I don't remember."

With that, he slipped into his room and slammed the door behind him.

23

During the night, a front of unusual warmth swept in from the southwest and clashed with the cold air that lingered over the Blue Ridge Mountains and a steady rain began to fall. With it came rumbling thunder and the occasional flash of lightning that lit up the countryside, casting long, black shadows of the skeletal trees across the snowy ground. When it stopped in the early afternoon, the gray ceiling of clouds did not part to reveal a crisp, blue sky but remained, having only grown darker.

Noah's mother announced that she had gotten some grocery money from his father and that she was going to head into town for shopping. She asked Noah if he would like to come with her but he declined, not feeling much like a trip into town or spending the long ride locked in an uncomfortable silence between them. In truth, the thought of staying in the house alone unnerved him more than a little but he decided to stick around nonetheless. Anyway, he reasoned, he could always go outside if the house became too oppressive or too eerie.

Before she left, his mother asked him if he would go and collect the last few days' worth of mail from the box at the neighborhood entrance, for she had neglected to do so with all the snow and ice that had been around. He told her that he would and then walked her to the door and said goodbye.

After she left, he flipped through the TV channels, but found nothing of more than passing interest. He sat and re-read some old comic books in the luxury of the living room, which was nice since he was usually forced to enjoy them on the sly, holed up in his bedroom. After reading the last of his *X-Men* comics for the hundredth time, he decided to get out and head to the mailbox. She would be home soon and would surely be disappointed if she discovered he had passed all of his time lying idly about the house.

The neighborhood road had been all but cleared by the rains, much of the black asphalt visible once again and soaking up the warmth. As he walked down the road, he looked around and found the snowy landscape diminished. The area around the mailboxes was covered by trees, though, so the soil there was still thick with snow.

As the metal door of the mailbox groaned open, he found a handful or two of envelopes and junk catalogs inside. He shut the box and started back toward the entrance, absently thumbing through the stack of bills and other envelopes until he came across a small, brown one that bore the return address of the Wrens back in Bedford. He forced the thick pile of other mail into the inside pocket of his jacket and then ripped into the envelope. Inside was a neatly folded piece of notebook paper and on it the familiar, blocky scrawl of his best friend.

The margins of the letter were adorned with Tommy's freehand illustrations. Drawings of cave painting quality that depicted Captain Red and Sergeant Black battling their enemies. Sharp blades and scribbles of Horde blood. The logos of favorite bands such as Metallica and the like. A crude drawing of Sergeant Black bending over and farting death to his enemies with lightning bolts and clouds of noxious gas. An abstract figure that sported enormous breasts and bore an uncanny resemblance to Laurie Wilson, a girl from school of generous proportions that was one year their senior and had long been an object of the boys' collective, developing lust.

Noah,

I got your letter. First off, I hope you know I think you are completely mental about the Von Trapp twins but your secret is safe with me, you nutjob. Since you've been gone, the Horde has taken control of Cady's Run and the valley. Thanks for leaving me in a lurch, comrade. I have no doubt they are headed in your direction haha! But seriously, folks . . .

The old neighborhood misses you. I miss you. I think maybe even Carl Wright misses kicking you in the nuts. Don't worry, though. I am taking the abuse. My dad says I should ask if we can come for a visit. He says to ask your mom and he made me write it in this letter. He's gonna read it when I'm done.

Happy now, Dad?

I'd love to come out to your new place and see what it's like. I bet it's waaaay more cool and interesting than here.

Give me a call and tell me when would be a good time. We're still at the same old number. Don't be a stranger, Captain Red.

Tommy

Noah brimmed with excitement. Practically trembled with it. He nearly skipped his way along the wet blacktop through the neighborhood entrance. As he did, he heard a curious sound from behind him. Just a rhythmic rustle of dry, fallen leaves at first. Then, as he stopped and listened, he heard the faint and labored cry of a man's voice.

"Help . . . somebody . . ."

As he turned, he was instantly disoriented. Something was different and for a moment he could not quite place what it was. Then he noticed the pure blue of the sky overhead.

Had the lingering clouds dispersed? There was sunlight falling on the branches of the trees alongside the road, illuminating the colors of the turning leaves even though those leaves had fallen away weeks ago.

They had fallen, right? Of course they had.

Across the road, he saw a man rise from the other side of the hill. His frame was thin and narrow and his clothes hung awkwardly in drab tones of gray and brown. His gaunt face was roughly bearded and his hair askew in all directions with leaves stuck in it here and there as if he had belly crawled through the forest to where he now stood by the side of the road.

He stumbled toward Noah, arms outstretched and a vacant, terrified look in his eyes. About his stomach his clothes were stained with something dark and wet. Noah was about to ask the man if he was all right when he heard the roaring sound of an engine as it came down the road. The man was nearly halfway across the pavement when a truck of faded green came sputtering into Noah's line of sight. It did not stop and its rusted bumper grazed the man's backside with enough force to unsteady him and send him whirling forward all the way across the road and onto the gravel entrance of the neighborhood where he crashed to the earth with a meaty scrape.

Noah's gaze followed the truck. It was an old one, older than his father's and older even than Clay's truck, with deep wheel wells that curved and bulged over the tires and a hood that was similarly bloated but narrowed toward the front. The back of it was an open bed but looked more like a trailer, the sides made of wooden slats that rose up from the frame a couple of feet. And there was no license plate. Noah watched as it motored on down the road, apparently careless of the man it had just struck.

Something was off, something not right. The wrought iron fencing at the neighborhood's entrance was not there, nor the mailboxes or the hard surface road. In its place was a narrow pathway of gravel upon which the man now lay, moaning and struggling to move. Noah tucked Tommy's letter into his pants pocket and moved to help him.

"Holy shit . . . sir, are you okay?"

A stiff wind rose up from the south, from the opposite side of the road, the trees popping as they bent with its force. The rush of warm autumn air carried a stench that Noah instantly recognized. He stopped in his tracks, and it was then that Noah noticed the strange fog of gray that lingered at the edges of his vision.

Just like the other night in his room.

His heart hammered inside of his chest. Noah turned and scampered into the nearby woods to hide. He found and took cover behind a tight group of trees that should not have been there, put his belly to the dry leaves and lay absolutely still as he watched the injured man and the road.

The opposite side of the road disappeared into a steep incline. From there, bobbing with climbing steps, emerged the top half of a weathered, wide-brimmed hat followed by the face and the burned, black cinders of the stinking man's eyes. Noah didn't look into them but shut his own and silently prayed.

No. No, no, no, no. Wake up. Wake up. Please, God.

But this was not a dream.

When he opened his eyes again he beheld the sight of the stinking man in the full light of day.

The man was every bit as tall as he had seemed before, thick and powerful in his appearance as well as the manner in which he carried himself. The brim of the hat he wore was folded up along one edge and Noah thought that, had it sported a feather, it would have closely resembled every illustration of the Confederate general, J.E.B. Stuart he had ever seen. His hair was long and greasy, darkened black with grime, and his square, stubbled jaw framed a face of chiseled cheekbones, a beak of a nose and other angular features. He wore a thin, filthy coat that came down to his knees and lingered at the top edge of the dull, brown leather boots he wore. Beneath his open coat was a button-down shirt that was dingy with age. A wide leather strap, the kind that would hold a rifle or a shotgun, crossed his chest and the stock of the long gun was visible just behind his left shoulder. Everything about the man seemed to convey that he had not bathed in weeks, if indeed he had ever bathed at all. His hollow, black gaze fell upon the injured man writhing on the gravel, mumbling indiscernible words.

To Noah, they sounded like pleas for mercy. Like begging.

The stinking man strode across and knelt beside the tortured soul.

With his left hand, the stinking man grabbed a handful of the man's hair and pulled his head up and back as with his right, he reached down to his belt line and drew forth a long, wide-bladed hunting knife whose point curved wickedly back toward its wielder. From its tip and halfway down, the blade was already wet with what must have been the man's blood. The knife itself was unusual but with its blade that curved eloquently before ending in the sharp tip, Noah recognized it as a deerslayer knife. Back in Cady's Run, there had been plenty of raw-boned men who brought dead bucks back to their trailers after a hunt, hanging and gutting the deer in their backyards. The blades those men had used were very similar.

The man let out a last, guttural cry as the stinking man slid the blade across his neck and pulled backward. A thin, red gash opened wide and exposed the bright crimson of his inner flesh as the man pulled on his head, sinews of muscle stretching to their limit and snapping, the blue-black walls of his throat and surrounding veins splitting open with an unimaginable flow of blood.

Noah, unable to help himself, gasped. His last-eaten

meal rose to the back of his throat. He swallowed it down along with the acid that accompanied it, but by then he had made too much noise, the leaf bed on which he lay cracking dryly beneath him.

The stinking man looked up from his kill and Noah could see the recognition on his face.

Noah did not wait nor did he think. He simply sprang up and darted between the trees. When his feet found the gravel road, he broke into a flat-out run toward the houses of the neighborhood, though they also appeared different than they should have. The buildings seemed squat and cold, colorless and even lonelier than he knew them to be. The dogwoods and pears and other trees that adorned the grounds, each easily eight feet tall or more, were simply not there. No snow, no wet ground, and the expanse of grass kept neat and trim by the old caretaker was hacked up from too much foot traffic and the scars of tire tracks and horse hooves. Fingers of gray smoke rose from the chimneys of every house and the culmination of these vapors was a dense fog that lingered about the rooftops and choked the air. Around the manor house on the rise there was no fencing and its painted siding of white and blue was the only bright color to be seen among the entire drab collection of buildings. The lake beyond glittered with afternoon sunlight and Cross Mountain sprawled to the west, callous and unchanged.

It's the past, he thought. *I'm seeing the past.*

Alien as the landscape was, Noah sprinted toward it. Then he slipped and his feet tangled together. As he fell, he winced and brought his hands up, ready for the sting of gravel and the crunch of it beneath his flesh. All with the stinking man hot on his heels.

But Noah tumbled forward and plunged headlong into a mound of cold, wet snow.

He righted himself, on his feet again at once, running down the road. He was more than halfway to Clay's house before he noticed that the world as he knew it had returned. Noah looked behind and, seeing nothing, slowed his pace to a jog as he veered left.

"Damn, boy, where's the fire?"

Noah planted his feet, skidded to a stop, and saw Clay Winston standing close by, shovel in hand, at the edge of his driveway where he had been clearing the last bits of melting snow.

"I . . . " he began but drifted off, his heart still pounding in his chest. "No, I . . . sorry."

The old man placed a hand on his shoulder to steady him.

"You all right, son?"

Noah breathed a sigh of relief.

"Yeah, I'm fine. I just . . . I don't know," he said, searching for an explanation that did not involve ghostly visions and murder. His mind suddenly seized on the letter in his pocket. "I got a letter from my friend back home and he wants to come for a visit. Guess I got excited."

Clay looked him over curiously and then offered a smile.

"Sounds like a good thing, right?"

Noah nodded, catching his breath.

"It is. But I'm supposed to call him to let him know when. And we still ain't got a phone."

"Use the office phone at the manor house. And give him the number in case he needs to call you back. I check the messages pretty often. If there's anything for you, I'll let you know."

Noah wiped snot from his nose and nodded his thanks to Clay.

"Really? That'd be great. Thank you."

"No problem. Tell your folks they can do the same if they need to take any calls."

"I will," Noah replied.

24

As Noah crossed the street to his house, he looked long at his father's truck in the driveway, and that hollow, heavy feeling of dread invaded his stomach. Then he remembered his father was gone and his mother had used the truck to go into town for groceries. But when had she returned? He had been at the neighborhood entrance where he had seen . . . whatever it was that he had seen. But he hadn't seen her drive through the gates.

He stepped in through the front door and kicked off his shoes.

"Mumma?" he called out without even bothering to look.

"Oh, well," he heard the lilt of her voice from the kitchen, looked in the pass-through and saw her unpacking the groceries from tall, rigid paper bags. "Looky here. The noble knight returns. Great timing, kiddo, since I've already brought in all the groceries."

In the presence of her voice and the normality it brought, he was suddenly flush with feelings he could not sort out. His resentment of her for tolerating his father's cruelty sank into the background and Noah went straight to his mother and wrapped her in a bear hug. He shut his eyes tight, longing to dispel the image of that poor man's throat opening up and the bright, otherworldly red of the blood.

She grinned wide at his embrace, pleasantly surprised.

"If you think this makes up for you not being here to tote these bags into the house, well, mister . . . it does."

He nodded against her and then broke free and began helping pull the groceries from the bags.

"Did you at least get the mail while you were out there? I saw you, you know. Hiding in the brush behind the mailboxes. You might need better camouflage, son."

She had seen him? How could she have seen him when

he had not seen her come through the entrance in the truck? Unless when these . . . visions . . . was that what they were? Unless when these visions came over him, his mind was plunged into another time and place while his body stayed in the here and now.

"So? Did you get the mail or not?"

"I did."

"Anything good?" she asked as she placed a couple gallons of milk into the fridge.

"Actually, yeah."

She stopped and looked at him. "Publisher's Clearing House check for a million dollars?"

Noah cocked his head and regarded her with a sour look.

"I got a letter back from Tommy."

"Oh? What'd he have to say?"

"He says they want to come for a visit, him and his dad."

His mother closed the door of the refrigerator and stood there a moment.

"Really? Is his father okay with it?"

Noah nodded. "Tommy said it was his dad that suggested it."

"That so?"

He watched his mother as she stood, considering it, her teeth biting into her lower lip and something like a smile at the edges of her mouth.

"So, what do you think?" he asked.

She tapped her foot on the floor for a moment and then went back to unpacking the groceries.

"I think you should write Tommy back and tell them that'd be just fine."

"Don't need to write," Noah said. "Clay . . . er . . . Mister Winston says I can use the office phone at the manor house to call them."

His mother nodded approvingly.

"So . . . ?"

"So then call Tommy tomorrow and tell them to come later this week."

Noah thought he might jump out of his skin, he was so excited. But there was a reticence there, a thing that could bring the whole idea crashing down before it ever really took off.

"Don't we need to ask Dad about it?"

Ada plopped a bag of sugar down on the kitchen table with a thud.

"Well, he's gone for the rest of the week anyway. And what he don't know won't hurt him, right?"

Noah nodded and grinned. He liked the idea of them leaving his father out of it.

That night, after supper, his mother loaded a selection of Elvis and Motown CDs into the stereo and goaded him into dancing with her.

"Some day, you're gonna have the chance to dance with a girl, son. You might as well have some practice under your belt when you do."

They shimmied and shuffled and gyrated and laughed until their feet fell from beneath them. He wasn't sure what had brought on her euphoric mood but he hadn't seen her that happy in a long time—if he had ever seen it. Noah imagined that's what their lives would be like without his ogre of a father around. He watched and clapped as his mother sang along at the top of her lungs.

And for once, Noah's thoughts did not dwell on his father or Black Billy. Nor were they fixated on the many phantoms of Cedar Banks, be they fair-haired, stinking, or dressed in a fine, blue gown.

25

Ada spent the following morning at the kitchen table with Noah, who was grinding through his school work, though his mind appeared to be elsewhere. He got up constantly, inventing excuses to do so; another glass of water, to go to the bathroom, to open the fridge and peer inside. All just to get a glimpse out front to see if Clay Winston was out and about so he could ask to use the phone.

She shepherded him through an English quiz, finished a math test, and he took notes on the next three chapters in his history book, though he did it all rather halfheartedly. It was going to be an early day, Ada had announced at the start of it, and when lunchtime rolled around at noon, Noah's school day was over. He sat with her a few moments longer and gobbled down a peanut butter and jelly sandwich and chips before going to the door to get his shoes and coat on.

"If you find Mister Winston to use the phone, Noah, see if they can come for a visit tomorrow. I'm sure Tommy's still on Thanksgiving break so maybe that'll work. If not, we'll have to call them back when we know what another good time might be."

Her son smiled.

"Okay," he said, lacing up his shoes.

"Now, I'm gonna go on into town again today," she continued from the kitchen, scrubbing the dishes from lunch. "Think I'll go get my hair done in case Tommy and his daddy do come to visit. Probably time I met some of the women in town anyway."

"Get your hair done?" Noah asked, surprised.

"Yes, son."

He looked surprised. Normally, they were not in the financial state to provide for such "vain luxuries"—Hugh's words—such as haircuts or brand new clothes or Ada getting her nails done. Usually, she cut her own hair as well as Noah's and his father's, which was easy enough with a comb and the electric clippers.

"I don't know why," he said. "Tommy's seen you in your nightgown and rollers in your hair, Mumma."

She sighed. "You want to come with me or not?"

"Naw." He slipped into the arms of his jacket. "I wouldn't want to miss Mister Winston if he comes around."

"Suit yourself." She shut off the water and came out of the kitchen.

She stood there a moment, hands on her hips and stretching her back, giving Noah a once-over.

"You know, you could use a haircut yourself," she said, reaching her fingers into his fiery red mop. "Getting a little scruffy up top."

Noah pulled away playfully and smoothed his hair back.

"I don't want to keep it short anymore," he said, then caught her eyes to make sure she understood. "Not like Dad's buzz cut. Not anymore."

"All right," she said.

Noah was in that stage of the early teenage years where he was asserting his independence. But it wasn't only that. After what had happened, she could see Noah was pulling away from his father, leaving behind a chasm that had perhaps always been there, just beneath the surface. Such independence was going to be hard for Hugh to swallow since he liked things only one way. *His* way. Without much room for deviation.

She watched her son zip up his jacket and go darting out the front door, then she went and started the shower. As the bathroom filled with steam, she stripped and stood before the mirror and wondered where it was along the path to adulthood and parenthood she had let herself get so frumpy. Her hair, once a brilliant, dark red was graying faster than it should be and hung flat and uninspired against her, just touching her shoulders. Even her natural curls, it seemed, had given up. She had put on some weight, yes, but not overly much. As a young woman, she had been thin and athletic, so the few extra pounds she had gathered over the years filled her out and gave her curves where there had been none before. Her breasts, once smallish and bouncy were larger—they had been since motherhood—but laid with a certain malaise against her flesh. The hallmark of having breastfed her son. Freckles dotted her body as they always had, as numerous as stars in the sky, though they had darkened with age. Altogether, she was not a bad-looking woman in her own estimation but when was the last time she put on make-up? It was not something Hugh approved of. He preferred her plain, and so that was how she had become.

But not today. And certainly not if Deputy Nicholas Wren and his son were coming for a visit. As she stepped into the shower and bent to lather her legs with shaving cream, she had to laugh. What was she? A twenty-two-year-old bachelorette getting gussied up for her big date? She seldom shaved her legs anymore. What was the point when it mattered nothing to her husband?

Ada couldn't remember the last time she had been alone with Deputy Wren where such concerns about her appearance mattered to her. It had been years upon years.

But there had been a time.

Nicky—as she had called him back then—was the one that got away. They had been high school sweethearts for a time and she still recalled the night when she found him necking with Mary Stuart in the school parking lot after a football game. She had cussed him out that night, and ever since then, many were the days she had regretted doing so. Her boyfriends after Nicky were a string of poor choices, one after another. Not that she and Nick would have ended up together and not that they would have married, though in hindsight and with a little imagination anything seemed possible.

No, she had ended up with Hugh. The only reason that she had ever been allowed to speak to the deputy at all was that Hugh had no clue about her past with him. Hugh had been home-schooled by his mother, just as she was doing with Noah now, and had not been permitted a social life that might have involved teenagers from her school.

In any case, if she was going to spend some time alone with her old beau, drinking coffee while the boys played outside, she wanted to look her best even if the deputy was long since past the point of noticing or caring. As she shaved her legs, she shook her head at her own ridiculous girlishness. It was silly, she knew, but even fifteen long years of marriage to Hugh Belton had not been enough to completely extinguish the torch she still carried for Nicky Wren.

26

With nothing to do but wait for Clay to come around, Noah wandered into the woods and down to the spot where he last encountered the little blond boys. The downed tree was still there, stretched over the shore and into the lake. He considered edging out over the tree just for the hell of it but with the recent weather and the runoff from the snow, the lake would be freezing cold and he had no interest in losing his balance and falling into it.

He kicked around aimlessly for a bit, wondering if the little boys were about. He neither heard the telltale laughter nor saw blurs of yellow hair go whipping by through the trees. Noah leaned against the stump of the downed tree and recalled that the last time he heard them, he had deliberately tried to do so.

It worked once, so why not try again?

He found the tree that he sat against last time and lowered himself onto the still damp ground, resting his back against the cold bark. A cool wind blew through the forest, and the trees swayed and whispered. He closed his eyes and tried to empty his mind just as he had done before. It was difficult, though, for there were many things that preyed on his thoughts—the vision of the stinking man and the murder from the day before not the least of them.

Perhaps he needed to get their attention. But how? He thought of the rhyme the older boy had been reciting, and Noah endeavored to enter a calm state of mind, eyes closed. After a few minutes, he tried singing the rhyme in the same way he remembered the boy had done.

"Wee Willie Winkie . . . "

But his doubts came gnawing at him. This was ridiculous. What was he doing? Sitting alone in the forest and singing a nursery rhyme in the hope of encountering two young boys who had long ago moved on to whatever the next world had to offer. Why should they care about his desire to find them?

After scolding his doubtful self, he calmed again and then resumed. He didn't know if he had the tune exactly right but he thought it was close.

"Wee Willie Winkie runs through the town," he sang, "upstairs and down in his burial gown. Scratching at the window, moaning at the lock. Where are the children? It's nigh on twelve o'clock."

He stopped and listened. No sound but the wind.

"Wee Willie Winkie runs through the town. Upstairs and down in his burial gown. Scratching at the window, moaning at the lock. Where are the children? It's nigh on twelve o'clock."

This time he did not pause but continued with another round of it. And after that, another and another, until he lost count.

"Wee Willie Winkie runs through the town. Upstairs and down in his burial gown."

The sound of a gasp, a sharp breath drawn in that was not his own. Still, he kept on.

"Scratching at the window, moaning at the lock."

Whispering. Words he could not make out but whispering all the same.

"Where are the children? It's nigh on twelve o'clock."

He paused and at first there was only silence. Then a voice, young and shrill.

"You ask him!"

After a moment, *"Where did you learn that rhyme?"*

Noah's heart beat fast, excitement surging through his veins. If he answered, if he opened his eyes, would it break the spell?

"I heard you singing it. That's where. Where did y'all learn it?"

"Daddy used to tell it to us around the campfire," one of them said. *"Now, Albie just teases me with it."*

The boys were whispering to each other again.

"So, your names are Will and Albie? I'm Noah. That's my name."

"Noah?" came the voice of Will, the youngest. *"Are you from the Bible?"*

"'Course he's not from the Bible, you dumb-dumb. That Noah is probably a million years old by now."

"I'm from here," Noah said. "Well, not *from here,* but this is where I live now. Where do y'all live?"

"We come here sometimes," the older boy replied. *"But we have the run of the lake so we roam all over."*

Noah nodded.

"Why do you stay here? Around the lake, I mean," Noah asked.

There was a moment of silence and Noah got the sense the older boy was thinking.

"We don't know," he replied. *"We just . . . can't seem to go anywhere else. Just the lake, the woods, and the mountain."*

"Albie! We're not alone anymore," the little one shrieked excitedly. *"We're finally not alone."*

"We're still alone, Will."

"But this boy can hear us!"

"It doesn't matter," the eldest brother said, a tone of despair in his voice. *"He's not like us. He feels different. Alive. Can't you tell?"*

Noah could not see but he could almost sense the young one's shoulders slump in resignation.

"If I open my eyes," Noah asked cautiously, "could I see you? Or will you just disappear?"

"Beats me. You're the only one we've ever been able to talk to."

Noah thought for a moment. It was working so well, he was reluctant to push it.

"Okay," Noah said finally. "I'm going to open them. Please don't run away."

Noah opened his eyes. He saw feet with beaten, muddy canvas sneakers that had gone out of style long ago. The boys' bare legs were pale and filthy, bruised and marred by scratches clotted with old blood. As he raised his head, taking in the full sight of them, he found them to be terrible looking. As if they had been lost in the woods for a hundred years and every twig and bramble, every jagged rock and muddy patch had touched their cold, white flesh. The upper leg of the youngest had been mauled, it seemed, the bone protruding white and chalky from the wound now black with age. He held a faded, stuffed yellow bear close to his chest, clearly a thing that brought him comfort. Their faces were filthy, their hair mussed and tangled. Although their mops of hair were dingy from the elements, they still shone with the golden blond color he had always seen as they slipped through the forest. Their eyes—while not black like the eyes of the stinking man—were pale and vacant, devoid of any life. As he looked at them, he detected again the gray at the edge of his vision. First it deepened and then receded. As it did, the sight of them faded.

"You all right?" Albie asked.

Noah calmed his mind and concentrated and after a moment, the gray returned and their appearance shifted from that of the tattered, injured boys he saw at first to young, healthy boys of unblemished flesh and golden hair. Their eyes shone a brilliant green and reflected amber sunlight. Then it shifted back again. It was as if he were both seeing them alive and healthy as they had been on the start of that fateful day and also in the state in which they had been when they had crossed the threshold into death.

The youngest, whose hair was longer and curlier than his brother's, gave his brother a playful jab in the side.

"*Say something, Albie!*" he whispered.

Albie's mouth opened to form words but hung there silently.

"Pleased to finally meet you," Noah said.

They regarded each other warily.

The wind in the trees picked up and a sweeping gust rushed in off the lake, broke on the shore, and somewhere in the forest, a heavy limb snapped and fell with a crash. Crows squawked and burst into flight. Noah's head jerked away instinctively toward the sound and when his gaze returned to the boys, he found that they had vanished.

Clay had his truck backed up close to the house and was unloading its contents when Noah came bounding down the road.

"Morning," the old man hollered to him.

"Afternoon, you mean," Noah said as he approached, his stride quick and purposeful.

"Right. Well, time gets away from me on occasion."

"I'll bet. Where you been?"

"Shopping in town." He extended his arm, making a show of his haul.

Noah looked in the bed of the truck and saw what must have been a dozen bags unimaginatively labeled "Rock Salt" along with a few paper bags that looked to be from both the grocery store and the town hardware. He fixed the old man with a quizzical look.

"You know the snow's melted, right?"

"Yeah, but it'll be back before too long. Old Man Winter's a vindictive bastard." Clay groaned as he reached into the bed and hefted another bag, set it down on top of the stack he had begun against the brick wall of the steps that led into his kitchen. "Besides, Herman down at the hardware overbought. Got these for half price."

Noah nodded.

Clay stood and placed his hands on his hips, stretched back a moment.

"Care to give an old man a hand?"

"Sure."

They unloaded the bags from the back of the truck, stacking them next to the house.

"Remember I was telling you about my friend back home?" Noah asked.

"Sure."

"Mumma wants me to call and see about them coming for a visit."

"Hey, that's great." The old man smiled.

"I was hoping maybe I could use the phone?"

"Sure thing. We'll head over just as soon as we're done here."

They meandered across the grounds to the manor house where it stood on the rise, lonesome and caged in chain-link. Clay fumbled with the keys and unlocked the gate that bore the faded sign of the construction company. *Parker Developments, Huttonsville, West Virginia*, it read.

Closer to it now than he had ever been before, the state of the old house surprised Noah. From a distance, it had seemed teetering and run-down. In truth, it stood proud and tall against the backdrop of the mountain and the gray expanse of the lake. Unwashed and uncared for, certainly, but it was clear that efforts to renew the place had once been underway not so long ago. Siding had replaced the old wooden planks, and the wraparound porch, with the exception of some peeling paint, still seemed solid even against the unrelenting abuse of the many seasons that had come and gone. As they climbed the steps to the front door, their footfalls scraped away tiny layers of the paint that went flitting away in the breeze. The front door was a large portal of heavy, dark wood whose center was an oblong, oval-shaped piece of stained glass. The old man plunged a key into the deadbolt and turned. The hinges groaned as the door swung inward and a rush of cold, stale air greeted them. Together, they stepped into the foyer and Clay leaned across Noah, flicked on a few light switches and several naked bulbs that hung from the ceiling blazed to life.

The renovation of the house had ceased with the work on its exterior, it seemed, for the inside was barren—subfloors exposed and the faded walls of old plaster riddled with hairline cracks. The only remaining thing that retained all of its historical charm was the staircase before them that led to the upper levels of the house. Though covered in the dust of years, the original mahogany was unmarred, the bannister and handrails incredibly smooth. The inside of the house seemed to convey a spaciousness that was not evident from the outside, especially not when observed from afar as Noah had seen it up until now.

"Whose house was this again?" Noah asked, his voice echoing off the empty floors and walls.

"You remember I told you about Lizzie Amburg?"

"The nurse from Cross Mountain? Yeah."

"Well, her local fame and reputation back in those days did well for her kin around these parts. Her father, who owned what passed for the town hospital and asylum back then, ended up buying a few of the farms around here after the war ended. Bought 'em cheap, made lots of money. Then he bought this place for next to nothing. Did right well for himself for a while. His oldest son even ended up owning the town newspaper."

The newspaper. Noah remembered that the article he'd read at the library said the boys, Will and Albie were camping near the old Amburg house when they went missing. This had to be the place.

"So, they got rich and built a mansion."

"Naw," Clay said, "this place was old when Miss Lizzie's daddy bought it after the war. It's been around a long, long time. Though it's changed hands and changed shape over the years."

Noah stared up at the grand expanse of the spiral staircase that ascended into the dark above, imagining what the place must have been like in those days.

"But," Clay said, "that's just more history. Go and call your buddy." The old man reached into his coat pocket and produced a flashlight that he clicked on and then off to test it. "Since I'm here, I reckon I better crawl under the house and check the pipes for cracks and leaks, what with the recent cold and all. Ain't like it matters but I reckon that *is* what they pay me for."

Before he went out, Clay directed Noah into the room off the foyer and told him to follow around until he got to another with lots of windows and a wooden table with a phone and answering machine on it.

"Okay," he agreed dumbly, but made no move, for the expanse of the place still enchanted him.

Noah had been in such houses before on school field trips. They had visited old plantation homes along the James River on the outskirts of Richmond as well as some within the city limits. Those homes were restored to historical accuracy over time, some ornate and some plain. But always it left him questioning how it was that one family could ever have need of so much space.

The layout of the Amburg house bore many similarities to those old manors. Following Clay's directions, the first room he came to, he guessed, had once been the parlor and the next, a drawing room. When he came to the room with the phone, he didn't know quite what to call it.

He thought it might be a salon. But, then, wasn't that a place women went to have their hair and nails cared for by others?

In the room, the windows stood nearly floor to ceiling and made up the entirety of the outside wall, giving the observer a wide and wonderful view of Ashwood Lake. In the yard between the house and the lake, there was little to be seen except for scraggly, untrimmed lawn space and a tall but skimpy weeping willow whose long, empty branches hung corpselike from the limbs. The willow stood between two much larger oaks that overlooked a small family cemetery with half a dozen headstones that jutted up from the ground, only a little higher than the grass.

Against the far wall of the room, nestled in a corner, was a wooden table with the answering machine and phone. As he drew near and got a proper look at the phone, he spat a bit of laughter.

The answering machine was a sleek, low-profile device that hugged the table upon which it sat. There was a alphanumeric display to indicate the number of messages—all standard fare. The phone was another matter.

It was a rotary phone, which Noah had seen before and knew how to use, but the very existence of the device gave him pause when approaching it. With all the phones available these days—even the wireless ones—he puzzled at the reluctance of the old man to make a further technological leap.

Apprehensively, he plucked the receiver from the hook and pressed it to his ear. The monotonous drone of the dial tone sounded and he plugged his index finger into the hole that corresponded to the first digit of Tommy Wren's phone number and wound the ring clockwise to the stop, listening as it ticked its way back with muted clicks in his ear. He followed likewise with the other numbers until he heard the shrill, electronic gurgle of the line ringing.

Noah glanced up and peered through the windows at the lake. Without warning, his sight grayed and shifted. He blinked twice to dispel it, but still the vision came.

The interior of the room was no longer cold and sparse,

for the windows were open and a warm breeze came drifting in off the lake. The plaster walls were whole and smooth, painted a bright peach color, and the sills and panes of glass were no longer replete with dust. In the yard beyond, the oak trees were thick with green foliage and the willow in between was smaller, green and supple with life. As its long, wispy branches swayed in the summer wind, he spied a woman standing in its shade. The brilliant blue of her dress was visible for only fractions of a second but her ivory skin was set against the backdrop of brilliant, scintillating waters and her dark eyes were fixed on him as he stood there in the room, the receiver to his ear, his mouth and tongue gone suddenly dry.

"Hello?" the voice said over the receiver, so true and familiar that Noah doubted his hearing and turned to stare down at the phone itself.

He glanced back to the windows and found the world had righted itself. Gone were the green tones of summer, the tall oaks, and the woman clad in blue.

"Hello?"

Noah pressed the phone closer to his ear, coming back to the here and now. "Tommy?"

"Well," the voice on the other end of the line replied, taking on a cool and collected air. "If it ain't Captain Red. To what do I owe the pleasure?"

"Quit screwing around. I got your letter, so now I'm calling you back."

"Oh, you got the letter? Good. I was afraid the mail out there was by pony express or something and it might take many moons to reach you."

Noah smiled. Dang he missed Tommy!

"Listen," Noah said, turning around to look at the room and realizing the vision had faded. "I'm calling you from the neighborhood phone, so—"

"*Neighborhood phone?* That's cute. When we're done, can I talk to John-Boy?"

"Seriously, Tommy. I don't have long to talk."

"Okay, okay. So, what's new?"

For a moment, Noah was full to bursting with a torrent of words, for there was so very much to tell. But now was not the time for all of that.

"Not much. Hey, I talked to my mom. Are you still on break from school?"

"Yeah."

"Awesome. She says you could come this week if you wanted to. Like tomorrow or even Friday?" He uttered the last bit with a wince, readying himself for a damning disappointment.

"That soon? Hold on."

Noah listened as Tommy dropped the phone to his side and spoke to his father. Then there was a crackling as his friend on the other end put the phone against his ear.

"I don't know, Noah," Tommy said with a reticence in his voice.

At this, Noah's shoulders slumped and he sighed into the phone.

"Of course we'll be there," Tommy bellowed from the other end of the line. "Dad gave me the nod of approval. So, yeah, we will be there tomorrow. Probably sometime after lunch."

"Yes!"

"Is that place pretty cool or what?"

"It's—" Noah began but cut short his words when he heard the front door of the manor house slam shut. Clay was done with his inspection.

"It's pretty cool, I guess."

"Whatever," Tommy scoffed into the phone. "All those woods . . . I bet it's awesome."

"Yeah," he said. "It's really something."

That was an understatement.

"Something?" Tommy asked. "What does *that* mean?"

He wanted to explain, but where would he begin? And how would it sound?

Crazy. That's how it would sound.

Clay came into the room then and Noah decided he had better finish up. "Listen, I gotta go. See you tomorrow, though?"

"Affirmative, Captain Red."

Noah dropped the receiver back onto its cradle.

"Everything all right?"

Noah nodded. "Sure is. My friend's coming tomorrow."

"Good. Let's celebrate, then. I got a mug of hot chocolate at my place with your name on it."

With that, the two of them set out from the Amburg house, pausing a moment to lock the gate behind them. Once he was on the other side of the fence, Noah dared a look back not at the house but at the willow tree on the banks of the lake. The branches swayed silently, and between their hanging boughs no phantom appeared.

Noah stood in the kitchen and watched as Clay put a pot of water on to boil for hot chocolate. His mother always made the mix from scratch and put it in hot milk, but mentioning that might have seemed rude and ungrateful so he kept it to himself.

"How's that book I loaned you?" the old man asked.

"Great. I really like it."

"Yeah, I rather enjoyed those stories myself when I was your age. Still dust off those books every now and then and read a little."

After a few minutes, the teapot squealed and Clay poured it into a mug of the cocoa mix, stirred it and handed it to Noah.

Noah sipped and leaned over to inspect the books on the entertainment center. He pulled out another dog-eared, paperback volume and began flipping through it. He didn't catch the title of the book but it had something to do with a Witch-house.

Noah turned the amber pages of the book, reading over

them. Clay pulled a beer from his fridge and sat down on the couch with a heavy sigh. The radio was turned off and Clay, for the moment, seemed content with the silence. It unnerved Noah, though, as he flipped through the book, so he began humming the only tune that was rattling around in his head—the blond boys' strange nursery rhyme.

"Where'd you hear that?"

There was an edge to Clay's voice and Noah looked up at his host, who sat on the couch, the beer dangling loosely from his fingers, with a look of bewilderment on his face.

"Oh," he said, searching, for he couldn't exactly tell the old man the absurd truth of it, "I don't know. I guess I just remember it from somewhere."

"Do you?"

There was no mistaking Clay's accusatory tone. He had heard the same inflection a million times from his father whenever Noah tried to explain away some transgression, be it real or imagined. It made him feel small and foolish, and Noah shrank into himself.

"Well . . . yeah, I . . . uh . . . " he stammered, still searching for the right words. "Why? You've heard it before?"

Clay took a long pull from his bottle of beer, so long that Noah thought he must have drained it. He set the beer down on the table and studied him.

"I know it very well. It was something . . . a song, I guess. More like an old schoolyard song. I used to sing it to my boys. Part of a ghost story I'd tell them whenever we'd go camping."

The words of Albie echoed in Noah's head. *Daddy used to tell it to us around the campfire.*

"I ain't heard it in a long, long time. Not since . . . " The old man drifted off silently into some distant recollection.

Noah stared wide-eyed at him. He swallowed hard and his pulse quickened. A cold sweat gathered on his skin as this new revelation washed over him. He didn't know for certain if the father of those boys—quite likely this very man sitting not five feet away—had murdered them, but since reading the article at the library and having seen their awful, broken ghosts, he had come to believe it. And here he was sitting in that man's house, drinking his hot chocolate and flipping through books like a fool.

Noah heard the book in his hands slam shut before he realized he had done it. When Clay's gaze rose to meet his, he turned his eyes away as casually as he could manage.

"I suppose it's a simple enough tune that it might be something else," the old man said, staring at Noah in a way that made him squirm in his seat.

"Oh, crap!" Noah cried, looking quickly to his arm, at a watch that was not there. Hopefully the old man wouldn't notice, though. "Mumma's expecting me back, so I better go."

He set the mug on the table, dropping the book to the floor. Ignoring it, he strode out of the living room and into the kitchen, heading straight for the door at as calm and casual of a pace as he could manage.

"You can take the mug with you if you like," he heard Clay call out. It was a gesture that was polite enough, but Noah suspected it was a ploy to get him to stop and return for the mug—to put himself back within the old man's reach. He thought of a fly buzzing through the air right into the waiting strands of a spider's web.

"No, that's all right." His hand closed around the doorknob. "Thank you, though."

Noah shut the door behind him and broke into a run. Across the street was his house and he couldn't reach it quickly enough. The truck was not in the driveway, so his mother had not returned from her errands in town. The old man would need only look out his window to see that.

Once locked inside of his own home, Noah went to his room and grabbed the Louisville Slugger. He positioned himself in the living room where he could see the old man's house. Noah watched and waited.

What reason did he have to suspect this man of such a terrible thing? This man who had been nothing but kind to him? None, he reminded himself, apart from his own suspicions about the disappearance and deaths of the blond boys. After all, the Rockbridge County police had found nothing to cast suspicion on Clay all those years ago.

So why should *he?*

But then he recalled his mother's instinctive wariness of the old man. A mother's intuition was a powerful thing. All along, she may have been right. And Noah could not shake from his mind the look on the old man's face when he asked him about the tune. There had been a darkly curious way about him, surely, but there had also been a reflective, hollow sadness. It had been regret that he'd seen in the old man's eyes.

When the truck, with his mother behind the wheel, came rumbling into the driveway, he ran outside to meet her. As she made her way into the house, Noah nervously gushed about the happy news—Tommy would come for a visit tomorrow.

"That's great! And thanks for noticing my hair, by the way."

She was right. In all the excitement, it hadn't even registered with him.

"It looks real nice, Mumma."

He followed her into the house, casting a glance over his shoulder at Clay's house. He was afraid he would see the old man staring at them from his kitchen window, his face a menacing scowl. But the windows were empty and Clay was nowhere to be seen.

27

Noah woke up early the next morning full of anticipation. Obscenely early, in fact. Christmas Morning kind of early. Except that he couldn't recall the last time he had been this excited about Christmas. In the Belton household, Christmas was a holiday observed with reverence but also an iron curtain of stifling silence rather than merriment. Christmas carols and songs having to do with St. Nick and sleigh bells and the like were banned, due to his father's disdain for non-religious elements of the celebration of the holy day. But this wasn't Christmas morning, it was just the tail end of Tommy Wren's Thanksgiving break and today, he would be spending it with Noah.

He busied himself in his room until his mother woke. Then he ate a quick breakfast before rushing off to shower and dress. His mother cautiously tried to temper his excitement with the possibility that the whole thing might fall through. Deputy Wren was a policeman, after all, and if he was needed and called on, he would have to go. But Noah wouldn't hear of it. He just knew it was going to work out. It had to.

When he emerged from his room dressed in his everyday clothes, he found his mother in a tizzy. She was flying about the house, dusting and vacuuming, fluffing pillows and straightening pictures. The place was fragrant with a sweet spice that was somewhere between vanilla and pumpkin pie and berries. She called it potpourri and the mélange of dried ingredients simmered low on the stovetop in a small pot of water. She sure seemed to be going out of her way to make things nice for the Wrens' visit, even though he and Tommy were likely to spend the bulk of it outside in the woods.

With nothing to do but wait, he read some more of the Poe book and glanced every so often out the front window toward the old man's house while his mother was bathing and getting dressed. The substantial amount of fuss she had displayed over the house that morning paled in comparison to the way she looked when she came striding down the hallway, still fastening an earring into place.

"Mumma," he gasped as she entered the room.

She was dressed in clothes that were casual enough but

somehow seemed cleaner and more pressed than he had ever seen them before. Her hair was styled and shaped, her graying red curls falling around her face with ease and she smelled of a sweet perfume he couldn't recall her ever having used outside of going to church. Her face was painted with make-up that he was not sure he had ever seen her wear before, her eyes delicately lined in black, the freckles and splotchy tones of her skin evened out with foundation and elegantly applied blush. Noah thought that his mother had the look of one of those models from the pages of her catalogs or women's home magazines.

"How do I look?" she stopped and asked, smiling at her son.

"You know it's just Tommy and his dad, Mumma."

She pursed her lips. "I know, but it ain't every day we have company, Noah. I just want to look nice."

She scurried into the kitchen and began wiping down the countertops for the umpteenth time that morning.

"You think Tommy's dad will take the boat here?"

She scoffed and shook her head. "Why, so you can con him into taking y'all fishing?"

Noah smiled and shrugged. "Never hurts to ask, Besides, they'd get here a lot quicker."

"Well, be that as it may, the boat belongs to the police and I don't reckon they just let him take it out on the lake whenever the mood strikes."

Noah supposed she was right. With a gentle sigh, he wandered over to the window and stood there, tapping his feet and looking often to the clock on the wall.

23

When the familiar Bedford County police cruiser pulled up in front of their house, Noah jumped up from his anxious perch on the couch and announced their arrival to Ada, who had been idly watching *Family Feud* on the television.

Her son raced to the front door and flung it open, rushing out onto the front porch.

Tommy came out of the passenger side of the cruiser with what looked like four or five backpacks slung over his shoulders. The boys rushed toward each other and they threw their arms around one another in an embrace that, if left to them, seemed likely to turn into a wrestling match that would end with one or both of them on the ground.

"Hey, hey now," Nick Wren shouted as he rounded the back of the cruiser and made toward the driveway and the front walk. "Thomas, those might not be your worst clothes but at least try to keep them from getting filthy in the first five minutes of being here. Don't make me shoot you boys."

Noah laughed.

"Yes, sir," Noah said and stood upright but grabbed the loose, green sleeve of Tommy's secondhand Army jacket as he pulled him through the yard toward and up the front steps of the porch.

They were just barely through the front door before Noah's mother was sounding the familiar reminder of "Shoes! Shoes!" Both boys immediately knelt and kicked off their sneakers before running off into Noah's room, her son leading the way. Ada watched them go, delightfully amused.

She turned back to the porch as Nicholas Wren climbed the steps.

"Ada."

"Deputy." She gave him a surly nod, making like she was in one of those old spaghetti western movies.

He gave a snort as he passed through and she closed the door behind him.

They stood there a moment, an awkward silence passing between them as they both listened to their sons in the nearby room, gabbing on like a couple of old hens at a social.

Nick, his hands lingering awkwardly on his hips, glanced over to Ada.

"Well, don't you look nice," he said. "Country living agrees with you."

She shrugged.

"You look good, too, Nick." She walked toward the kitchen. "Coffee?" she asked.

"Coffee sounds good," he said.

Ada took a deep breath, a little surprised at how easily her coyness with him had returned. Almost as if she had caught him necking with Mary Stuart in the school parking lot just last week and she was still making him pay for it. Again, it was not as if they hadn't seen each other many times back at Cady's Run but they had never really been alone with one another as they were now.

Ada thought Nick looked amazing. How was it that someone in law enforcement—light duty though it might be in Bedford County—looked as if he hadn't aged a day since high school? He still had the same slim, taut build. Instead of the drab tan and brown of his uniform she had grown so accustomed to seeing him in, he wore faded denim jeans and a button-down flannel shirt blue-black in its pattern and beneath its open collar peeked the faded white cotton of his undershirt. The only sign of his older years was a light salt-and-peppering of his thick, dark hair.

Ada directed Nick to have a seat at the kitchen table. She was in the process of scooping coffee grounds into the basket when the boys came rushing out of Noah's room with a clamor, dropping to slip their shoes back on.

"We're going out, Mumma," her son offered before she could even ask the question.

They were strapped with backpacks and gear for their war games.

"Y'all be careful with those things, now," Nick said, though he never took his eyes off Ada.

"We will," they assured him in unison as they bolted out the front door, slamming it shut behind them.

She finished preparing the coffee pot and clicked it on.

There was the familiar gurgle and drip as she sat down at the table across from Nick.

"Be careful with what things?" she asked.

"Pellet guns," he replied, and grinned. "Don't worry, there's no ammo."

Ada raised her eyebrows in feigned surprise. Boys and their weapons.

"So," Nick said, leaning in, his fingers interlocking on the table. "How are things? How's your new life out here? How's Hugh doing?"

It was only then she noticed Nick was sitting in the seat Hugh normally occupied. The very one he'd been sitting in only days before when he had turned the table on them all and begun another bad patch in the slow, grinding storm of hostility that was the ruin of their lives.

"Oh," she said, determined not to betray the despair the last few weeks had instilled in her. "It's a special place we got here. And things have been good as ever."

Ada wondered if he could tell she wasn't being totally truthful with him, though. He was a policeman after all, and probably had a very developed sense of sniffing out a lie.

"Where did you get these?" Noah asked, admiring the smooth, black contours of the pellet gun. It looked so real, he doubted anyone could have told the difference between it and an actual firearm.

"This one," Tommy said, bringing the bulk of his own weapon to bear and sighting it as he pointed the barrel into the trees, "I got for my birthday."

Noah winced, suddenly feeling like an ass. Tommy's birthday had been in early November, but with the move to Cedar Banks and everything since, it had slipped his mind.

"I'm sorry, man. I forgot about your birthday."

Tommy glanced over at him from the sight of his rifle. "Don't worry about it."

Noah smiled a moment, then raised his own gun up and sighted it.

"And this one?"

"That I bought from Carl."

"Carl Wright?" Noah asked, shocked and recalling the bully from back home.

"Yep."

"He actually sold it to you?"

"Well, I had my allowance to spend and it turns out Carl likes money even more than he likes kicking my ass, so . . . "

Both guns the boys held were styled more after weapons from *Star Wars* than the Gulf War. But they were still cool as all-get-out in Noah's estimation.

"Pellet guns," Tommy explained. "No cocking like the old BB guns. There's a cylinder of gas in the stock that shoots the pellets out."

"Sweet." Noah admired the weapon. "Where's the ammo?"

Tommy raised up a bit from his sitting position and let go a sharp little fart.

"Speaking of gas!" Noah waved his hand in front of his face and scrunched up his nose.

The boys laughed.

"Naw," Tommy said. "Seriously, my dad made me promise I wouldn't bring any of the pellets. Didn't want us to shoot each other's eyes out, I guess."

"So . . . " Noah stared at the weapon cradled in his arms, "what then?"

"Just sounds cool." Tommy turned his weapon on his friend and let go a volley of fire that escaped the barrel of his gun in loud, harmless pulses of air.

Noah swung his rifle around at the ready, but not at Tommy. He aimed it at the dark thicket of woods along the base of Cross Mountain, instantly becoming Captain Red.

"They have the high ground so they'll come from that direction."

Tommy turned and dropped down behind the cover of the fallen tree. "Tell me more, Captain Red."

Noah smirked as he steadied his rifle. "Up just below the ridge, there's a low spot called Bishop's Gap."

"Yeah?"

"They'll be camped there."

"I see. So, we should take the mountain?"

"No way. Around these parts, no one takes the mountain. No one *has the mountain*. Not even the Horde. If anything, *the mountain has them*."

Tommy raised an eyebrow.

"Oh," Noah said. "There's one other thing."

"What's that?"

"If they come off that mountain, they'll be an army of the dead."

"Like zombie alien insects?"

Noah nodded.

Tommy grinned, loving this new dimension to their make-believe world. "Then how do you kill what's already dead?"

Noah paused.

"I wish I knew," Noah replied, though there was a dreadful truth in those words that had nothing to do with the war games they were playing.

The short, rapid report of the rifle sounded out as he squeezed off round after round, decimating the imaginary alien Horde that teemed from the dark mountainside. *If only it were this easy*, Noah thought as the memory of the vile, stinking ghost blackly invaded his pleasant fiction.

How do *you kill what's already dead?*

29

After the coffee brewed and Ada poured the first cups, she couldn't have said how much time had passed. Once she and Deputy Wren had gotten to talking, it had been just like falling off a log. It was effortless how she laughed around him, recounting memories from the days of their youth.

"And I remember once, one of the girls that used to hang out with us, Brenda . . . oh, what was her last name?"

"Platt?"

"Yes." Ada grinned, jabbing her finger into Nick's forearm. "Platt. Although all us girls called her Brenda Flat."

She illustrated the meaning by motioning straight up and down over her chest.

"Anyway, we were having a slumber party over at Layla St. Paul's house and she had snuck into her old man's stash of bourbon and brought a bottle for the party."

"See, I knew it," Nick said with a wide smile. "All you're doing now is confirming what all teenage boys think goes on at slumber parties, Ada."

"Well, wait 'til you hear this, then." She squealed and took another sip of coffee. "So, we were all passing the bottle around and giggling, talking about boys and such."

"Boys? Wait. Was this while *we* were dating?"

"Shut up, Nicky. I'm talking."

He bowed his head in mock shame. "Yes, ma'am."

"We'd killed . . . I don't know, maybe half a pint of Old Grand-dad and out of the blue, Layla just pulls off her top and starts shaking her boobs." Ada watched as Nick's eyes widened. "The rest of us are just watching with our jaws on the floor, not laughing, not saying anything because Layla clearly had too much to drink and I think she was hoping we'd all join in for some reason. Well, we didn't. Except for one of us."

"Who?"

"Brenda Flat stands up and just rips off her entire nightgown, almost goes over backwards before she can pull it over her head, she's so doggone drunk, and then she starts shaking *her* chest like some stripper. Only—unlike

Layla—she ain't got nothing to shake. Still, ain't a one of us saying anything, so when she's done shaking her thing, she stops and looks at all us girls and says, 'Well, what do y'all think about *that*?' Layla doesn't say a word, just runs into her bathroom and starts rummaging around, then comes back out with a pink bottle in her hand and says, 'Brenda, I think you'd better put some calamine lotion on those two mosquito bites before they get to itching.'"

They both burst out laughing.

Lord, she hadn't thought about that slumber party in years. Having Nick around seemed to loosen the surface of these old memories she thought had long ago been buried by her adult life.

Nick gulped the last from his coffee cup and stood.

"Suppose I could use your bathroom?"

"Sure. Just through the living room and down the hall."

Ada watched him as he walked out of the kitchen, unable to look away. As he disappeared around the corner and into the dimness of the hallway, she hollered after him.

"Second door on the left!"

She sat there a moment, smoothing her jeans with her hands and wondering what she should do next. More coffee? Should she offer to fix them some lunch? Her head was buzzing with caffeine and she was flush from spending time with her old beau and all the carrying on. It was good seeing him, sitting and chatting. To be laughing again, it felt . . . what was it? Nourishing? Yes. Nourishing and normal.

"Ada?" she heard him call from the other end of the house.

"Yes?" she said, rising and making her way toward him.

The hallway was dark as always except for the end, where light spilled in from the windowed bathroom. She had closed all the doors except for the one to the bathroom, but as she passed by Noah's door, she saw warm electric light glowing from the open doorway of the worship room.

Nick was standing just inside the door when Ada approached. He stared wide-eyed at the altar and the grisly metal cross that could have only been fashioned and judged beautiful by an unhinged mind.

"What the devil is this, Ada?"

She looked away from him and over at the cross, but said nothing.

"I'm as church-going as the next man," Nick said. "Not like Hugh, I know, but maybe that ain't a bad thing. But this is just . . . strange."

He looked to her with a furrowed brow.

"I thought this door was closed," she finally whispered, an emotional unsteadiness in her voice.

"It was, but—"

"This door was supposed to stay closed!" she shouted, though she did not meet his gaze.

She trembled, her hands balling into fists.

"Ada?" Nick said gently, touching her cheek and tilting her head toward him. "You want to tell me what's been going on here?"

She contemplated how to answer the question, her lips quivering and body shaking. No logical answer came to mind. She couldn't answer what she didn't know.

"Ada?"

Tears flowed from her eyes then and she whimpered as she leaned toward him and he took her in a comforting embrace. When his arms brushed down her back, grazing the bruises still tender, she winced and jerked reflexively away from his touch.

Nick looked her up and down, eyes full of concern, and his jaws clenched. Ada's back was still tender with bruises and she could see in the face of her old flame that he had a pretty good idea who had put them there.

She laid her head against his chest, the wet of her tears soaking into his shirt.

"Tell me, Ada. Tell me what's happened to you."

The blasts of their rifles were a volley of whispers. Airy pulses echoing through the trees. Noah still had his finger near the trigger, knuckles tight, when a hand landed on his shoulder. He turned and raised the butt of his rifle, more startled instinct that anything.

But it was Tommy.

"Jesus! I almost clocked you."

"Look." Tommy pointed toward the mountain. "We got 'em. We got 'em all."

Noah stared out and saw his friend was right. The mountain had been emptied of the foul things. They had prevailed against impossible odds once again. He leaned over and clasped hands with his comrade.

They rested their weapons against a nearby tree and tore into the rations of Snickers bars that Tommy had in one of his packs. Noah was halfway through his when he noticed something moving at the edge of his vision—the boys, maybe. But he didn't look. He didn't want his friend to catch him staring out at something Tommy couldn't see.

"So," Noah said, "did you ask your dad to check for anything about those blond kids?"

Tommy finished his candy bar and crumpled the wrapper, shoved it in his pocket and looked at Noah with a degree of resignation.

"What am I supposed to say to him, Noah?" he asked, holding out his hands helplessly. "He's gonna want to know why I'm asking such a thing. Am I supposed to tell him what you think you saw?"

Noah dropped his eyes, looked down at his feet.

"Okay, I'm sorry. *What you saw.*"

"Thank you."

"And if I tell him that," Tommy continued, "he'll think you're off your nut. Then he might talk to your mom about it. And then what?"

It made sense, Noah knew, and he didn't blame Tommy, wasn't angry at him for it. Especially considering what Noah had discovered about the boys recently. Not only about the boys but about their father, who—it turned out—lived right across the street. He badly wanted to share all of this with his friend but he knew how crazy and ridiculous it would sound. It was too weird and Noah had more than enough weird in his life these days. He would enjoy the rest of the time with Tommy just being normal for a change.

"You're right." Noah said. "It's probably nothing."

They picked up their rifles and packs and ambled along the shore toward the house and the dock that reached out over the lake. Neither of them said much on the way there, especially Noah, who was lost in thought.

In the time since his last encounter with Clay, he had wondered if maybe he was rushing to judgment about the old man. But strange things about him kept coming to mind—things that he hadn't thought twice about before. The old man's willingness to befriend a young, teenage boy like Noah struck him as very unusual now. Then there was his obsession with the past, with war, and with death itself.

Noah and Tommy walked to the end of the dock and sat. A breeze stirred and rose off the water.

"This dock is pretty sweet, man," Tommy said. "Dad almost brought us in the patrol boat today but he didn't know if there'd be a place to tie up."

"Well, now you'll know for next time," Noah said. "And the dock is nice. One of the perks of the house."

Tommy snickered. *"Perks,"* he said, shaking his head.

"Hey, speaking of perks!" Noah slipped his hands under his shirt and pushed out from beneath to mimic two large and pointy breasts. "How's Laurie Wilson these days?"

Tommy shook his head and grinned.

"Man, she's looking better than ever. I think her boobs are getting bigger by the day."

"Yeah?"

"By the time we get to high school, she ain't even gonna be able to stand up."

At this, the boys roared.

Tommy breathed out a long sigh. "Dang, I'm thirsty."

"What? No water rations in one of those packs of yours?"

"Guess I didn't think of everything."

"I'll go get us a couple Cokes from the fridge."

"Yes," Tommy said, sitting upright and putting on airs, summoning a voice that sounded a lot like Thurston Howell from *Gilligan's Island*. "Why don't you do that, Jeeves? We'll take our . . . coke-tails on the dock by the lake."

Noah stood, shaking his head. "Coke-tails. I bet you think you're funny."

"I *am* funny."

"Yeah," Noah said with a sardonic grin as he turned and headed up toward the house. "Funny-looking."

"Nice place you got here, Noah," Tommy shouted after him.

It was a nice place, Noah thought to himself, and the bit of envy in Tommy's joking had not escaped his notice. A new house and a dock by the lake right next to the mountain. It sounded picturesque. Like something out of a story or a painting. It sounded like *somebody else's* life—not his. But what was the cost? As Noah was learning, every good thing in the world came with a price. Something was always paid, something always sacrificed. Cedar Banks was a nice place to be sure but he would give it all up in a heartbeat to be back in the double-wide at Cady's Run. To be living a normal life full of regular people, not one where every passing day seemed populated only by specters of days long past.

Deputy Nick Wren reckoned that Ada had wept in his arms until she was plum out of tears. At one point, with her face so close to his, their cheeks grazing and their lips agonizingly close to touching, they had almost given into temptation. But Ada had stood and excused herself to the bathroom to wipe the streaks of eyeliner from her face.

Nick had long suspected that Hugh was abusing Ada and possibly even Noah. He had always been on the lookout for the tell-tale signs. But the sonofabitch had been clever about it, never leaving marks where they could be casually observed. More than that, his abuse was also psychological as much as it was physical. Hugh Belton had frightened them both to death of going to anyone to complain. Certainly not the police—even though the deputy had once lived mere steps away from their doorstep.

He had suspected it, but done nothing about it. Not that there was anything much he could have done. Even now, there wasn't much. The law was very specific on the criteria required to separate a child from a parent or get a restraining order on a husband, none of which they would ever meet because Hugh Belton had the two them so spooked, they'd just given up.

Ada had explained to him that after moving to Westlake, here on the outskirts of Whitetail, things had gotten worse. Hugh's wrath had become hard to bear and his punishments were increasingly more violent. She'd even shown him the narrow, dark space behind a crawlspace door where Hugh imprisoned Noah to teach him a lesson.

My God, he thought, shaking his head.

How had she not gone crazy from all the years of uncertainty and abuse? How had she not just up and left the bastard? But love was strange that way, he supposed. Strange and dangerous. As a cop, he had seen it firsthand. Domestic disturbance calls where the wife came to the defense of the husband who had been smacking her around just moments earlier. No charges pressed, just promises made. Until the one time the domestic disturbance became a homicide—as they did all too often.

But it wasn't just Hugh tormenting them, she'd told him. Confused, Nick asked her what she meant. Now that she had explained, he found himself no less confused. Nick knew she wasn't crazy.

Well, he didn't think she was anyway.

In his professional opinion as a police officer who had seen his share of crazy, he didn't see any of it in her. Other than the strange occurrences she had detailed for him, of course. It was a . . . what? Ghost? Spirit? *Poltergeist?* Some kind of thing that wasn't made of flesh and blood. Something that could drift in and out of the house on a whim and terrify her whenever it had a notion to do so.

The first thing he'd asked her was if Noah had shared any of these experiences. Ada had answered no—she would have known if it was happening to her son. Whatever it was, it only seemed interested in her.

It sure sounded like the wild imaginings of a woman so terrified by her husband that even when he wasn't there to threaten her, her mind created threats from raw, unformed shadows. He would have dismissed her claims out of hand and pleaded with her to see a therapist, to go to the Rockbridge Sheriff's Department and get herself and Noah the hell out of that house. Except Nick knew things about Cedar Banks that Ada didn't—things she couldn't have known.

Because of that, he had no choice but to believe her.

Ada came back into the room and sat down on a bench across from him. She had pulled herself back together quickly. He placed a comforting hand on her shoulder.

"Better?"

"Yes, thanks."

Nick leaned forward. "Ada, what do you know about this place? Not the house specifically. But Cedar Banks. What do you know about it?"

"Tom Marley, the agent who showed the house, said it was an old Work Projects Administration work camp from the Depression days."

Nick nodded. "Well, I didn't mean to be nosy but I was curious about where y'all were moving to, so I did some checking into Cedar Banks after you moved."

"You did?"

He nodded, turned to look at her. "Yep. And your agent was right. It was a WPA work camp. But I don't suppose he told you it was a prisoners' work camp, did he?"

The vacant look on her face was all the answer he needed.

"I didn't think so," he said. "Except for the locals, probably not too many folks remember it, but this narrow spit of land they've named Cedar Banks used to be called Crow Neck. It was owned by the Amburg family, who lived in that manor house across the way. The government leased the land from them to build and run the work camp."

Ada stirred in her seat. "Why would they let prisoners work out here?"

"It was part of a government program. A convict with only a few years left on his sentence could have it commuted if they worked for the WPA. Not the most elegant way to sort out a bunch of convicts, though, because it put petty criminals working right next to stone-cold killers and sociopaths."

Ada swallowed hard.

"At Crow Neck Camp—that's what they called it back in those days—there was some trouble. In the 1940s. Right when the WPA was winding down."

"Like what kind of trouble?" Ada asked.

Nick moved over and sat next to her. "The head cook for the camp, like most everyone else, was a convict. The police suspected him of a lot of things. Everywhere he went, people went missing. Men, women, children. From Texas to Tennessee and as far north as Ohio. Around here, they arrested him for killing a man during a brawl at a tavern in Clifton Forge. Had him cold, and locked him up."

He stood and stretched his legs, crossing the room to where that awful crucifix stood. He gazed over it and continued. "Anyway, he was a real raw-boned sort of fella. Some said he could live in the woods all alone for months or even years at a time. That's probably how he managed to avoid getting caught for so long. By trade, he had been a huntsman and he had quite a knack for hunting and trapping wild game, dressing and cooking it. So, when he came to Crow Neck, that's the job he was given. He was damned good at it, too. They never went hungry around here. But there were some men that went missing during that time."

Nick fixed her with a grave look, and Ada drew in a sharp, shallow breath.

"Of course, convicts going missing didn't surprise anyone. Pretty common in work camps, really." He turned to her. "But when a human finger bone turned up in the stew one day, they finally got suspicious about the huntsman."

"Oh, Jesus, Nicky," Ada said, a hand over her mouth.

She looked pale to Nick—like she might be sick. "You all right, Ada?"

She cleared her throat and motioned for him to go on.

"They couldn't prove anything unfortunately. A finger bone didn't equal a murder back then. So, nothing came of it. Sometime after that, though, the huntsman was caught with the Amburg family's seventeen-year-old daughter, Clara. Caught with what was left of her anyway."

What was left of her. Those awful words hung in the air a moment.

"Do I want to know?" Ada asked.

Nick sighed and sat back down across from her. "I think

you need to. So, you know what it is . . . maybe . . . that you're up against."

"All right."

"When they found the huntsman, he'd already raped and killed the poor girl. He was nearly finished—" Nick took a moment and cleared his throat. "Finished butchering her for the next day's meals. They knew it was her by the dress they found with the remains."

Ada's mouth was agape, her hand held up to her face. "Sweet Lord."

"They locked him down in his own quarters. They didn't even involve the police until after."

"After what?" Ada asked.

"Next morning, they took the huntsman out, threw a rope over the limb of a tree and hung him dead. He was still strung up when the police finally got out here to the camp."

Ada sighed and rubbed her hands down the legs of her jeans. "The huntsman . . . what was his name?"

"Dekker. His name was Clyde Dekker."

Nick and Ada sat in stunned silence for a moment as the tale he just told sank in. Then Ada excused herself to the bathroom and left him there in the worship room, listening to the sound of her retching and dry heaving, as if she could expel all of the awful things she had just learned.

God Almighty, he thought. *If only it were that easy.*

Noah had walked into the house to retrieve the Cokes and was surprised when he didn't find his mother and Deputy Wren at the kitchen table, chatting over coffee. He opened the refrigerator and pulled two bottles and was turning to leave when he heard voices reverberating from down the hall. Moving through the living room, he saw the light on down at the end, coming from the worship room.

He couldn't conceive of any reason his mother would have taken the deputy into that awful and embarrassing part of their new home. But they were speaking in low tones, so whatever they were talking about, it sounded serious. Naturally, he decided to stay and listen.

Starting with the real estate agent having held back the detail that the work camp was full of convicts, Noah got an earful. While the Cokes grew warm and beaded with droplets of water in his hand, Noah listened with rapt attention to Deputy Wren's grisly history lesson on Cedar Banks and the terrible things that had happened here.

He listened right up to the part where the deputy said the huntsman's name. Noah had to steady himself, his knees suddenly shaking like twigs in a gale, and the cokes about to slip from his grasp.

So, it had a name. The ghost . . . the stinking man . . . it had a name.

Clyde Dekker. Huntsman. Cook. Killer. Dead man.

Noah's mother excused herself to the bathroom and one of the benches groaned against the floor as she stood up. Not wanting to be caught eavesdropping, he turned and padded away quietly, through the kitchen and down the stairs into the yard.

His feet now on the soft earth, he walked to the dock. A fire raged in his head, as if the things he had just learned were burning him from the inside. All at once, he was terrified, sickened, but also felt strangely vindicated. As unreal as it all was, he was not imagining it. There was another sensation taking shape within Noah also. Empowerment. Just knowing the name of the stinking man's ghost seemed to confer power upon him.

He has a name.

He has a name.

Over and over he repeated it under his breath as he approached Tommy, still sitting on the dock. The sun was low now and a fading orange sky set the edges of the clouds alight all along the horizon to the west.

When Ada returned, she found Nick standing at the window in the living room, watching the boys sitting together at the end of the dock out back.

"Sorry," he offered. "That room was giving me the creeps."

He didn't need to explain, least of all to her. She sat down on the couch and drew her knees to her chest. "You think this man, this Dekker. You think he's the one I've . . . " She couldn't finish it, though. Couldn't bear to.

"Honestly, Ada?" Nick sighed. "My first inclination is that you're imagining it and you should go get some help. Except your description of the . . . thing . . . matches the description of Dekker. Matches him exactly."

"Well," she said, hoping to find a way out of this conclusion, "I haven't actually *seen* anything."

"No," Nick replied. "But it's all there in what I read. Right down to his famously unwashed stench and the hand-rolled cigarillos he was known to smoke."

He turned to face her.

"And that ain't from the history books or old newspaper articles, Ada," he said. "Those details were only recorded in the police report at the time."

They stared at each other, unsettled and uncertain.

"What should I do?" she asked, fretful tears coming to her eyes.

Nick came across the room, sat, and took her hands in his own, locking eyes with her.

"Ada, I can tell you all day long what to do about Hugh, but this . . . " he drifted off a moment. "I specialize in things and people I can put in handcuffs. Things I can read Miranda rights to. Things I can lock in a cell. This is something else altogether. I haven't a clue what to tell you to do other than to get the hell away from this place."

She gulped down a fit of sobs and shut her eyes.

"And how you do that," he continued, "is by first doing something about Hugh. If you can get away from him . . . if you can leave this place, then maybe you'll get away from this thing. Whatever it is. Go to the Rockbridge Sheriff's Department, Ada. File a complaint against that sonofabitch. Get a restraining order."

She was already shaking her head before he even finished. "Those things don't happen overnight, Nick," she said. "Me and Noah will still have to live with him . . . *after* he knows what I've accused him of."

"Ain't you got somebody you can stay with?"

Ada shook her head. There was no one, no one in the world except for maybe Nick. But that wouldn't look very good to a judge later on. It might look like something it wasn't and like they'd all cooked up this story to get rid of Hugh.

"I'll find you somewhere to go," Nick said. "I promise I will."

She had no doubt that he could. And maybe they'd be all right for a little while—her and Noah—but eventually Hugh would find her. Short of locking him up, there would be no stopping him. And once he did find them, well . . . Lord have mercy. She and Noah had made it this far under Hugh's iron rule. They would just have to last a while longer until Noah was eighteen. What she didn't understand, though—what she couldn't wrap her mind around—was what to do about the huntsman, Dekker. What defense did she have against something like that? And why had Dekker picked *her*?

"What do you think he wants?" Ada asked Nick. "Dekker, I mean."

Deputy Nick Wren exhaled a long sigh and considered it, then shrugged. "I don't know. Maybe, in death, he wants the same things he loved and wanted in life. Like maybe we all would if we were damned to be wandering ghosts."

Ada nodded, turning this idea over in her mind, recalling the unmistakable lust that had hung thick in the air that night in the kitchen with the entity. The way it had caressed her flesh.

"What do you think that is?"

"For Dekker?" Nick said, his eyes darkening as he looked away from her. "Killing. I supposed he must've loved killing more than anything else in this world."

"Jeez, what took you so long?" Tommy asked Noah when he returned to the dock.

Noah's thoughts were elsewhere, though, so he said nothing—just handed the soda bottle to Tommy and stared intently out at the lake, turning things over in his mind.

"You all right, Noah?"

"Huh?"

"I asked if you're okay. You look sick or . . . I don't know. *Something.*"

"Do I?" Noah replied, running his fingers over his face. "I don't know. I guess I just got too warm going into the house."

Tommy nodded and twisted the top off his bottle for a swig. "You fished off this dock yet? I mean I know it's real cold and all, but . . . "

Noah sat down on the dock beside his friend, their feet dangling over the edge, just inches above the gently moving water. "Naw, I haven't yet."

"Shit, I'd be fishing every day if it was me."

Noah smiled. He opened his bottle of Coke and the two sat at the end of the dock, reflectively studying the water and the failing light of the day rippling of its surface. He very badly wanted to tell Tommy of what he had heard in the house. But he was afraid the whole thing would just come off as odd, and right about now Noah felt like the world around him was about as odd as he could stand. So, he sat and drank his soda and said not a word.

After a few minutes, Noah heard the kitchen door open and Deputy Wren hollered out for Tommy.

"Yeah?"

"Y'all come on in and say your goodbyes. We gotta get going, okay?"

"Okay," Tommy groaned.

They both sat there a moment longer with nothing but the silence of their imminent parting between them.

"Maybe you can come back next weekend," Noah offered, though he knew that wouldn't happen.

"Yeah, maybe. But if not, definitely on Christmas break."

Noah nodded, but he doubted it would happen. His father would be around.

They shuffled down the dock toward the house, neither boy trying to get there with any speed.

"Hey," Tommy said quietly, leaning in and elbowing Noah. "Let's go back to your room before I go. I got a few more things for you."

"Oh?"

"Yeah," his friend replied, a certain gleam of mischief in his eye. "Call it an early Christmas present."

Noah forced a smile and tried to muster some excitement at the idea. Tommy having come for a visit was all that he could have hoped for, though it was the worst kind of gift—the kind that didn't last, on account of having to give it away.

30

From a dense stand of trees near the entrance to Cedar Banks, Hugh Belton stood in the shadows and watched as the tail lights of Deputy Wren's Bedford County cruiser lit up and it drove around the far side of the neighborhood. As it turned toward the entrance, he stepped back into the deep, black cover of the night and waited for it to pass.

Just that morning, Hugh and Bobby Ratsinger, the other driver, had offloaded the materials from

Poughkeepsie a full day ahead of schedule at the last stop in York, Pennsylvania and had hit the road. They had made good time getting back. When Bobby pulled the flatbed diesel up to the neighborhood and carefully slipped the wide vehicle through the narrow entrance, Hugh had seen the police cruiser parked in front of his house. So, he'd told Bobby to let him off there and back out of the development. He would walk the rest of the way, he told him.

Instead, he had stood and watched.

His first thought had been that it was the Rockbridge County police come to pay him a visit—that Ada had finally gotten fool enough to call them about Hugh exercising his God-given right to discipline his household as he saw fit. She was awful sore at him from the last licking he'd given Noah. He had seen something in her that night that he'd never seen before.

Hatred in her eyes.

Hugh supposed he knew then that she was getting it into her head to leave him. It was only when he saw Deputy Nick Wren and his good-for-nothing son come bounding out of his house that he understood the whole of what was going on in his absence.

While the cat's away, the mice do love to play, he thought.

From his spot in the trees, he leered at the faces of the deputy and his son illuminated by the headlights that bounced off the road and the trees—smiling and laughing. It boiled his blood. When the cruiser turned right and went disappearing down the dark country road, Hugh stepped out and onto the street at a brisk walk toward his house.

His house, by God.

He wondered how many times Ada's old boyfriend had been over to visit while he was away and working to put food on the table. Oh, she didn't think he knew about her and Nick Wren being high school sweethearts but he wasn't nearly half the fool that Ada took him for.

How many times has that man been in my house?

He imagined the marriage bed that belonged to him being soiled by long and lustful writhing. He imagined the sound of their ill-gotten pleasures echoing off the walls of his bedroom. On their wedding day, Ada had sworn before God to cleave only to him. Tonight he would remind her of that sacred vow.

Black Billy, strapped to his ankle beneath his denim jeans, itched to be loosed from its sheath as he stood at the edge of his driveway and watched. The house was warm with light and he could hear the TV blasting inside as his wife and son went about their evening, happily ensconced in the comfort that Hugh afforded them. All without a thought spared, or respect shown for the husband and father to whom they belonged. Climbing the steps of the porch, he placed his hand on the doorknob, twisted, and opened it.

Hugh stepped across the threshold into his house and Hell followed with him.

31

Ada came back to consciousness just as she had been, her face pressed down into the pile of pillows, the bedspread and sheets tossed haphazardly about from the struggle. The fabric and her face were still wet with tears and blood. The wound on her scalp stung like a swarm of hornets. She lifted her head a little, the pain vibrating through her body as she did so, and caught a glimpse of her clothes scattered about the room. On the bedside table, her brassiere hung over the picture of her and Noah taken when he was a baby. A pants leg of her jeans stretched over the table, the button and zipper torn, dangling somewhere below. Her body ached and her muscles were useless, atrophied appendages.

For a passing moment, Ada wondered what had happened. How had she ended up like this? No sooner had the thought come to her than it was answered. With a rush, her memory returned, and with it a headache that quickly slithered around her brain. It squeezed from her mind the visions of the night's events and did so with a sharp and throbbing agony. She descended into a dreamlike fugue and remembered.

She and Noah had been in the kitchen. Nick and Tommy Wren just left minutes before and she was microwaving something for their supper when the front door swung open and in walked Hugh Belton with a fire in his eyes the likes of which she had never seen before.

"Well, now!" he shouted as he slammed the door behind him. She heard the click of the deadbolt falling into place, for it sounded to her as lone and loud as a single, fatal gunshot.

"What's for supper?" he continued as he stepped into the kitchen with them.

She and Noah stood aghast with blank, stupefied looks on their faces.

"What?" He feigned surprise, though it was tinged with real bitterness. "Nick Wren didn't bring any of his world famous fried fucking turkey?"

Noah made to move past his father toward the living room or the house beyond it, maybe for the front door, but Hugh froze him with a look.

"Still your bones, boy, or I'll rap them so bad that come the morning, you'll wish I'd just gone and killed you."

Then he turned his gaze to her, sneering and accusatory. She steeled herself and tried her best to look him right back in the eye. She hadn't done anything wrong, despite what Hugh might be thinking.

"Well, Missus Belton, don't you look pretty," he spat at her. "How did he like it, your old boyfriend?"

"How did he like what, Hugh? He brought Tommy for a visit, that's—"

"How did he like your whore-paint, woman?" he shouted over her. "Made up like the harlot I should have known you are."

She hung her head, shamed, wondering how he knew about her past with Nicky Wren, though it hardly seemed to matter at that point.

"Lord, I was blind, but now I see," he whispered, raising his hands and open palms as if in a prayer of offering, his gaze aloft for a moment before settling back onto her. "Forgive my woman for her trespasses, Lord. Forgive her . . . because I sure as Hell won't."

Heedless of his imposing father, Noah ducked low and made to go quickly around and beneath Hugh's reach. Going for the door, Ada supposed, where he would cross the street and speed away to the old man for help.

Whatever his goal, it would not be realized. As he tried to slip by Hugh, the man reached out and grabbed his son by the shoulder. They struggled for a moment, grappling, and then he lifted the boy up into the air. He was suspended for a moment before Hugh sent him hurtling across the living room. Noah flailed in mid-air, then crashed face-first into the upholstered arm of the easy chair. From there, he slumped to the hardwood floor, his neck like a wet noodle, the back of his head cracking against the floor. That sound sent a wave of motherly terror through Ada.

"Dammit, Hugh!" she screamed. "That's our son."

He turned slowly and regarded her without remorse. "You," he whispered venomously. "I give you everything and this iniquity is what you bring into my house?"

Before she could even form a response, she saw him reach down his leg to his ankle, pull up the denim. From a sheath strapped there, he drew forth Black Billy.

Upon seeing it, she tensed up in preparation for the blow, but when he brought it down, it surprised her. It cut a black ribbon across her vision and met first with her cheek and then scraped across the rest of her face. Her nose bent far to the side, skin straining and then tearing, blood vessels breaking, sending a shower of crimson down her face.

Hugh had always been careful not to batter her face. He'd always kept the bruises to places where they could be hidden. Not anymore.

She teetered, trying to keep her balance and her vision even as both slipped away from her. When she went limp and fell, Hugh caught her in his arm, though it was not to lend support. He crooked his elbow around her neck and squeezed, stepping forward and dragging her along with him by the throat. She reached out for anything she could but succeeded only in knocking over lamps and pictures. Her airway was constricting more and more with every step he took through the living room and down the dark hallway.

With a toss, he released her onto the bed where she landed belly-up. She lay there for a moment, so dazed that she did not perceive him removing her pants until they were at her knees. She struggled against him, clawing at the bedspread and the sheets to get away, even though there was nowhere to go. Frustrated with her resistance, he took hold of Black Billy and rapped her across the forehead. At first there was the pain from the blow and then the steady ache dulled only by her shaken consciousness. As she lay there, confused and limp, he pulled the remainder of her clothes from her body. What he could not remove, his huge, thick hands tore away with abandon. Naked and vulnerable, she flipped over and clawed at the headboard to gain a grip.

"You are mine," he seethed from behind her. "I might could forgive all you've done but you have to—"

She kicked out and struck him in the stomach. For a moment he lost his breath and paused, but it only seemed to double his strength and resolve as he grabbed her hips. He leaned in and pressed himself against her, the rough, greasy denim scraping her bare skin.

Pressing his mouth to her ear, he whispered, "You have to be taught a lesson."

She shook her head and growled and he eased off her for a moment, though that brief respite was followed by a hail of blows from Black Billy that landed upon her back and arms with a thundering force that seemed likely to pummel her bones to dust.

"You are mine," he bellowed, sounding to her as if he spoke through tears of anguish.

"You—"

Thwack!

"Are—"

Thwack!

"Mine!"

Thwack!

She no longer had the strength to resist or to crawl away from him as he approached her, pressed against her backside once again. Ada knew well what he had in mind but judging from the fleshy, limp thing pressing against her thighs, Hugh was not up to the task.

A snicker escaped her lips and the sound of it made him go even softer.

"You can't even get it up now, can you?"

"Damn you, woman," he snarled.

She heard the snap as he opened the folding knife he kept on his belt. As he leaned over her, she just knew that this was it. He was going to cut her throat and leave her there to bleed out. And Noah? Would Hugh kill his only son? Or would Noah be the one to find her in the morning, lying cold in a red-soaked bed?

"When the cat's away, the mice will play," he whispered.

The blade pressed into the soft flesh just to the side of her nose.

"Let's see if Nick Wren wants to play with your ugly ass after this, little mouse."

Hugh dragged the sharp blade in a line across her

cheek, and as it bit into her skin, she struggled against him. He doubled up on her and jammed his knee down on her neck as he pulled the blade from her nose across her face again and again, crisscrossing. Red strokes, like a drunken butcher cutting meat.

The pain was red-hot, but she was slipping away from it. She was sinking.

Ada was shutting down.

To make it through this, to come out on the other side of it, a primal and merciful part of her brain set itself about burying the horror right away. Her perception was hazy and impossibly gray and the strokes of the blade were met with numbness as the world swam away from her in a swirl of crimson on white cotton sheets.

Now, as she struggled toward consciousness, her ears still rang from the blows he had laid upon her—deafening her to the world with a persistent ringing. Her face burned with the lacerations from his knife, the cuts now stiff with coagulated blood.

Hugh wasn't there in the room anymore, and thank God for that.

Before she had blacked out entirely, she had seen him striding away down the hall, his heavy work boots like thunderclaps on the hardwood floor. Then the thud of the front door slamming shut, which echoed throughout the house and rattled the windows.

There was something else, though. Something she needed to remember?

Noah.

Her son had fallen early under her husband's assault. She remembered the sharp crack of his head on the hardwood. Terrible things flashed through her mind. Concussion, brain bleeding, aneurysm, skull fracture. The surge of a mother's adrenaline in Ada's veins demanded that she see to the welfare of her child. She tried to rise from her prone position on the bed, but her body was spent and would not allow it. With a shudder, she came to rest again, flat on the bed with nothing but the lonely silence of the house for company.

That was when she smelled him.

How long the thing had been there, she didn't know. Had he only just materialized from the blackest depths of Hell's Pit or had he been there all along, watching and slathering like a hound?

After her conversation with Nick, she had gotten the notion that it was Hugh's violence that attracted the thing. Maybe it was that alone which gave him the power to be perceived at all. She didn't know. But she could feel his presence now, growing like a cancer within the walls of her bedroom, intensifying. Ada turned her head and thought she saw a hulking shadow but before she could fix her watery eyes on it, the lights of the room flickered and then gave out, plunging her into a waking night.

Then there came that guttural chortle of amusement.

Last night, in the moments between Nick's departure and Hugh barreling through the front door, she had been considering just how bad a spot she and her son were in. There was nowhere for them to turn, nowhere to go. They were beset on all sides by violence and fear. Even her best ally—a policeman—knew that this was something that she alone had to deal with. And the system wouldn't help them. They wouldn't even survive the attempt to get away from Hugh—she had no doubt about that. Ada whimpered as terror crept over her like the legs of a thousand tiny spiders.

And in that moment, she remembered Nick's words.

If you can get away from him . . . if you can leave this place, then maybe you'll get away from this thing.

When Nick said that, she'd had a simple thought. So simple and ignorant and foolish to her own mind that she had dismissed it.

Now, though, with Hugh's new brand of violence and the iron scent of her own blood lingering in the air, mixing with the huntsman's foul reek, that foolish notion now seemed the best of a precious few and terrible options.

She needed to use her two tormentors against each other—Hugh and the huntsman. Only then would she be rid of them both.

Broken and bloodied, Ada summoned all the courage and resolve she had left. For her own sake and for Noah's she had to try.

"I can smell you, you know," she said dryly, suddenly aware of the croaking of her voice and how very thirsty she was.

Despite the fact that she could not see him, Ada could feel his desire in the air as surely as she could feel his evil. He wanted her but he was no longer of the flesh, and even the worst of their pain and fear wasn't enough to give him the strength to simply take it. There was something she could offer, though. Something powerful that might just make the difference—consent.

As unthinkable of a prospect as it was, she could offer herself willingly.

"I know who you are, *Clyde Dekker*."

At this, she sensed genuine surprise, though it in no way daunted him. Rather, it seemed to feed his ego and only served to deepen his desire.

"Oh, yeah," she said. "Couldn't get yourself a woman like a real man, I hear. Always had to take one. Like that young Amburg girl they found you with at the end. She wouldn't have nothing to do with your stinkin' ass, so you had to take her by force."

She managed a dismissive scoff. "I bet you couldn't even get it up then, could you?"

The walls and the table and the bed seemed to tremble and swell . . . or was it just her imagination? It hardly mattered.

"Well, come on, *little man*," she taunted. She would offer herself up to him, but it would not be without a price.

In the darkness there was a seething but impotent silence.

"But you can't, can you?" she spat, then laughed. "As impotent now as the day they swung you by the neck."

She couldn't see him but his presence evoked an image in her mind's eye of a caged animal, pacing back and forth, unable to get at the quarry that lay just beyond its reach.

Yes, he wanted her but she knew what else the old wraith craved. Nick had said as much.

Killing. I think he must have loved killing more than anything else in this world.

Ada could offer him both.

"I know the appetites you have," she said, trying hard to control her voice and the sobbing that threatened at the edge of every word. "And I can give you what you want. *Everything* you want."

At this, the presence swelled with such animal enthusiasm that the very walls groaned and a pressure filled her head, increasing the throbbing pain tenfold.

"I'll give it to you, you son of a bitch," she said. "You can take as much of me as you like. But that's the price for what I mean to purchase from you, understand? The thing you want most of all."

There was no need to speak it. She had already let the thing get its foot through the door. The presence of Dekker was there, awful and invasive in her mind. She thought of Hugh and all the memories she had of him, both good and bad. Then she thought of his tyranny falsely clothed in faith, and the unending anguish and alienation it had brought to her and to Noah.

They should never have come to this place. In this dark corner of the wilderness, in the shadow of the mountain, there was no deliverance to hope for. No one to rescue them. Even God had forsaken them.

There was a disquieted stillness as the offer was considered.

Ada waited, breathless, her heart beating wildly in her

chest and her head half-buried in the pillows still moist with her own tears and blood. When, in the darkness, the bedroom door creaked on its hinges and latched closed, she knew a deal had been struck.

The bargain was made.

In the darkness, the huntsman breathed and took on a more substantial form. Not flesh, and not exactly physical. It was like the pulse of sound she remembered when she used to linger near the speakers at the church dances of her youth, a forever wallflower. The thing was stronger now, though. Empowered by her consent. She bristled at its cold touch on her skin. Ada lay still and resolute as she allowed the vile thing to climb atop her, to invade her most intimate places. She didn't know if Noah had yet awoken, but she prayed he hadn't. Ada didn't want her son to hear the muffled, wailing sobs to come, as the thing took unholy, carnal liberties with her.

PART III:

RECKONING

"Some rise by sin, and some by virtuc fall."
—William Shakespeare, *Measure for Measure*

32

NOAH AWOKE WITH a shock. He twitched and instinctively raised his hands to defend himself. But things had gone calm. Groaning, he rose up on one knee, holding onto the chair for balance. He looked around, expecting to see his father there, but the house was dead quiet. A thunderous pain throbbed in his head. He doubled over, placing his head on the cushion of the chair, cradling it with both hands. He remained there until the searing spikes dulled to a persistent ache. He got unsteadily to his feet and took a good look around. The living room was a mess. Lamps were still lit but were overturned and the skewed positions of their shades cast weird, angular shadows about the walls. Looking through the picture window, he saw that it was absolute dark outside and he wondered what time it was. He shuffled into the kitchen, moving like a horror-show zombie to steal a glance at the clock. It was 4:13 in the morning.

Noah's head was aching, his memory fuzzy. He struggled to recall the night. They had been getting ready to eat when his father came in, he remembered. Then all Hell had broken loose. He had tried to escape, to make it out the door. But his father had stopped him cold, picked him up, and tossed him across the room like a bail of straw.

That was all he could remember, but the rest was easy enough to guess. Without a doubt, his father had taken out his rage on Noah's mother. Although he hadn't witnessed it with his own eyes, he was sure the man's fury had been unchained.

As he shambled about the kitchen, trying to get his head right, his gaze fell on the table. There were two place settings there, empty and unused. But there was now another plate, too, where his father usually sat. It was dark with gravy, drying noodles going stiff, and slivers of beef from the Stroganoff they were going to have for supper. Unlike the other chairs left askew, his father's was neatly pushed in against the edge of the table.

He ate, Noah realized. *He beat her like an animal, then sat down and ate supper.*

Noah trembled with anger, with fear, with uncertainty. Where was his mother?

It was so very quiet in the house. Had his father finally crossed the line and killed her?

The thought sent Noah into a panic and he tore through the living room, down the hallway, his eyes searching every space for some indication of her. In his bedroom, he saw nothing. In the worship room, he saw nothing.

All that was left was the bedroom his mother and father shared. The door was closed. He approached it tenderly, needing to see what lay on the other side, but also afraid of what he might find.

He sneered some courage into his guts, turned the knob, and burst in.

It was a mess. Clothing was tossed about carelessly, things out of place, knocked over, lying on the floor. Noah's father was nowhere to be seen but his mother lay naked and face-down in the pillows of their bed. A wide, crimson stain had gathered around her head.

"Mumma?" he called, his voice weak as he approached the bed.

No answer, no movement.

"Mumma?" He placed a hand on her shoulder and gently shook.

She stirred. He shook her with insistence, calling to her over and over again.

"Noah?" Her words were slurred and groggy, her command of speech not yet restored. She turned to him. Her face was pale and sallow but for the marks; there were dark lines of crusted blood that streaked across from one cheek to the other, her skin swollen along the wounds where a blade had opened the flesh.

"Mumma! Mumma, Jesus, are you—?"

"I'm fine, baby boy." Her voice croaked. "Just fine."

Her naked back and bottom were covered with fresh red welts that would soon blossom into dark bruises. The marks of Black Billy—these were the fingerprints of his father. Seeing his mother there in that moment, Noah swore to himself this would never happen again. A vivid scenario flashed through his mind and he imagined his father sleeping in bed beside his mother. Casually sleeping, after all that he had done, after all the misery he had visited upon them. Noah thought of the baseball bat in his room. The Louisville Slugger. When his father came home—and Noah was sure that he eventually would—he could take the bat and creep into their bedroom. Standing there beside their bed, he would split his father's head wide open. Blood for blood.

"You're hurt real bad," he said, trying not to stare at his mother's face.

"I know. I'll be okay. Just got to clean myself up is all."

Noah couldn't believe what he was hearing.

"No. It ain't okay, Mumma. I've got to go get some help. I'll go across the street and get Clay. Maybe he can—"

At this, his mother's eyes widened and her voice went stern.

"You can't do that, Noah. You can't. He sees me like this and he'll call the police. He won't be able to help himself. And once they get involved, son . . . " There were tears at the edges of her eyes, cresting over and down her battered face, her voice shaking. "Noah they'll split us up. My heart couldn't take that, son."

Noah remembered what she'd said before. How they would send him to a foster home. Away from his mother. Away from his only family.

"We can't lose each other, baby boy," she said. "You don't want to lose me, do you?"

He shook his head.

She managed a smile.

"You're a good son. Now, help me up and into the bathroom so I can get cleaned up."

"All right, Mumma." Noah took his mother's hand and guided her out of the bed into the bathroom, though he didn't flick on the light switch.

"Go on now," she said, shooing him away.

He hovered there a moment, wanting to protest.

"Go on," she hollered, but smiled, then closed the door.

Ada paused in the darkness before turning on the light. When she finally switched it on, she gulped and whimpered at the sight of herself. A score of dark, jagged wounds crossed her face.

When the cat's away, the mice will play.

Hugh's attempt at whiskers, perhaps, for his unfaithful little mouse.

He had nicked her nose with his blade, too. A few strokes of his knife had made her a monster.

Ada wet a cloth and dabbed at her face through tears, gentle with the scabs so as not to make the blood run again. When she was done, she returned to the bedroom and found clean sheets stretched across the mattress. It was a small thing her son had done, but she was thankful for it—even if Noah had put them on the wrong way.

Bless his heart, she thought, as she slid beneath the covers.

Ada lay there on her side, looking at the wall where there was nothing at all to see. It was strange. Before, she had always preferred to face the doorway so that she could see if Hugh came in. Now, it hardly seemed to matter. Sooner or later, one of her tormentors—either the living one or the phantom—would darken that doorway and there was nothing in the world she could do about it. She was resigned to these terrible fates.

At least for now.

Ada was spent, utterly and absolutely. She closed her eyes and let her mind drift. Strange noises came to her then. Muffled whispers of movement. Not from inside the room but close. Very close. She was falling hard into an engulfing rest, though, and could not spare the energy to wonder at it further.

Still, it was there; that sound. Like something moving in the walls.

33

Noah was munching on a peanut butter sandwich when he heard his mother settle into the bed. After a few minutes, when the gentle purr of her snoring drifted down the hallway, he balled up the bloodied sheets he'd stripped off the bed and shoved them into the washer. Standing there, though, faced with the dials and buttons and settings, he realized he didn't have the slightest clue how to wash a load of anything. So, he closed the lid and set about cleaning up the mess from the previous night's melee.

There were things scattered about the floor in pieces— trinkets and knick-knacks that had shattered. He scooped them up into the dustpan and dumped them into the trash. All the things that were broken beyond repair.

It reminded him of his entire young life, and something in him longed to just sit down right then and there and have a good cry. To wallow in the awful things and wait for his mother to come and comfort him. But that was a child's want and it occurred to Noah then that he hadn't been a child for many years, even if he was only now catching onto that fact. Adulthood was being thrust upon him whether he was ready for it or not.

His father was a coward and a monster. Noah was the man of the house now. It was high time he started acting like it. Without so much as a single tear, Noah straightened and cleaned until the remnants of the previous night's violence were cleansed from the house.

How long? he wondered. *How long until I'm picking up the pieces again?*

His father would return. There was nothing he could do about that. But he wouldn't let him have at his mother like that again. He'd stop him, even if it killed him.

Weary from the cleanup—weary from it all—Noah needed to rest, but was afraid to let his guard down. In the end, his fatigue won out, but before he stretched out on the couch, he pulled a big knife from the block in the kitchen and slid it beneath the pillow and between the cushions.

He pulled the chain on the living room's ceiling fan and lay down. Noah clicked on the television and scrolled through the few channels until he landed on some reruns of *The Rifleman.* He leaned back on the pillow and watched for a while. Above his head, the blades of the fan—unbalanced in its socket—circled round and round, wobbling with a steady swish and thump.

Swish, thump, swish, thump.

He didn't intend to think of it but that sound reminded him of Black Billy cutting the air and crashing into Noah's flesh and bones. He couldn't help but recall Thanksgiving night, when his father had locked him in the crawlspace.

Beneath the pillow, his fingers grazed the cold steel of the kitchen knife, reminding him that it was there if he needed it.

The crawlspace. The dark and the cold. Black Billy. These things floated on tumultuous currents of thought and his tired mind, heavy with sleep, sank into a memory and rendered it as a dream.

Swish, thump, swish, thump.

Noah stirs out of a heavy darkness, like a tremendous weight about his head. His father is dragging him down the hallway by his feet. To that room, that room with the hideous cross and the strange, black chamber in the wall. The crawlspace, the secret place. His head lolls to the side and consciousness threatens to disappear once again. He holds onto it, but just barely. He is detached from the world. It plays before him as if he were seated in a theater, watching.

He's shoved into a cold place. The sudden change in temperature goes a long way toward clearing the fog from his mind. He is in there now. In the crawlspace with its metal floor and walls like ice against his skin, with its lingering stink of sweet, rotten meat. One last shove, the hard sole of his father's work boot pushing against his hip, and the light cutting through the opening diminishes. Then it's gone. Before the door closes and the lock clicks into place, though, Noah can hear his mother in the worship room, sobbing into her hands with hitched breaths.

Then all the world is darkness.

He flails about inside of the space, his knees, hands and feet bumping against the walls. Even though he is small and the space is larger than his body, it is becoming difficult to breathe.

When Noah was only a toddler he was dropped off at a daycare by his mother. After being left that morning, he became suddenly ill. Coughing at first and then vomiting. The daycare people fell into a panic, as if a deadly virus had snuck into the place. They quarantined him—but not in a nurse's office or even a classroom.

They locked him in a storage closet.

In that closet there was a single bulb with a pull chain. The bulb was on the fritz and very dim, flickering on and off constantly, randomly plunging him into blackness. The four walls lined with shelves of balls and toys closed in on him—the balls were featureless faces, the action figures looming menaces. He beat against the closet door and cried out for release but no one came to free him. Not until hours later when his mother finally arrived to pick him up—furious.

The crawlspace is just like that, except multiplied by a thousand.

Noah feels the air thinning, the walls encroaching. In the room that is only inches away, his mother and father are talking. The sound of their voices comes through the wall as a deadened hum. Then there comes a sound that he cannot account for. A shuffle of movement that doesn't belong to him. A prolonged drag and shudder, as if something massive is slithering within the walls.

He remembers the matches in his pocket from lighting the candles for dinner. Strike-anywhere matches. His spirits lift as he digs a hand into his pants pocket and fishes one of them out. He flicks it against the metal above him and it flames to life, filling the dark space with a dancing, amber light. His shadow convulses on the walls. He tries to calm his breathing, to control it. Then, all too soon, the match burns down to his fingers and he drops it. The light flickers and gives out. He digs for another one but then there is a different sound. The rasp of many voices—a storm of whispers. Unsure if he is hearing it with his ears or only in his mind, he shakes his head to make it go away. But it does not. And through the chaos of it, two words emerge. He perceives them as clear as a bell.

"Hear us."

There is a tug on his sleeve, an unknown touch brushing against his skin. Colder than the icy metal walls around him. The breath goes out of him and with a trembling hand in his pocket, he searches for another match. He draws one out but it slips from his unsteady fingers.

Outside the crawlspace door, in the worship room, the muffled conversation has stopped.

Noah exchanges some words with his father. From Noah's lips they are words of supplication and apology. It doesn't matter that he knows his words are hollow. It only matters that he flee from this dark and shrinking place.

Why won't they just let him out? He's learned the lesson. Why doesn't his mother do something?

"Don't . . . don't leave me in here, Dad. I'm sorry, so sorry . . . " he says in a loud but trembling voice, gasping for breath.

Finally, his fingers close around a match that does not slip his grasp. He reaches up, flicks it against the metal and it roars to life in a plume of smoke and sulfur stink that is absolutely lost in the bad meat odor of the suffocating crawlspace. But this is not what troubles him the most.

It's what he sees in the meager light.

Bodies surround him. Pale, dead skin marred by crimson wounds, faces with missing eyes and ears, jaws locked open in rigor. Limbs hacked away from their torsos. And they are moving—all of them. Clawing at him.

"Hear us."

Their chilled, rotting fingers grasp at him like fat, writhing worms. How many of them there are, he has no idea but there is no space in this dark hole that they do not occupy, and for a moment he is reminded of the congregation crowding around him as they did back at the Pentecostal church. Laying on hands, constricting and terrifying him into a numbing paralysis.

With a final, sputtering gasp of flame and smoke, the match gives out and he is alone with the darkness once more.

Except he is not alone—not at all.

Noah screams. It is a high, pained sound, like a roll of barbed wire being ripped out of his mouth through his throat, his lungs emptying like a bellows.

His mind struggles to flee, to disconnect from this horror. It fails.

He sucks in a deep breath and there is more screaming as he feels the dead upon him, a putrid blanket of cold, necrotic flesh.

They cling to him, all of them filled with an ache for something that is beyond their reach. Comfort. Justice. Retribution. Their loved ones now long forgotten. Even life itself—especially life. All of them wanting something he cannot provide.

Noah sinks into himself, burrows deep to weather this storm, and does not emerge until hours later, when he is at last free from the crawlspace and his mother is by his side, watching over him.

He stirred out of the last tendrils of his memory-as-dream and was just awake enough to catch himself whimpering, breathing shallow. He needed to put a stop to all that. Reaching his hand further under the pillow, he closed his grip around the handle of the kitchen knife. It was only then that his breathing eased and a sort of icy calm came to settle over him, bearing him gently back to rest.

34

The next morning, Noah found his mother in much better spirits, even if her body had not quite caught up yet. He fixed her coffee and a plate of toast with jelly—all that she could manage to eat, she said.

He sat there in the bedroom with her while she ate, until she shooed him away.

"Lord, Noah," she said. "It ain't like you're on deathwatch, son. I just need some rest is all. Go on and be a kid for a while."

Reluctantly, he did as he was told and strapped on his shoes and coat. He sauntered down into the woods where he busied himself, mostly knocking around the old, dead trees, pausing often to look out onto the lake and consider all that had been going on of late.

Beneath the growing anger at his father, Noah was tired of it all; tired and sad. They were all alone out here, with no one to help and no one he could confide in—no one with whom he could share his burden.

The stark loneliness he felt had him considering calling for the boys, Will and Albie, but their presence would probably only unnerve him and turn his thoughts to Clay. The old man was the one person he had thought was his friend, but who Noah now suspected was just another shady figure to be dreaded—one among many—here in the shadow of the mountain.

When his stomach began to rumble, he judged it close to lunchtime and so he made his way along the lakeshore back toward the house.

Rounding the last bend in the forest, though, he spied his father's truck in the driveway and it froze him in his tracks. What would be waiting for him there once he stepped across that threshold? Another beating? Another lecture infused with scripture? Perhaps something worse? Maybe his father had returned to finish the job and Noah would find his mother there, cold in the bed, and his father waiting patiently so that he might give his only child the same dark ending.

The thought of that man in the house with his mother sickened him, though, so Noah screwed up what little courage he had and pressed on. Up the steps and into the house.

Inside, it was quiet. Not even the television was on, and his father was nowhere to be seen. Still, Noah could feel his presence in the house. It was a heaviness in the air to which he had long ago grown accustomed.

He stepped into his room and grabbed his Louisville

Slugger before going up the hallway and easing open the door to his mother's room. A bedside table lamp was on and she was in the bed on her side, her back turned away from the door, snoring. Gently latching the door behind him, Noah went to the only other place there was to look.

The door to the worship room was cracked open, the light on inside. His father was on bended knee before the cross, his hands joined together and his head bowed in silent prayer. Noah's lip curled in disgust at the sight of him. Part of him wanted nothing more than to charge in and take a swing at the back of his head with the business end of the Slugger, but he supposed that beating someone—even a very deserving someone—in front of a cross was probably some form of sacrilege. He let the tip of the bat thump on the floor as he leaned against the doorframe.

The fear melted away and left only raw contempt for this man in its wake.

His father turned and regarded him. In his eyes, there was an even calm that was so human and so normal that Noah was reminded this man was not entirely a monster— even if he often was. There was a time when Noah remembered him as just a normal dad, although strange and tyrannical in his own way. He recalled flashes of such moments. His father patiently teaching him how to make a paper airplane and launch it into the wind. The way a smile crept across his face whenever Noah requested spaghetti for supper—his favorite meal, and his father's also. That Fourth of July at the Bedford County Fair, and how lofty he'd felt, perched atop his father's shoulders as they watched the dazzling fireworks display. That same night, he had inexplicably allowed Noah to stay out well past his bedtime so that he might devour cotton candy and fried, sugary elephant ears. So much so that Noah had crawled into bed with a full and aching tummy.

He wanted to hate the man that knelt there before his own twisted cross, but he simply could not. No matter the

Hell he'd made of their lives, he was still his father. And in that moment, Noah understood something of the complexities that his mother must have always wrestled with, though she never spoke of it to him. Nor would she—ever. He was her baby, her only child, and she didn't reckon him capable of understanding.

Still, his mother was in bed now, recovering from her wounds, and this sonofabitch was playing at piety.

"You praying for forgiveness?" Noah asked.

"There something I need to be forgiven for?"

A flurry of angry replies to the question flew through his mind, but he settled on one his father used on him time and again whenever Noah asked a similar question.

"If you have to ask, then it's not yet time for forgiveness."

His father stood, looked him hard in the eye. Noah had spoken some bold words, and he'd meant them. Now, though, his knees wanted to knock together as the man stared him down. His grip on the Slugger was moist from his sweating palm.

They stayed like that for a moment, their eyes locked. It was his father who broke, though, and glanced over at the crawlspace door.

"I see you patched up the latch and put a new lock on it."

Noah nodded.

"Where'd you get the hardware?"

Noah considered giving no answer but silence. After all, who was his father to question him about that damnable place?

"Not that it matters, but I took it from the tool shed in the backyard."

"*My* tool shed?"

"It ain't yours no more."

The words fell out of Noah's mouth before he could second guess them, but he didn't flinch, and wouldn't take them back.

His father sighed. "I see."

Noah backed out into the hallway a little more, though his eyes never left his father. He watched him, as wary of the man as he would be a copperhead snake loose in the house.

"Dad," he dared. "Mumma don't want you here."

"No, I expect not. Not yet anyhow. She's still pretty sore at me, I bet."

Sore? Noah thought. *Oh, she's sore all right.*

"What'd you come here for?"

Hugh plucked his duffel bag from a nearby bench. "Gotta make another run up north tonight. I need to at least wash these clothes."

Noah considered it for a moment, fighting the urge to bend.

"No," he said, shaking his head and raising the bat a little in case he had to swing it. "They got laundromats in town."

At this, Hugh Belton's nostrils flared. Noah could see the anger building in his father's reddening face and that telltale vein bulging on the side of his neck. He tightened his grip on the Slugger.

"All right then," he growled and walked past Noah, down the hallway, stopping just as he crossed into the living room. "You know, son, when I'm back home—and she will let me back, don't you doubt it—we're gonna put all this behind us. *All of it.*"

The icy threat was not lost on Noah, but he raised his chin in bold reply.

"Lord, yes," his father continued as he walked to the front door. "When I come back home, there's gonna be a reckoning around here, boy. As God as my witness, there's gonna be a reckoning."

Noah's sweaty fingers trembled as they grasped the Slugger. He followed his father to the door, determined to see him out.

"See you soon," his father offered in parting, flashing a poisonous smile.

Noah closed the door and locked it, then went around

to the kitchen and did the same. He waited until the truck was gone, its red tail lights diminishing far into the night, before be breathed a sigh of relief.

Then, with all his anxiety and fleeting courage formed into an acid rock in his stomach, he ran to the hallway bathroom and threw up.

When he finally slept that night, it was not in his bed. He lay on the couch, instead, facing the front door, with a white-knuckled grip on the handle of the kitchen knife tucked beneath the pillow.

35

December

Ada dragged herself up to a sitting position. All things considered, she was doing much better than expected. She still ached a bit, but she discovered that normal movement itself was much less painful than it had been the day before.

On her bedside table, the clock read 10:24 in the morning. Three days since the night Hugh had dragged her into that bedroom. Next to the clock, there was a new plate with toast and jelly, a cup of coffee, and a note from Noah.

Morning, Mumma. Made you some breakfast if you want it. I'm outside messing around.

Beneath his scrawl was a smiley face with tiny hearts for eyes.

"Sweet boy," she remarked as she sipped the coffee and found it cold.

She put her feet down on the cool floor and stood. The soreness in her limbs abated with every step she took through the house to the kitchen. The coffee in the pot was still hot, so she splashed the cold cup into the sink and poured herself a new one.

Glancing about the house, she was pleased to see Noah had cleaned up all the mess. She knew he would have done so by now. But for the horrible memory, it was like nothing ever happened. At the sight of it, Ada was awash in a flood of love and appreciation for her son, though she wasn't sure how deserving of him she was.

She wiped at her eyes and looked around.

The calendar tacked to the kitchen wall was still turned to November. Above the grid of days was a lovely picture of a grist mill by a river shrouded in a canopy of autumn foliage.

"Hell of a Thanksgiving that was," she remarked bitterly, thinking back. So, she flipped the calendar over to December and smiled.

December had always held a special place in her heart. With all the trappings of Christmas time and the anticipation of yule festivities that permeated the very air, she had taken quite a shine to it ever since she was a little girl—as most all children do. Her affinity for the season had not waned with adulthood, though. It was still very much a part of her.

It was a great pity that Hugh's disdain for celebrating the holiday in traditional ways had always been something of a wet blanket on her spirit. Even though she feared him—perhaps now more than ever—his wishes meant much less to her now. Especially after what he had put them through.

After what he's put our son through.

Well to Hell with Hugh, she decided. Why not breathe a little life back into the holiday this year? She recalled an old box at the bottom of her closet whose contents she had not yet culled. In it was a string or two of Christmas lights from the last tree she'd had and a collection of decorations that had been her mother's favorites long ago.

Why not? she thought. Trimming the house with a little holiday cheer might even go so far as to brighten her dismal mood.

If it could be brightened . . . with the dead thing hanging about.

Even now, she could smell him near, skulking in the background just out of sight. Ada had made a pact, and now he was with her always. Dekker lingered nearby whether she was asleep or awake and his constant presence drove her into such dark places of the mind that in the days since, she had slept more often than not—a means of escape as much as it was for her body to heal.

At times, he spoke to her of foul things that she could scarcely bear to hear and when he did, she tried to counter his taunting by covering her head in pillows or humming familiar tunes loudly, that she might drown out the sound of his gravelly voice in her mind.

Sometimes it worked, other times it did not.

He had also been at her again since the night of the pact, climbing inside her with all the charm of a rutting hog. He reminded her of Hugh in that way. She had suffered his assaults in silence, digging a hiding place deep in some part of herself where she could find sanctuary. But the most abysmal horror always came afterward, when she awoke in her bed and found him still there in the corner of her bedroom, his black eyes upon her, leering. How much more of her he would take was a thing unknown, for she had no measure of how much more she had to give. And in those dark moments of wakefulness, she wondered when the stinking phantom would honor his part of the bargain. When would she be rid of Hugh so that she and her son could make another life for themselves far away from all that was cursed and damned?

Ada stood in the kitchen with sagging shoulders, alone but not alone. She spared the evil thing a look as he stood in the corner of the kitchen, stropping a wicked blade on a length of leather over his knee and smiling horridly.

She hung her head in her hands and wept.

After a morning walk around the lake in hopes of catching the blond boys as they roamed the woods, Noah was headed back home when he came upon Clay standing idly by the lakeshore. He was uncertain of how to behave, but decided it was best to act as if all things were normal.

"Hey," Noah said.

Clay looked up into the wide, gray sky and sniffed.

"They say one hell of a storm's coming."

"Yeah?" Noah replied.

"I come down here to see if they're right," Clay said. "The lake . . . it gets a certain smell coming off the water whenever there's big weather headed this way."

"Neat," he said.

Neat? That sounds stupid and fake, he thought. Noah didn't want to seem too nervous.

"Anyway," Clay said. "What's doing, young man?"

The old man didn't look surprised to see him. Not one bit. Had he been waiting for him? There was no other reason for him to be out here, just milling about. He had no line in the water, wasn't scavenging the shore for relics or whatever it was that kept the old man crisscrossing the grounds at Cedar Banks day after day. And that stuff about smelling the weather sounded like bullshit to Noah.

He was waiting for him. Noah was sure of it.

"Just out for a walk out in the woods," he replied.

The old man flashed him a casual smile that cooled Noah's blood.

"Me, too."

Noah looked beyond Clay to his house. It seemed so far away. Then he noticed the bits of freshly shaven wood scattered all around the old man's feet. In one hand was a stick of wood he'd been carving on, and in the other flashed the long blade of a Bowie knife.

He shifted his feet nervously when he saw it.

"Carving something up?" he asked.

Clay looked down at the bit of oak and nodded, though

Noah got the sense that his mind wasn't entirely trained on it.

"I never told you why it is I spend so much time wandering these hills, did I?"

Noah shook his head, his breath going shallow and his heart starting to flutter.

"I didn't think so," Clay said, tapping the knife blade against his thigh. "Which presents me with something of a conundrum."

Noah blinked, shoved his trembling hands into his jacket pockets.

"Conundrum?"

"A mystery," Clay clarified.

He swiped the knife blade against his trousers and it made a ringing sound as it came away.

Noah skirted around closer to the forest, keeping his distance. Clay turned, too, never taking his eyes from him.

"See, I think you know something, Noah," the old man said, then snorted. "Only I don't see any way you could know it."

Shit, shit, shit. Noah's knees were going wobbly.

"Me?" he replied. "I don't know—"

Then, looking past the old man to the far shore of the lake, Noah saw the two fair-haired figures standing by the water. Albie and Will. Clay's murdered children. A secret the old man had thought was safe until Noah went rushing out of his house that night like his feet were on fire.

Clay noticed him staring off into the distance. "What?" he asked and turned to see.

It was the brief distraction that Noah needed. He took off like a shot and passed by the old man, making a beeline toward his house. His feet pounded in the soft earth. When he looked back, he fully expected to see Clay coming— stalking toward him like some slasher movie villain.

But the old man stood where he had been, watching him flee, a steely look in his narrowed eyes.

"Gotta get to supper," Noah shouted. He wasn't sure

why he bothered with the lie, though. The cat was obviously out of the bag. Even once inside his house, the worry wouldn't be over. This place wasn't safe anymore. Maybe it never had been.

When he scrambled into the house and slammed the door behind him, he was struck by the otherworldly light that bathed the room. Along the tops of the walls were strung . . . Christmas lights?

He didn't even know they owned any Christmas lights. But there they were. Red, green, blue, amber—all glowing brightly, their luminescence blending together to form an ethereal rainbow border around the ceiling.

His mother had gotten only so far, though. Where the living room ended and the hallway began, the last string of lights hung limp against the wall, the rest of them gathered into a ball on the floor in the hallway. The kitchen chair she had used to string them up was on its side.

His heart shuddered and just as he wondered what had happened to her, he heard his mother whimpering from down the hall.

Leaping over the chair, he scurried down the hallway toward her room. Halfway there, he stopped. Through the half-closed bedroom door, he could see her lying face-down, naked on top of the bed. Her eyes were tightly shut and her lips curled up in anguish. She was moving on the bed, repeatedly, writhing as if crawling away from something.

Noah had never seen the act of sex. Not even so much as a Playboy or Hustler magazine, let alone a dirty movie. As a sheltered boy of fourteen years, sex was some strange and faraway thing that took on a peculiar and awkward form in his imagination—awkward but pleasurable, perhaps even beautiful. What he beheld now was none of those things.

"Mumma?"

She opened her eyes, so filled with tears. Wondering how it was that his father had managed to return home without his noticing, Noah called out to her again. But before he could move, a figure appeared in the bedroom doorway.

The dark silhouette of the stinking man.

Noah started for the bedroom but no sooner had he launched himself down the hallway than the door slammed shut. Noah thrashed against it, flinging his body into it, but it would not give.

He sank down to the floor, leaning against the door.

"Mumma," he cried. "Mumma, no."

Inside, his mother sobbed and begged for it to stop.

With her tortured cries ringing in his ears, he knew he had to get inside. Rising to his feet, he tore into his bedroom and grabbed the Slugger. He rushed his mother's door, swinging the bat high over his head.

It came down hard on the wood and splintered it down the middle but the door still would not budge. Noah stepped away and took aim at the door handle instead, brought the bat down. The wood by the jamb splintered and cracked, breaking away. Again and again he thrust the Slugger down until the handle fell from the door and rolled away down the hall.

He swung again and the remains of the jamb and the lock gave. He kicked the door and it swung open into the bedroom.

Noah stepped in with the bat raised. It would do no good against the phantom, but it wasn't something he could help. Instinct and adrenaline surged through his body.

But the room had gone quiet. Even the lingering chill from the huntsman's presence was dissipating like smoke. On the bed, his mother groaned. Noah dropped the Slugger, pulled the sheet over her lower half, and knelt beside her.

"It's okay, baby boy," she whispered to him. "I'm okay."

He shook his head and grabbed at her to pull her from the bed. He had to get them out of this place.

She rolled away from him and he collapsed at the bedside, staring at her, unbelieving.

"I told you, son," she said, sitting up, reaching for her clothes. "I'm okay. Ain't the first time it's happened."

In her eyes, Noah saw defeat and he swallowed hard as an awful realization came over him. How long had this been going on? All this time, he thought Dekker had been tormenting him and him alone.

"I'll—" he stammered. "I'll go get help."

They had no phone, of course, but the manor house had one. And even though he couldn't go to Clay, he could get to that phone. He'd take the Slugger and bust in if he had to.

"No," she hollered at him. "I made a . . . I made a deal. With that thing."

He shook his head. "A deal? Mumma, what're you—"

"A pact," she said, slurring the words. She was fading from consciousness. "To get rid of your father. For both of us."

"I don't understand."

She had gotten her bottoms pulled back on, but she was wavering unsteadily. And she wouldn't look him in the eye.

"Got to see it done," she muttered. Then she went limp and fell back onto the bed.

But Noah did understand. Suddenly, with awful clarity, it was plain to him. They were alone out here. They always had been—with no one to turn to, just like she'd said. And when the vile killer's spirit had come looking, his mother had given it someone to murder.

To get rid of your father. For both of us.

From Dekker she had purchased a way out of their living Hell. And the currency was the most intimate part of herself that she could offer to him.

As he stared down at her, breathing softly, the salt of her tears drying on her cheeks, he shook his head.

"But, Mumma," he whispered, feeling suddenly frail. "The cost . . . the cost of it . . . "

36

With his mother now resting comfortably, Noah found himself unable to rest at all. He paced back and forth in the living room, nibbling at his fingernails and thinking. They needed to leave before his father came back, and before Dekker returned. Not just their house—they needed to leave all of Cedar Banks behind. It wouldn't be tonight, though. Not in the shape his mother was in, and since his father had the truck, they had no means of getting away from this place anyway. Unless they walked out.

The manor house had a phone he could use to call Deputy Wren. The trouble was there was no way of getting to it—no way of getting past the chain link, razor wire fence. Unless he went to Clay, but that was not an option. He knew Clay's terrible secret, after all. Probably the only thing keeping the old man at bay was his thinking that Noah's father could come home at any moment.

Could he sneak in?

Noah considered it. The fence that surrounded the old house was trimmed at the top with razor wire, and there was no getting over that. So, the only way to get in would be to cut the lock on the gate. But what could do that? Their tool shed had a pair of garden shears but even Noah knew that wouldn't work.

He was quickly coming to the disheartening conclusion that there was no getting out. Not until something shifted in their favor anyway. For tonight and tomorrow—and maybe longer—they were trapped in their home at Cedar Banks. Prisoners in a cage.

There was also Dekker to consider. The evil thing was

gone for now but how long would that last? Until he gathered enough strength to return? There was no way to defend against him, and no way to get rid of him, was there? If there was, he certainly didn't know it, and Noah could think of no one who might even have such an answer.

No one alive, came the notion, like a whisper.

Noah looked down the dark hallway to the worship room, but the sight of it filled him with a paralyzing dread, and he uttered the words, "Please, no."

In that room was the terrible portal into the crawlspace. That tiny metal box from Hell where he'd been locked away. The thought of returning to it soured his stomach and weakened his knees. He turned away from it and sat down on the couch.

Still, he reasoned, if there was some way to be rid of Dekker, who better to ask than the tortured souls of the ones Dekker had killed and kept there in that tiny space? They existed on the other side, apart from the world of the living, and knew things Noah did not. And their desire for vengeance from beyond the veil of death was strong indeed. He had felt it that Thanksgiving night.

Were they tormentors like the stinking man or might they be allies? The hard truth of it was that Noah had no idea, but if the spirits in the crawlspace were at all like Albie and Will, then he could speak with them. That was the only way to be sure.

Quaking and heartsick at the very idea, but seeing no other way forward, Noah summoned some courage from deep inside, rose from the couch, and went plodding down the hallway to the room that lay waiting at the end.

He flicked on the light and stared at the small, terrible door cut into the wall. On the other side of it, a teeming mass of dead and awful things lingered. Murdered spirits trapped in eternal agony—but also quite possibly the only hope left for Noah and his mother.

He choked down the fear as he fished the tiny, jagged key to the new lock out of his pocket. With trembling fingers, he opened the lock, grasped the edges of the door, and pulled it forth. The yawning blackness opened before him and a blast of cold air came rushing out, chilling the room and all in its wake.

He patted his pocket to make sure his penlight was there, then crawled inside feet-first. In the freezing cold space, his breaths escaped him in long, smoky plumes, and he tried very hard to distance this moment from the memories of that Thanksgiving night and the daycare closet when he was but a child.

Reaching up, he fingered the edges of the door. He hesitated, closed his eyes, whispered a prayer, closed the door, and was plunged into a dark and frigid night.

Lying there, he opened his mind, pushing aside the noise of everyday thoughts. Just the way he'd done the first time he'd spoken with Albie and Will. It wasn't long before the dead came—pawing at him with their cold, blood-wetted flesh, their many voices blended together like the raucous sound of cicadas in the summer trees.

Noah's fear screamed at him to go. The door was there. *Right there.* All he needed to do was kick it open, climb out, and never return. He wanted to run, wanted to be far away.

But instead he knuckled down, fought hard against the revulsion, and found his voice, however unsteady it was.

"D-d-do you remember the one wh-who murdered you?" he asked them.

"*Dekker,*" they replied, though they called him other names as well. Names that were unfamiliar and unlike any words Noah had ever known.

"What . . . um," Noah struggled, unsure. "Why is he . . . why does he stay here if he's dead like you?"

Out of the storm of voices, one rose above the din and came to the fore.

"*Eyes,*" the voice hissed, "*Must close eyes. Follow us down. See so many things.*"

Noah wasn't sure he wanted to see, but he closed his eyes all the same.

In the black, the face of a man came floating toward him. A face he had seen before, out by the mailboxes, when the stinking man had chased him down. The grim countenance was stoic and devoid of expression.

"I know you," he said. Then Noah was drawn into its eyes, where the knowledge was revealed.

The man's name was Abner Whitman. Long ago, during the time of the work camp, he had stolen six bags of grain from a neighboring farmer to feed what was left of his family. After having been caught and arrested, the judge had given Abner ten years for his crime. An example to others that even during the Depression and no matter how desperate the circumstances, crime and theft of property would not be tolerated. After a brief stint in the county jail, he'd been given the opportunity to come to the work camp and serve the rest of it; maybe even get his sentence shortened. Abner had arrived at Camp Crow Neck in the thick heat of the summer and by the following autumn, he was dead. Dekker had come upon him one day as Abner made his way back to the camp after a scouting assignment. The huntsman caught him near the road and slashed his throat. Then he shoved him into a large burlap sack used for toting wild game back to the camp . . . back to Clyde Dekker's kitchen.

"She keeps him here. The girl."

Abner's old-timey, mountain drawl rolled so thick Noah could barely understand him.

"He looks for her, always looks for her."

The lady, Noah thought. *The blue lady. Clara Amburg.*

"Yes."

Noah was near to tears now. "He's . . . my mother . . . he's hurting her. Will you help me?"

At this there was a stir and loud voices protesting, voices filled with anger and reluctance. Even though they were long dead and bound to the in-between place where they languished, Noah could feel their fear of the huntsman.

Abner's voice, which had faded, rose above the din.

"*. . . ties him here, too. This one thing. The bone braid. A talisman. Like an anchor.*"

He was about to ask, but then a vision of the object came to him from Abner.

The bone braid was long. Nearly as long as a man was tall. It was made of small bones—like those of a finger—joined to one another by short lengths of fabric in between. Noah sharpened his focus on the object. No, not fabric. Not yarn, either. They were stolen locks of human hair in a wide array of colors and textures, wrapped around the ends of the bones, joining them like links in a chain.

These were Dekker's trophies, the only bits of the people he had killed that he hadn't discarded or eaten. These he had kept for himself. At the top of the braid, the first bone was capped with a bit of leather and black hair, sealed in wax. The huntsman's first kill. On the opposite end of the braid was a petite, white bone—a lady's finger—and hanging loose from its end was a long, flowing lock of auburn hair.

The blue lady's hair. His final victim.

The voices of the dead were a chorus of incomprehensible ravings. The vision of the bone braid disappeared. The one called Abner struggled to be heard and, although fading in and out, he hissed into Noah's mind again.

"*Find the braid. It goes with him . . . all the way to Hell . . . we will cast him, all of us.*"

Noah opened his eyes and saw only darkness. But he felt their cold flesh all the same. He twitched against the clawing dead.

"Where?" he called out to them, panicking. "How do I find it?"

But there came no reply. Only voices. Only that symphony of anguish.

They were grasping him now and Noah was being pulled down into the dark hole—to the in-between place where they lingered. His heart was thundering in his chest and he just knew it would burst. He was going to die in here.

"*The mountain . . . cave of bones . . . the young ones know,*" he heard Abner's voice shout to him above the others. "*The fair ones!*"

Noah had more questions but he couldn't summon the breath to ask them. The darkness squeezed him. His lungs were collapsed balloons. He kicked the crawlspace door open and inched his way out until he fell forward into the room, gasping for breath.

In that awful moment, lying there before his father's twisted cross and drooling onto the cold floor of the worship room, Noah knew exactly what he had to do when the morning came.

He knew it with a heavy heart, and rasped a simple prayer.

God, help me.

37

Although he had spent only a few minutes in the crawlspace communing with the dead, the experience had worn Noah to the bone. After picking himself up from the floor in the worship room, he had shuffled off to his bed and collapsed. Opening his mind to Abner and the others had been much more taxing and frightening than his experiences with the dead boys in the woods.

Waking the next morning, he found the weariness gone, though, and as he sat up in bed, rubbing sleep from his eyes, he wondered at what he was about to do. He wondered if he would meet with success or failure and if any of it would actually work or simply leave him and his mother exactly where they were—trapped in this place with no way out.

First, he went in to check on his mother. He found her

resting. He might even say she was doing so peacefully were it not for the horror that he had seen the night before and the dark, heartbreaking resignation in her eyes.

The things she had endured for his sake filled Noah with shame.

Outside, the sharp pellets of ice mixed with the falling snow, striking the windows in quick, sharp clicks that sounded for all the world like the second hand of some great clock swiftly ticking by. With no time to waste and his mother's life—perhaps even her soul—hanging in the balance, Noah dressed in layers for warmth and pulled his boots on.

If he could find the cave Abner had told him of and find this thing—the bone braid—he would need to bring it back. Noah had no wish to carry such a thing in his hands. So, he rummaged in his closet and produced a worn, olive green duffel bag that must have once belonged to his father. He bunched it up and shoved it into his backpack, then slung the straps over his shoulders and stepped out into the gray of the icy morning.

After descending into the woods around the lake, Noah went to the spot where he had spoken with the boys before and called to them. Many moments passed with no sign of them, no feeling of their presence, and he began to worry that this was all pointless. Sitting still as he was, he was growing cold in the chill wind, and was not sure he would last much longer.

He resolved to try a few more times before giving up and returning defeated to the house. He closed his eyes and went deeper into himself than ever before, reciting the rhyme about Wee Willie Winkie. Noah's lone voice did not echo among the trees, but was absorbed by the brewing storm as the snow and ice blanketed the forest floor and the naked limbs of the trees.

Over and over he sang out the rhyme, but felt nothing besides the cold of the day creeping into his flesh and bones. Finally, ready to yield, he opened his eyes.

And there they were, standing before him, phantoms of summer in their shorts and t-shirts. Without a moment's hesitation, he apprised them of his plan and the boys listened closely. By the end of it, his teeth were chattering and Noah's limbs shook violently from the cold.

"Cave of bones," Albie said, his bright eyes dimming. "Yeah, we know it. Not sure about any kind of braid, though."

"We don't like that place," Will chimed in, his voice mousy and delicate as he grasped his yellow bear, dangling it at his side.

"I'm s-s-sorry," Noah said. "But I need y'all to take me there. Something awful's happening to Mumma and I have to stop it."

After a moment of grave consideration, Albie agreed to Noah's plan. After all, it was bold but it *was* simple—perhaps deceptively simple.

And maybe more than a little foolish, Noah thought.

He was just a fourteen-year-old boy after all and, despite having lived among hill folk all his life, he was not much of a woodsman. He gazed up at the mountain, wreathed in the dense fog of snow and ice, and was suddenly terrified that he would never return from this trek—that he would be swallowed whole by the long, dark ridge that dominated the western sky.

Still, Noah reckoned, it was the only hope he had of getting rid of the huntsman.

There was simply no other choice.

38

The freezing rain fell, cutting through the air and coming down hard, thousands of tiny needles pricking Noah's bits of exposed flesh with every passing moment. For most of the journey, his spectral guides had kept to simple paths that zigzagged up the slope with long, gentle climbs but now he was picking his way up a wide, steep rock field. With the wind and the sleet pelting Noah hard, coating the treacherous rocks with a layer of ice, it was as if the mountain was snapping at him, eager to add yet another soul to its collection. At best, the slightest misstep meant being immobilized by a sprain or broken bone, and from there the possibilities only worsened. Even dressed as he was for the cold, it seemed unlikely he would last the night if he became stranded here.

The flat of the ridge loomed above. If he could only walk there, he would make it in just a few minutes. But there was no such direct way upward. On the path he had come, scrambling over the rock field, the only way of getting to sure ground was across the deep fissure before him that stretched out like an evil grin across the face of the mountain. Albie and Will stood there on the opposite side already, looking on and beckoning him to follow.

Noah peered down and reckoned the chasm to be just shy of twenty feet deep, with boulders at the bottom more jagged and lethal than the snow covering them let on. It wasn't all that wide, though—maybe seven feet across, probably a little less.

He thought back to gym class, back to his best attempt at the standing long jump. Because that's what this would be. There was no room on this side of the fissure to gain speed or momentum. It was either jump and make it or jump and don't.

"Five and a half feet," he said out loud. "I can make it."

He grinned, his teeth bared in raw determination. Noah squatted and stood, squatted and stood, loosening his muscles. He tried not to look down as he counted off the launch in his head.

5 . . . 4 . . . 3 . . . 2 . . . 1.

Then he jumped.

39

The sleet coming down on the aluminum roof of Kemp Metalworks reverberated through the building like an endless round of applause from some unseen audience. Men standing only feet away from one another had to shout to be heard over the noise.

Hugh was bent low, his hands inside of the access panel of the large press brake machine. He was fumbling with a loose power coupling, the connection so far up inside the panel that he couldn't see what he was doing and had to feel his way through the task.

"Belton!"

Hugh turned to see the slight, short man called Little Jimmy Billings standing close by, cupping his hands around his mouth as he shouted. Hugh looked at him questioningly.

"Bossman wants to see you!"

Hugh nodded and glanced up at the second floor office lined with windows that looked out onto the workshop floor. He stepped away, wiped his hands clean with a rag, and then climbed the steel frame stairs up to the office. The second he opened the door and stepped in, removing his grimy ball cap, the cacophony of the icy rain was muted by the insulation and layers of wood and framing that enclosed the office and the other rooms below. Behind the desk sat Henry Kemp, his nose in a ledger. He didn't even look up when Hugh entered, just motioned for him to take a seat in one of the chairs set before his desk.

He endured a long silence, sitting there and repeatedly pinching the bill of his filthy hat with his fingers, waiting. When Mister Kemp was done with whatever it was he was so engrossed in, he closed the ledger and folded his hands before him, smiling cordially at Hugh.

"How are things, Hugh?"

What is this? A social visit?

"Things are fine, Mister Kemp. Just fine. Thanks for asking."

"You sure about that?"

Hugh shifted awkwardly in his seat. "I ain't sure I understand . . ."

"Hugh," Henry Kemp began with a heavy sigh, "I know you been bedding down nights in the break room, sleeping on the couch. You been cleaning up in the showers here, too. Troubles at home?"

Hugh nodded. "You could say that, yeah."

"Been there, buddy. Believe me. I understand, and I was willing to let it slide for a few days because I'm sympathetic to how a woman can beat a man down, drag him down to the dregs."

Hugh grinned.

"But I ain't running no goddamned bed and breakfast here. And seeing as how you never even came to me about it, what you've been doing ain't nothing but taking liberties, Hugh. Sends a message to the other men, you know? And that I cannot allow."

Leaning forward in the chair, Hugh wondered how quickly he could reach across that desk and snap his boss's neck like the hen-pecked chickenshit he was. He opened his mouth to say something but before he could get it out, Henry Kemp continued.

"Go on with the day, put in your hours, and then go on home. Straighten things out with your wife. Or . . . hell, I don't know . . . find some other woman and shack up with her for a while. I don't care. But you've got to get your living situation under control. If you can't then I just can't use you here. Understand?"

Hugh swallowed hard. "Yes, Mister Kemp. I hear you."

His boss leaned back, apparently satisfied that he'd given Hugh a stern enough talking-to. He sighed. "My advice, though, is to go on home and work it out with your old lady. Gotta face the music at some point, you know?"

"Yes, sir. I reckon that's the gospel truth."

"Good. That's all, Hugh. I hope to see you tomorrow. Best of luck to you, buddy."

Hugh stood and hesitated a moment. He considered saying something else, muttering some obligatory words of thanks for Mister Kemp's candor and his understanding, but the truth was that Hugh was embarrassed at having been called into the office to be lectured on his own personal business. This was Ada's fault. If she wasn't such a disloyal bitch . . . if she wasn't in the habit of driving him to the brink . . .

That red feeling was growing inside him, though. A glowing ember of anger and wrath. So, Hugh thought better of it and walked out of Henry Kemp's office. The roar of ice upon the roof returned, invaded his ears, ceaseless in its onslaught.

But his thoughts were on his troubles at home.

It was *his house* anyway, wasn't it? *His castle.* Why should he be loath to return to it just because of his uppity wife and his ungrateful whelp of a son? He smiled darkly. It would soon be time for Ada and Noah to face the music.

And oh, how Hugh would make them dance.

40

Noah cleared the gap, but just barely. His feet hit the rocks on the other side, his arms still spinning like propellers as he tried to keep his balance. But the rocks were just as slick with sleet and snow, and the moment's sure footing went out from under him as he slid backwards and down the craggy side of the gap.

He grabbed and slapped at the rocks in front of him, his gloved hands searching to find purchase somewhere . . . anywhere.

Catching the lip of a wide, flat boulder, his arms screamed with the shock of bearing all his weight, and his head slammed against the rock face in front of him, filling his vision with bursting stars. His fingertips slid a little, leaving Noah certain that any moment he would go tumbling down into the fissure.

Now, flattened against the side with the dark, yawning space looming at his back, he kicked his feet about to find a toehold. With every swing of his legs, he felt his grip weakening. After a few tries, his boot slid into a small cubby in the rocks and he pushed up, taking the strain off his arms.

And he finally breathed again, unaware that he'd been holding the air in his lungs until he felt some small amount of safety.

Holding on tight, his head ringing and the ice pellets knifing him in the face from a gray and indifferent sky, he declared that today was not the day Cross Mountain would claim him. Just like his alter ego, Captain Red, he would complete his mission and win the day, no matter the odds or the obstacles.

He hadn't slid down far—a few feet at the most. It shouldn't be a tough climb but it was made so much worse by the glaze of ice covering everything he could grab onto.

Summoning his strength and a bit more courage, he began his ascent slowly, choosing each grab and foothold with care. It took much longer than he would have liked, but he shimmied up and over the lip. He rolled onto his side, unable yet to stand, and lay there breathing heavily. The boys, whose phantom shapes stood waiting, assured him it would be smooth sailing the rest of the way. He liked the sound of that very much.

Getting to his feet and taking a first stumbling step, Noah noticed the pain in his hands. Even inside the gloves he wore, they were cracked and bleeding, cold and red. Looking at the boys who stood in the center of the ridge, he could not help but think parts of him were starting to look a little too much like the deathly parts of them. On the other side of the ridge, there was a dense stand of tall pines, so he made for them, wanting to get out of the weather's constant assault—if only for a moment—before going any farther.

Once there, the pines provided a shrouded canopy that blocked the ice and wind. He went to the ground and slipped the backpack off his shoulders. In it, he had packed a Swiss Army knife, matches, a flashlight and a few packs of crackers. The space in the rest of the pack was taken up by the green Army duffel bag.

Noah sat for a few moments and gnawed on the food as he watched the nasty winter storm wailing around him. In the darkening mid-day light, in the midst of the tall, dormant grass that lined the flat, narrow ridge, he noticed something jutting up. It might have been a tree except that there were no other trees, big or small, mixed in with the grass. Curious, he rose and went trotting out to have a look. Noah realized what he had found before he even saw the whole of it.

As he neared the protrusion, he noticed smaller ones that dotted the landscape, visible only because the grass was bending low with the weight of the freezing rain and snow. Small, worn stones with jagged angles.

Headstones.

They were sparse, and even though the sky was still filled with subdued light, he could not have made out the inscriptions. The one at the center was large with a base that rose up from the grass. A column of stone stood erect atop it but was roughly broken off from years upon years of exposure to the harsh mountain weather. He was standing on the very ridge where the battle had occurred, where the cross had been erected that had given the mountain its present name. Looking down into the grass at his feet, he saw the edges of the top half of the cross, covered by earth and growth, snow and ice.

That strange, gray feeling niggled at his mind, and for the first time he recognized that it was the dead reaching out to him. It was a sensation that set upon him with such profound longing that he was nearly helpless to deny it. But his attention was drawn to the blond boys at the far edge of the ridge, beckoning him hence.

In his reverie, Noah had forgotten about the storm and the stinging rain. He sprinted back across the ridge to the shelter of the pines. He shouldered his pack and followed the boys as they led him down another wide path of tall grass. The mountain slanted down toward him, jagged, rocky and imposing on either side of the pass. From Clay's descriptions of the battle, Noah knew that he was skirting along the edge of Bishop's Gap.

Even on a fine spring day, with the usual mountain breeze, the air currents would have funneled through this break in the massive mountain. But in the midst of the storm, it was as if a small tornado was trapped between two towering walls of rock. Noah could barely stand but struggled along the edges of the pass, faithfully following his guides, gritting his teeth against the elements. It must have been only a hundred feet or so before he stopped, but his body declared it something more like a hundred miles.

Noah wiped the sheen of freezing rain from his face and looked to the next point forward. He saw the two boys standing side by side, each of them with an arm outstretched, pointing down to a patch of deadfall. Not understanding, Noah rushed toward them.

"What is it? Is this the place?"

They nodded their heads in unison, a strange and unearthly gesture, and Noah looked down to where they pointed.

What he saw was a barrier of small dead tree limbs and branches that had fallen haphazardly, some new and others old, all covered with a layer of earth and muck that filled in the many spaces. He took hold of a sturdy limb and began plunging it into the snow and the mud beneath. Stabbing it into the earth over and over, he was rewarded with nothing but the resistance of the hard turf. He had been nearly at the breaking point, about to shout at the dead boys for wasting his time, when his spear failed to bite and went plunging into the ground so far that he lost hold of it. On his hands and knees, he dug at the spot, pulling deadfall and mud back until a man-sized chasm opened up. The dark space that lay beyond smelled of cold and earth.

Noah reached back and pulled the penlight from his pack. Shining it down into the dark hole, he saw that beneath him was a hollow space whose sleepy, subterranean night had not been disturbed in decades.

"This is it?" He looked up at the boys.

Again, they nodded in unison.

"Y'all gonna come down here and show me?"

At this, Will clutched to his brother, hiding his face.

"This is as far as we go. It's as far as we ever go," Albie said. "We . . . just can't."

He studied their faces for some kind of explanation but found nothing but grim, determined countenances.

"Okay," Noah said, positioning himself over the opening into the cave. "Wish me luck."

Without another word, Noah slipped down into the hole feet-first. Above him hovered the ghostly forms of the blond boys, watching with rapt concern.

After sliding down the cold stone beneath the opening, Noah dropped the backpack and clicked the flashlight on. Despite the dim and stormy sky, the daylight coming in from the mouth of the cave above was sufficient to illuminate most of the space, although details were hard to make out. He shined the light around the cave and was relieved to see that it was spacious enough not to send him into a claustrophobic panic. The chamber he dropped into was large enough to hold a couple of cars. The floor was uneven and rocks jutted up from the earth here and there. On the wall to the right, a natural ledge of stone ran nearly the length of that side of the chamber and Noah gasped as his light fell over what remained there.

The top halves of two skulls, one large and one small, sat amidst a pile of smaller bones. Below the drop of the natural shelf in the rock, other bones lingered. Tangled in their midst were the ragged, half-eaten threads of summer clothes. Shorts, t-shirts, tube sucks, and rubber-soled sneakers whose leather or canvas had grown dull with mold.

There wasn't much left of these things, just bits and pieces, but it was enough that Noah recognized them. A few feet away, though, as if removed from the scene of death and decay, there lay Will's precious yellow bear. While it was a bit worn and thin, the cave had not taken it like it had taken the clothes. Time had not claimed the little thing so prized by the little boy. Noah felt a lump grow in his throat, though he could not quite articulate why.

Looking away from it, he took a careful step toward the bones, his penlight glinting off the shine of the rounded skulls.

He reached toward the larger one.

"Albie," he whispered.

As his fingers grazed it, that sensation came barreling toward him—the world going gray at the edges, the things before him transforming into a vision not of the present but the past.

He saw the two boys before him, huddled together on the cave shelf. Will was sniffling through tears. Albie reached down and wiped them away every so often, hugging his brother a bit tighter every time even as Will closed his arms around his bear. Their injuries were as plain as they had always been to Noah, but even as Albie grimaced with pain, he looked out of the cave's mouth to the scant daylight flooding in. Along with the sound of Will's gentle sobbing, there was the rushing wind and thunder of a storm that raged somewhere above.

And Clay Winston was nowhere in sight.

Not standing over his boys with a blood-darkened blade, not rolling them down into this earthen tomb, to be forgotten. Then, and only then, did Noah understand. The knowledge came to him like the rush of a remembered dream to his waking mind.

Albie and Will had died here but they hadn't been murdered. A storm had snuck up on the lake as the boys played among the forests of the mountain late on a summer afternoon, and when they had tried to get back to the campsite to find their father, they had gotten turned around. In the rains and punishing wind, Albie slipped and fell among the rock field, badly fracturing his leg. With his little brother's help, he was able to get back to Bishop's Gap, where they searched for shelter. Unwittingly they stumbled upon the open mouth of the cave covered by deadfall and clay that had softened in the storm. They fell right through. Once at the bottom, and now both injured, they had been unable to make it out.

That was why they didn't want to return to the cave, Noah realized. This was the place of their earthly demise and even after decades of wandering, death had not numbed them to their own passing. Noah wondered who had been the first to die and how long the lingering one had clung to the lifeless corpse of the other, weeping and aching for rescue.

Clay Winston had spent the last twenty-some years searching these hills for the remains of his sons, restless and heartbroken.

And Noah had thought him their murderer.

He hung his head in shame and turned to glance up through the mouth of the cave, but as his flashlight swept across the other side of the cave, he froze.

Bones, he thought. *So many bones.*

They littered the floor on the opposite side of the cave, too numerous to be counted at a simple glance, though Noah had a suspicion their numbers would equal however many men had gone missing from the Crow Neck work camp a half-century ago. This was Clyde Dekker's true place of murder. Like some fairy tale monster on the mountainside, he brought his kills to his den in the hills, dressed them to butcher later and discarded what was left.

As Noah inspected the field of morbid debris, the

flashlight's beam swept over the walls, and it was there that Noah noticed strange markings. They were so utterly unlike English or any other kind of writing he had ever seen, it was difficult to say if it was writing at all or nothing more than curious shapes scratched into the surface of the stone. As he gently picked his way among the bones, he also saw at the far end a break in the stone which formed a short entrance to a dark hole leading deeper into the body of the mountain. Shining his light into it revealed only that it was a long, cramped, and blackened passage. The sight of it made him uneasy, his flesh crawling. Despite his curiosity, he judged it too dangerous to investigate further.

Noah shined his light over the cave, suddenly wanting to be out of there more than he had ever wanted anything in his life. The death in the chamber was overwhelming and he found it hard to breathe. Bones upon bones, so many that he would surely never find the braid that Abner had told him of. Along the floor, he saw a rusted knife, a canvas pouch of what might have once been tobacco but was now little more than a pile of threads on the cold stone. Shining the beam along this edge of the cave, he spotted something long and pale draped over a jutting rock.

His quarry hung there, covered in decades of dust, dull ivory bones strung together with twine and human hairs in a multitude of shades. At the sight of it, Noah's lips drew back in disgust. It might as well have been a venomous snake.

Unzipping his pack, he removed the green duffel bag. He snatched up the old knife and scooped the bone braid up with it, hovered its length over the opening and dropped it in. As if it might escape, he quickly zipped the bag closed.

Outside, the freezing rain sounded like it had lightened some. Noah strode away from the skeletal remains of the huntsman's victims but stopped just below the mouth of the cave. He looked back at the remains of the boys, their lonely skulls lying next to each other, empty sockets staring out at the darkness of this place as they had for so many years.

Their restless spirits drifted about the lake while their

undaunted father still roamed the mountain in search of some trace of them. Perhaps Noah could bring some peace to all of them.

He owed them all at least that, didn't he?

Noah unzipped the duffel bag, moved the huntsman's braid to his backpack, and set about the task of packing the bones of his two new friends into it, laying them down gently and with a reverence they had long deserved. As he did so, he thought of the journey back down the mountain and decided he would walk the ridge a bit to find a way down less perilous than the gap he'd leapt over.

An hour later, as he made his way down the mountain by way of an easier but much longer path, the torturous rain of ice ceased, and in its place, large, thick flakes of snow began falling. It was a boon to the mission Noah had set himself on, and the hike down benefited from it. Even with the bag slung over his shoulders, heavy with the remains of Albie and Will, he was able to double his speed. When he finally stepped onto the level ground around the lake, his legs felt weird and wobbly.

More than that, the sky was darker than he expected. By the time he made it to the edge of Cedar Banks, with the sunset hidden behind gray clouds, it was nearly full dark.

Noah's muscles burned with exhaustion as he trudged up the steps of Clay's front porch. With a heavy sigh, he knocked on the door and waited a minute or two for the sound of the old man coming to open it.

But that sound never came.

Noah went around and peered through the windows of Clay's garage, shining the flashlight beam in, but didn't see his truck.

Where in the world was the old man on a night like this? The weather was beyond awful and had been all day. He had no business being out on the road.

Nevertheless, Noah knew he had to do *something*. He needed to get back home and see to his mother. He had moved the bone braid to the outer pocket of his backpack and, although the duffel bag was much heavier, it was the weight of the huntsman's talisman that darkened his spirits the most.

He tried the side door of Clay's house and found it unlocked. It didn't surprise him. He didn't suppose the old man believed in locking his doors. Why would he in a place as remote as Cedar Banks? Noah stepped into the warmth of the house, leaving his backpack and its dreadful contents out on the landing. He carried the green bag inside, the remains of the children clacking together as he closed the door behind him and prepared to write the strangest note he would likely ever leave for someone.

41

Clay Winston wasn't much of a drinker now but, boy, there had been some times in the past that the old man could barely remember, and not many of them with pride. He had the sense today would be another one of those times. They'd had to practically peel him from the bar stool down at the Shamrock, a roadhouse outside of town where the interstate ran as close as it dared to these hills.

He had protested, of course, making his argument as eloquently as he could through slurred speech, but the fact of the matter was the weather had gotten damned nasty, and since they hadn't seen a single trucker stop in for a meal since lunch, they were shutting the place down.

The owner had suggested that Clay turn the heater on in his truck and snooze the rest of the night but that sounded like an awful silly waste of gas and the battery, didn't it? Bidding them farewell, he pulled the wool cap onto his head so it covered his ears, and staggered out into the dusk with a belly full of draft beers and shots of Cutty Sark whiskey.

He started up the truck and, after a moment, rolled down the window and turned on the radio in the hope that the loud music and cold rush of air would help keep him alert. Pulling out onto the highway and making his way to the exit back to the state route, he wished he'd had the good sense to ask for a cup of coffee to go. But it was too late for that now.

Too late for many things.

As Clay's truck ambled slowly along the icy road, he turned the radio up higher, but no wall of sound, no distraction could keep the vexing thoughts from his mind. He hadn't even managed to drink them away down at the Shamrock—not like he had hoped.

He drummed his fingers on the steering wheel.

Noah had been acting strange of late. Awful strange. And then there was the way he had been humming that tune a few days ago—the tune there was simply no possible way he could know.

Except . . . there was one way, wasn't there?

Clay wasn't the kind of man to believe every odd thing he ever heard or even those he saw with his own eyes, but he understood there was more to the world than the banal veneer of everyday life. There was more to it than just waking, working, eating, crapping, and going to bed. There were extraordinary things and extraordinary folks in the world.

Like those with *ghostsight*, who could see past the veil of this world and glimpse the ones who had passed on, or the ones who remained here still.

A rumor handed down to Clay when he was a young man told that his grandmother had been gifted in such a way. She had even used her gift in a traveling carnival, so the story went. It sounded like the stuff of some Ray Bradbury yarn to him, but what did he know? Anything was possible. Then there was old Witch Wilkins up on Duncraven Knob. He had gone to her after his boys disappeared, desperate for anything that might help find them. She hadn't been able to offer much, but all the same, Clay *knew* she had the sight. That was no mere rumor.

Perhaps Noah had it, too. And if so, maybe he had been seeing—even speaking with—the spirits of his boys. What Clay wouldn't give to lay eyes on them again! If it was true about Noah having the sight, then he envied the boy. Clay, himself, was not possessed of such a gift and the last time he had seen them alive would forever be the last time he would see them until he was standing there at the pearly gates himself.

A chill gust of wind blasted into the cab of the truck and the radio blared a hiss of static, both of which snapped Clay out of his musings. He had been on autopilot, he supposed, because he had driven deep into the mountain roads since leaving the Shamrock, and hadn't hardly noticed. Hell, he was only a mile or two from Cedar Banks. Nor had he realized that the gray sky above had gone full dark and, now that he was paying attention, he could barely see the road.

"Jesus!" he shouted out loud, his own voice sounding unfamiliar.

Clay reached down to the dash and pulled the knob for the headlights.

When they blazed to life, though, he saw more than just the road before him, more than bright white snowflakes rushing toward him like stars in space. And what he saw overrode his common sense, causing him to slam on the brakes, sending the truck into a spin that quickly landed it with three wheels in the snowy ditch, one tire up in the air, still spinning.

There, bathed in the pale glow of the Chevy's headlights, he had seen his children, Will and Albie, standing in the middle of the road, staring right at him with horribly empty eyes.

42

After Noah removed his wet, soiled shoes, he stepped inside his house. The television was on and there was the sound of water running in the kitchen sink. Dropping his backpack by the door, he hollered out to his mother that he was finally home and sorry he was so late. As he turned into the kitchen, he slipped for a moment on something cold and wet.

The floor of the kitchen was covered with a shallow layer of water. The faucet was running, the sink overflowing. The refrigerator door was wide open and his mother sat at the kitchen table, staring blankly in his direction, but not actually looking at him. There was a troubling distance in her gaze.

"Mumma?"

When she didn't respond, Noah tiptoed through the water to the sink and shut the faucet off. On his way to her, he reached out and slammed the fridge door shut. Standing next to her, he leaned down and put his hand on her shoulder.

She was cold to the touch.

Thinking the worst, he whimpered a moment and went to his knees in the chill, standing water. But he could tell her chest was rising and falling with slow, steady breaths. He took hold of her shoulders and shook her.

"Mumma, what's wrong? Mumma?"

After a minute or so, her wide stare broke and she blinked her eyes and looked over at her son, confused.

"Mumma, it's me."

"Noah? Back so soon?"

So soon? He'd been gone nearly all day.

"Mumma, are you all right? What happened?"

She looked about the room as if searching for some memory that eluded her, the creases of her brow deepening. Then she turned back to him. She still seemed dazed.

"My heart was troubled, son," she said with a voice that was nearly a whisper. "I was in him and he was in me."

Noah narrowed his eyes and studied her. It made no sense, what she had said. The words were similar to something from the Book of John, but neither their order nor their context was the same. He pulled the other chair closer to her and sat down, leaning forward and holding her hands in his own.

"I don't understand, Mumma. You mean God? You think that God was in you?"

Once again, her eyes fell haphazardly over the walls of the kitchen, then settled darkly on Noah.

"No, son. It wasn't God."

Noah sopped up the kitchen water with bath towels from the closet, but did it quickly and with distracted thoughts. He was more concerned for his mother now than ever before. She wasn't making any sense. He had to wonder if the last brutal thrashing by his father—or even the visits from the huntsman—had damaged her mind. It seemed as likely as anything.

After helping her to the couch to rest, Noah watched her warily. She was not only dazed, but seemed physically weakened. Her eyes closed the very second she lay her head down on the couch and she drifted immediately off to sleep.

As he stood there, watching over her, he sniffed the air and found a familiar, pungent scent in the room. Sweat beaded on his forehead and his heart began to race. That stench heralded the coming of the huntsman. He was coming or perhaps was already here. No matter, Noah would stand his ground this time—stand by his poor, tormented mother and face down the evil thing.

He waited and waited. The huntsman did not come. Nor did the awful stink dissipate.

Remembering the bone braid, he pulled it from his backpack and held it aloft as if to show it to the unseen spirit. The strength of the stink in the room increased and a sense of immense pressure filled the house, even Noah's ears, muffling all sound.

But still the huntsman did not come. Noah hadn't known the phantom to be shy, but that was precisely how it seemed now. Not because Clyde Dekker's power had lessened, though. Noah's intuition screamed that it was more like the huntsman's energy was divided, and a great portion of his presence was concentrated elsewhere.

Noah glanced back down at his mother—at the rapid movement of her eyes behind their lids, her chest rising and falling in quick, panicked breaths. He bent low and sniffed the air near his mother and his stomach turned cold.

He knew where the huntsman was—the very place that the spirit had been trying to get to since Noah and his family arrived. Slowly, with each assault, each terrifying display of his power, the huntsman had been slipping into his mother's skin, crowding her mind and damning her soul.

Taking a careful step away from her, Noah turned to the front window. Outside, through the snowstorm and the darkness, he could see Clay's lights burning inside the home. He shoved the bone braid into his pocket and laced his boots back onto his feet.

Ghosts and demons and bone charms be damned, it was time to leave.

Whatever happens to Mumma from here on out, Noah thought, *let it happen in a hospital. Or even a church. Just not here.*

He stalked across the grounds in the falling snow. It was time for some honesty with Clay Winston and, regardless of what Noah's father might do to them, it was time to get the hell out of Cedar Banks once and for all.

43

Noah didn't bother with knocking, just went barreling into the house through the unlocked side door. He found Clay sitting at his kitchen table, a beer can gripped in one hand and Noah's note in the other, staring down at the bag of bones on the floor.

The old man barely looked up when Noah entered.

"Clay?" Noah called to him. "Mister Winston?"

"You've been seeing them, haven't you?" the old man asked.

Noah paused a moment. "Ever since we been here. Before, even. Back in Eastlake."

At that, the old man glanced up. "Eastlake?"

"They wander all over, it seems," Noah added quickly, growing impatient. "Clay, I promise I'll tell you all about it soon, but right now—"

"I saw them, too," Clay said, still dazed. "All these years and I never seen them . . . not once. Then tonight, there they were. Standing in the road just as pretty as you please. Why did I see them tonight, Noah?"

He shrugged. "I don't know."

"Swerved and slid right into the ditch, almost straight down. I climbed out and looked for them again but they were gone. I called and called for them. After a while, I walked on back and here they are waiting for me. Well, what's left of them, anyway."

Clay wiped away tears as he stared down into the open bag, the ivory remains of his children there like a scattered jigsaw puzzle.

"Where did you find them?"

Noah sighed. "There's a cave at Bishop's Gap, up on the ridge."

"Been walking the mountain for years, Noah. I ain't never seen a cave."

He thought about how many times Clay must have been up there and walked right past his boys, maybe just a few feet away, buried under the mud and rock and debris that slid down the mountain in the storm that night so many years ago, entombing them.

"I know," Noah said. "You never could have seen it. No one could have. They showed me where it was, your boys."

Clay smiled at that and the fog seemed to lift from his gaze, as if he finally noticed Noah's anxiousness.

"What . . . what's going on, Noah?"

"It's Mumma," Noah said, his voice breaking. "She's in real trouble. Bad trouble."

Clay slid the other kitchen chair out with his foot.

"Have a seat, young man. And tell me *everything*."

Noah sat down. Clay was certainly owed some explanation, but he also made it clear to the old man that there was no time to lose.

He hardly knew where to begin, but he started with the first night he had seen the huntsman, Clyde Dekker. He told him all about the things he had seen since, the way the demonic old haint had been tormenting them. In a rush of sometimes incoherent details, he told him about the spirits of the murdered dead, about his father, the things that Dekker had been doing to his mother, and about the deal she had made with the evil thing. Lastly, he told him about what he feared was happening to her—that the huntsman was settling into her, consuming her soul as he dug in like a tick, deeper and deeper.

He explained that none of that mattered anymore. They just needed to get out, get away from Cedar Banks. Tonight. He needed Clay's help to get them out of there in his truck.

The old man chugged the rest of the beer, and when he crushed it on the table, a dark look came over him.

"Christ Almighty, Noah, I'm sorry," he said. "My truck's a mile or so back up the road in a ditch."

Noah had heard him say that before, but hearing it now and seeing that helpless scowl on the old man's face froze his heart. They were more trapped now than they ever had been, all of them.

They sat in silence as the wind moaned outside.

"Ain't no way out," Clay said. "Not tonight. I don't reckon even emergency services could make it out in this. Not unless it was something godawful, something life and death."

"But it is godawful," Noah shouted, slamming his fist on the table. "What's happening to Mumma is life and death!"

Clay placed a gentle hand on him.

"You know it, Noah, and I know it," he said. "But convincing the sheriff or the rescue squad is another matter. More than likely, they'll tell us to watch over her and they'll be out as soon as this storm passes to take her to the hospital."

When Noah gave no reply, Clay continued.

"It's only a few hours until morning. Maybe she'll be all right until then."

Noah heard the old man's words but he wasn't really listening.

. . . convincing the sheriff or the rescue squad is another matter . . .

"What if someone else could convince them?" Noah blurted out.

Clay cocked his head. "Like who?"

Noah pushed away from the table and stood. "I've got an idea, but I'm gonna need your help."

"Anything," the old man replied. "Just say the word."

"Think the phone at the manor house is still working?"

"Maybe."

"Then I need the keys to the gate and the house. And I need you to watch over Mumma while I'm gone. Can you do that?"

Clay stood and fished in his pocket for the ring of keys, handed it to Noah.

He left the old man standing there as he rushed for the door, opening it and letting the cold, dark night rush in. Before he charged out, he looked back at Clay.

"Just make sure she's all right, okay?"

"I'll watch over her like she's my own," Clay replied and placed a hand over his heart.

Satisfied, Noah turned his back on the light and warmth of the old man's house, and closed the door behind him.

44

His greasy old barn jacket had barely warmed in the house before Clay put it back on to cross the street and look in on Missus Belton. He stepped into his boots and paused a moment just inside the doorway.

He glanced back into his house with the nagging feeling he was leaving something behind. As his eyes searched over his cluttered den, they landed on the leather belt and holster coiled on his desk. His reproduction 1849 Colt five-shot revolver beckoned to him. Clay didn't know what use a gun would be against the kind of things Noah had told him about, but to go without it seemed foolhardy. He flicked open the cylinder of the pistol, emptied the blank rounds onto the table and replaced them with live ones.

Outside, the pistol was heavy in his coat pocket as he walked toward the Belton house. On the front porch, he kicked the threshold to knock the snow from his boots, opened the door, and went inside, shutting it lightly behind him. A lamp on the other side of the room shone dimly and a string of Christmas lights along the wall imparted an otherworldly glow to the place. Missus Belton was stretched out on the couch in her nightgown. She lay on her side, facing the front of the room, hands clasped next to the pillow beneath her head.

Jagged scars crisscrossed her face from where her husband had cut her, and to look upon them made Clay wince. It was a hard thing to behold, and it left a lump growing in his throat that was formed from both anger and pity.

He watched her breathe, though she made no other movement or sound.

Clay walked the house, checking the rooms. He told himself that it was for safety's sake, but in truth, the old man simply had a curious nature. He wanted to see the place in which the boy had survived during his stay here, wanted to know if it bore the signs of a broken family or if it seemed completely normal and average. Mostly, he found the latter to be true, but when his eyes fell upon the twisted cross in the worship room and the squat door beneath the wainscoting, he could not deny the troubling shiver that ran through him.

"There is nothing of God here," he remarked, then clicked off the light.

He went to the kitchen and pulled a chair, where he sat at the table and waited for Noah to come tramping in from the Amburg house.

He rubbed his freezing hands together. It was woefully cold outside, the kind of chill that was hard to shake from old bones. Clay fancied a steaming cup of dark brew and decided that, were Missus Belton up and about, she would not begrudge him a little coffee. So, he rummaged through the cabinets and drawers in search of filters and grounds to brew a pot. He longed for its deep warmth and was so consumed by the notion of it, he didn't notice the change in Ada Belton's easy breaths or her body stirring on the couch.

45

Noah trudged across the landscape, each footstep through the snow heavier than the last. Ahead lay the chain-link fence surrounding the Amburg manor house. With its dark and empty windows suspended in the structure, the entire house appeared far too much for his comfort like a bony skull with shadowed eye sockets.

Noah was a little surprised when he plunged the key into the lock on the gate and it let go with only a slight resistance. The gate eased open and he pushed inward against the deep snow, making a gap wide enough to fit through.

As Noah emerged on the other side, it seemed the temperature dropped by a few degrees instantly. The skin on his neck tightened, the hairs standing on end. It wasn't the cold wind that was to blame, although it rushed across the land with nearly arctic ferocity. Instead, it was a sign that he was familiar with by now that something was close. Something dead, something restless.

The blue lady, Clara Amburg.

Gazing up at the house, he saw her inside, her image distorted by the rippled glass of the old windows. He drew his hood tighter and lumbered through the white toward the porch.

Noah muttered a curse under his breath as he stepped into the manor house and shut the door, silencing the howling, frigid wind. He shivered.

"I swear I think it's colder in here than out there."

He fumbled in his coat for the handle of the penlight he had brought, then clicked it on. There was a light switch somewhere close, he knew, so he shined the flashlight over the wall to find it. A panel of four switches hung suspended in a cavity in the wall and he reached over and flicked all of them on. A string of lonely overhead bulbs flickered to life and flooded the dark space with weak, yellow light.

Still, he was grateful for it. Noah followed around, through the parlor and the drawing room, into the white-walled room with so many windows.

The black rotary phone sat on the table. He crossed the room, placed his hand on the cold curve of the receiver and froze. Panic overtook him and awful, hopeless thoughts crowded his mind.

The lines were down. They had to be. The storm had swept in and crippled everything. There would be no getting out of Cedar Banks tonight. Maybe not ever.

Oh, God, please. Please, please, please . . .

He gulped an anxious breath and picked up the phone, held it to his ear.

When he heard the steady hum of a dial tone, Noah calmed. He dialed the Wrens' phone number and listened to the first few rings.

Would they be home? Where else could they be on such a night? Then a terrifying thought entered his mind; just because the lines weren't out at Cedar Banks meant nothing. There were miles upon miles of phone lines stretched through the mountains between here and Cady's Run. In fact, it would be a miracle if the phone lines weren't down somewhere between Eastlake and Westlake, cutting off all communication.

The line clicked and Noah jumped, sure that the call had gone dead.

"Hello?" came a voice crackling through the speaker.

"Tommy?"

A moment of silence passed and Noah wondered if it was all in his mind.

"Noah?"

"Oh, thank God," he said, almost going boneless.

His friend immediately sensed something was off, something was urgent.

"Noah, what's going on?"

Noah struggled for a moment, overwhelmed at the friendly, concerned voice on the other end of the line.

"It's bad . . . real bad . . . Mumma's . . . she's in bad shape. Is your dad home?"

"Yeah," Tommy said, sounding confused. "Hold on."

The sound garbled and Noah could hear Tommy calling for his father, telling him who was on the line. Then the sound of fumbling as the deputy took the phone.

"Noah, what's going on, son? Tommy says it's about your mom?"

"She's real sick, Mister Wren. Bad kind of sick. She's . . . not acting right. Not like herself."

"Is she conscious, Noah?"

"I don't—" Noah looked back in the direction of his house. "I don't think so."

On the other end, silence.

"Mister Winston says no one will come to help us in the storm, that no one can get here," Noah said, tears now streaming down his face.

"I'll—" he heard the deputy stammer on the line, "I'll call the Rockbridge sheriff, Noah. I'll do everything I can."

Then silence. Noah listened.

"But it might not be until the morning, son."

Noah sank onto the floor, the receiver still pressed to his ear. The world was closing in on him. A pit of despair was opening up to swallow him.

"Mister Wren," he said, his voice shaking. "When you were here, talking to Mumma, I was in the kitchen and I know what she told you."

Silence.

"She wasn't lying and the thing that she told you about . . . it's done awful things to her, Mister Wren. Awful things. I think it's doing something to her right now. Getting inside her somehow."

"Dekker," Noah heard the deputy croak.

"Yes, sir. It's him."

"Noah? You listen to me. Take care of your mother as best you can. I'm coming to you. Me and everyone else I can muster."

"Okay," Noah replied, the grip of doom easing a little.

"We are going to get you and your mom out of there tonight. I'll find a way. Understand?"

"Yes, sir."

"Sit tight, son," the deputy said. "And be brave."

"I . . . I'll try."

The line clicked and went dead, leaving Noah there on the floor, still clinging to the phone as if it were a lifeline and he a lost soul, adrift on stormy seas.

46

The first traces of dull awareness came like waves washing upon a shore, cascading over her body and waking it slowly, sensation creeping back into every limb and supple breadth of skin. Ada's legs stretched and a shudder ran through her belly. The house smelled of brewing coffee and the couch bore the heady scent of her family, all familiar aromas. She wanted to pick up her head, open her eyes and have a look around the room. She willed it, but her body would not respond. Again and again she tried, but in the end she was nothing more than a transient, screaming voice in the darkness of her own mind, where she had been mired for what must have been an eternity. The sleeve of the nightgown slipped up her shoulder as her arm pushed forward clumsily. It was a motion meant to stretch her muscles, though it was not one she had chosen. As her hand slipped into the crack between the couch and cushion, her fingers stretched out and, to her surprise, found something there. Something cold and familiar to the touch, and as her fingers dragged along a thin, metallic ridge, they found the gentle taper of the bolster, the curving scoop of the finger guard of the knife.

In the impotent darkness, Ada couldn't understand what the object was doing there, and she puzzled over it for a moment. If she hadn't put it there, perhaps Noah had—most likely in case Hugh returned in the night while her son lay asleep in front of the television.

Now her fingers were grasping the worn handle, their grip not yet sure, still waking. A lurid smile cut a crescent across her face. In this black and confusing corner of her mind, she was not alone. Something terrible stank and slithered in the twilight of dawning consciousness, and it had taken control.

Her body lay there quiet and unmoving as nerve endings sparked to life and the huntsman came fully awake in this new vessel, this new flesh, molting like a serpent shedding one skin for another.

Clay had been sitting at the kitchen table for some time now. He had polished off two cups of coffee and just poured a third. He meandered into the living room and stood before the window, watching the snowfall. Behind him, he heard a soft grunt and the sound of movement, sounds that might otherwise be lost but cut through the silence of the house. He turned to see Ada Belton moving on the couch and he relaxed a little. She was awakening. This would go a long way to assuaging the boy's fears that she was locked deep inside a kind of sleep from which Noah feared she might never emerge. He set his coffee down and went to her.

"Missus Belton, it's Clay Winston. Noah asked me to look after you."

Her eyes snapped open and she glared at him warily, like she didn't know him or maybe hadn't expected to see him here in her home. Clay could hardly blame her.

"Where's . . . where's the boy?" she spoke in a frail, dry voice.

The old man stepped closer and bent to her level, contemplating what half-truth to tell her that would allay her concern. Her arm jerked forth from beneath the pillow then and something shiny flashed, then whistled through the air. It met with the side of his neck and dug in.

In that instant, with his eyes locked on hers, Clay understood. It was Ada Belton's hand that wielded the blade, but the woman herself was imprisoned somewhere inside. The look in those eyes belonged to something else— something cruel and malevolent.

With his warm blood spilling down his neck and soaking his shirt and jacket, Clay stumbled backwards into the television, nearly knocking it over. He clawed his way along the wall toward the front door, instinctively seeking the exit even though there was nowhere to go and no one to call on for help. Behind him, the huntsman in Ada's skin stood and rounded the couch on the other side and came upon Clay just as he kneeled at the front door, struggling with the knob, smearing crimson as he tried in vain to open the door and escape. His knees were going weak, and his head was light and woozy. When the huntsman grabbed him by the collar of his jacket and dragged him back into the room, Clay found what little fight he'd had in him was now greatly diminished. His soul would soon be liberated from his flesh.

Strangely, the idea didn't trouble him all that much.

Dekker wrapped an arm around his neck and held him close. He reversed his grip on the knife and kept it low.

"You think I don't know nothing about you, that it? Well, I know," the huntsman snarled.

With that, he plunged the blade deep into Clay's gut and ground his fist in slow, firm circles. Clay groaned with nearly mute agony as his insides were shredded.

"I been here a long time, old man," the huntsman whispered, his breath foul. "I know you couldn't look after your own. I know that." Then he sighed. "Wish I could say it was me that took them boys from you, but you lost 'em all on your own. And now, even after all 'em years you ain't got no goddamned better at looking after what's yours."

The blood ran dark from Clay's abdomen now. His

mouth struggled to form words, his voice only a whisper choked with gurgling blood.

"Our Father who art . . . " was all he could manage.

"Oh, you want to say a prayer?" Dekker asked, smiling. "Well, how about this? Heavenly Father, there ain't nothing on the other side. *Nothing*, ya hear? I been there and I seen it. Just a cold, dark nothing. You'll see for yourself."

Clay wanted to offer a retort, but his thoughts were hazy, thin, slipping away.

Instead, he focused on the Christmas lights strung along the wall. How beautiful they were. The finest he had ever seen. Like shimmering, neon flowers. Like stars frozen in the act of becoming.

The huntsman watched as the last glimmer of light faded from the old man's eyes and when Clay Winston was gone from the world, the huntsman dropped him to the floor like a slab of unusable meat.

"Pray on that, old fool."

Dekker stood there, the knife slick in his grip with warm blood. He felt like a man fifty feet tall, alive and absolutely bestial in the world again. Overcome with a primal need to kill, to eat, to fuck.

But here he was in a nightgown.

He sighed. It was a pity it had to be a woman's body but it would do for now. When the old man slumped dead to the floor, his jacket crumpled up around him. Out of one of the pockets slid a pack of cigarettes and a book of flimsy matches. The tightly rolled sticks of tobacco had spilled across the floor, a few of them soaking up the dark red that pooled around the body. He had never cared much for cigarettes, being the puny and tasteless things that they were, but seeing as how there was no other tobacco around, he couldn't be picky.

Trapped inside, Ada looked upon the carnage with her own eyes, sickened by it. As she screamed into the void, Clyde Dekker smiled wide, smoked, and looked through the window at the black night outside and the endless barrage of stark, white snowflakes.

47

Nick Wren hung up the phone and stood there a moment, chewing his lip. His son hovered nearby, shuffling his feet, waiting.

"Dad, what's going on? Is Noah's mom okay?"

He shook his head, still chewing. "No, she's not. Ada's in trouble. They're both in trouble."

It was the wrong thing to say and Nick saw Tommy's face go white at his words.

"Now, just calm down."

"Jesus, Dad!" Tommy shouted. "We've gotta help them."

"I know," he replied, "but this storm . . . "

"Damn the storm, Dad."

Nick turned on his son, leveling a pointed finger. "Watch your mouth, young man."

Tommy stomped his foot and twisted away, his long hair flinging from his eyes. His son was pissed off, but more than that, he was scared. Scared for his friend. Nick was scared, too.

"I bet it's his asshole dad," Tommy growled.

"He didn't say that. Just that his mom's in a bad way and needs help."

Tommy said nothing. The old silent treatment.

I'm afraid it's worse than that, though.

"I'll call the Rockbridge sheriff," he said. "I'll call everyone I can to try and get them some help."

His son whirled around on him then and let him have it.

"Dad, Noah didn't call the Rockbridge sheriff. He didn't call 911. He called *you*."

Nick threw up his hands.

"Dammit, son, don't you think I know that? But this storm's shut everything down. It'd take hours to get there in this. If I made it at all. There's eighteen inches of snow and ice on everything from here to Norfolk. The roads are frozen and the whole state's shut down."

Tommy hung his head and turned away, leaning against the window that looked out onto Ashwood's cold waters.

"I don't want to argue about this, son, so let me get on the horn with—"

"What about the lake?" Tommy asked.

"What about it?"

"Is the lake frozen, too?"

Nick had lived on the banks of Ashwood lake all his life. He'd seen hard winters on it, too, and much to the chagrin of local children hoping to ice skate, in all those years it had never frozen over. Not once.

He knew then what his son was driving at and was ashamed he hadn't thought of it himself. What would take hours by the road would be a fraction of that by way of the lake. Nick's patrol boat didn't see much action during the cold months of the year, though, and he'd never taken it out in such foul weather as this.

"It'd be foolish to go out on the lake in this storm," he remarked. But his mind was working the problem, ticking off the challenges, evaluating the dangers.

Tommy eyed him with a profound disappointment. The kind that only sons and fathers ever knew.

"But, Dad—"

"It'd be foolish," he interrupted. "But it would be cowardly not to try."

Tommy's face lit up as Nick strode across the room, plucked his winter department coat from the hook by the back door and shoved his feet into his boots.

"I'm coming with you," he heard his son say.

"Tommy, there ain't no time for this and I—" he began, then looked up at the face of his son, stone-stubborn and resolute.

Out on the lake during a winter storm was no place for a child. But then Tommy wasn't a child anymore. Nick had to remind himself of that. Still, he wasn't a man yet, either, so he was still prone to rash and reckless judgment. If he didn't allow the boy to come with him, his son would try to get there some other way. And Lord knew what would happen then.

At least this way he could keep an eye on him.

"Fine," he said. "But dress warm, son. It'll be colder than a witch's tit out on that lake."

43

Noah stood on weary legs. He sighed, thinking of Deputy Wren coming to the rescue, waking every lawman and country boy with a four-wheel drive between Eastlake and Westlake to get them out to Cedar Banks.

But that was just a hope. It wasn't time to celebrate. Not yet. God willing, they might get his mother out of there tonight, but there was no telling what it would take to get rid of the huntsman's ghost. Noah had the bone braid, just like the dead Abner told him, but he hadn't a clue how to use it. He could only hope someone else would know.

Noah was striding through the house back to the front when, out of the corner of his eye, he saw a soft, glowing blue shape pass between doors in a long hallway downstairs.

He stopped and stared down the dark passage.

An idea came to him. Abner had guided him to the bone braid. Maybe the Blue Lady could tell him what to do with it.

"Hello?" he called out.

He crept down the hall to the room where she had disappeared. The yellow light from the bulbs behind him didn't penetrate the gloom there. He plucked his penlight from his pocket and shined it into the room.

There was nothing.

"Miss Amburg, I just want to talk to you. I don't think you underst—"

Behind him, the blur of another blue glow as she slipped into another darkened room at the end of the hall.

"I'm just trying to help my mother," he called out and followed.

But there was nothing in this room either.

Noah wondered why she wasn't letting him see her, why she was evading him.

"The one who hurt you . . . the one that stays in this place . . . he's hurting her now. Hurting Mumma and I have to stop him."

If the dead girl had any empathy, she would have to help him now. Wouldn't she? He waited and checked the other rooms, all dusty and empty. No sign of her.

He didn't have time for this. He'd have to find out about the bone braid some other way.

Frustrated and short on patience, he turned his back and barked to the empty house. "Fine, then. I hope you rot out here, damn you."

Noah hurried back up the hallway, through the drawing room and when he stepped into the foyer, he found her facing him, floating there between him and the door.

He made no movement, just watched her there with her soft, glowing form and cold eyes. Was she waiting for something from him? Was there a certain way he needed to ask? This was all so strange and unthinkable.

"I don't know—"

The ghost of Clara Amburg placed a finger over her lips and hovered there a moment.

Then she rushed forward, enveloping Noah in a cold

embrace, and the gray gathered at the edge of his vision. It was different than the other times with the huntsman. This was more like a knock on the door, and it was up to Noah if he wanted to answer it or not—to let her in.

She wanted to show him something, and he wanted to see it.

Like looking through an old spyglass, the grounds at Cedar Banks come into view, although this is another time, when this place was known as Crow Neck. Men mill about the encampment with long, brooding faces. They steal glances at him from behind narrowed, self-righteous eyes.

Noah sees the world as Clyde Dekker did, perched upon a rock near the main road, like a crow, like a killer, surveying the camp before him. They move about like ants, these others, and though his bloodlust constantly demands he cull their ranks, he finds the predictable routines of the men curious and amusing. Always, they move in the same pattern, before and after the call for chow. Every swinging dick shuffling to and fro, onward to the next objective, and all of them utterly unaware of the weird symphony of their labors.

All except for him. The huntsman sits and smokes and considers the world before him. He is beyond their paltry toils. If not for him and his skills, they would be reduced to eating bean slop and dry bread. In the hard winters, when the supply trucks could go as long as a fortnight between deliveries, without the huntsman, many would have wasted and wanted. But they had not. Because he always provided sustenance for them. Meat. Flesh. Their breath of life, which most seemed to take for granted. It was his alone to bestow or take away.

Life in this wilderness was a courtesy, not a right.

Up at the Amburg house, Clyde sees the young girl come out into the yard with a basket of laundry to hang on the line. He watches from afar as she bends to pull the clothing from the basket and he feels his blood getting up. The pretty thing has long been the object of fantasy for all of the men in camp, especially himself. He thinks of her often when he is alone but in his imaginings, she is not his wife, not even a steady girl. He cares nothing for such conventions. In his fantasies, he knows her as no other could. Carnally, of course, but he also knows the sound of her screams and the precise placement and amount of pressure required to snap her spine—paralyzing her but keeping her awake for her disemboweling. Ah, the way the brilliant red of her insides contrast with her pale, freckled skin and the sudden cascade of blood down her breasts as he slides the knife across her slender, aristocratic neck. These things he imagines. These things he longs for.

There is a jostling of his vision and Noah feels himself propelled forward in time.

Dekker is approaching the steps of the building that serves as both his quarters and his kitchen. Though it looks radically different in many ways from the land around it, Noah can tell it is the same house his father moved them into. The huntsman has something large and unmoving in the sack he carries over his shoulder.

Forward again, but not very far.

The huntsman is in the camp kitchen, standing naked before a large wooden table that Noah has seen before. Only this time, he is not sharpening a knife—but using one. He cleaves scarlet meat from a ruined pile of flesh and bone. Unthinkable amounts of blood and fluids drip from the table's edge, pooling onto the floor below, sinking into the fibers of the floor. Among the scraps there were bits of auburn-haired scalp and a blue dress, crumpled and soiled. Not far away behind a small door in the lower part of the wall, in the cooler, Noah knows there are slabs of cured meat that were once men. The sound of the knife edge sliding over bone is a sound that Noah has never *known and never cares to hear again. Dekker works away, so fervently lost in his butchering that he does not hear the others coming until they are upon him.*

Finally, he turns to see them standing in the doorway, a crowd of men with shovels and picks and axes in their hands, the expressions on their faces replete with horror and disbelief.

The huntsman glances down at the charnel display he has wrought with something akin to loss. He wears the bone braid draped around his neck like the vestments of some savage warrior, commemorating his many kills. It is never far from him, that charm, and it must go with him, all the way to Hell. He would not pass through the veil without it.

Noah tore himself from the vision and found himself on his knees on the cold floor, staring up into the light bulbs above, his mouth opened wide and dry. Awake now, he lurched forward, gasping for breath.

The vision imparted to him by way of Clara Amburg was gone now. He sat alone in the foyer of the old house, trembling and struggling to regain his bearings. It was over. But he had gleaned two things from the vision.

One; the huntsman and his charm were one and the same, and in order to send him into the next world, he would have to figure a way to send the bone braid, too. At least, that's what he thought it meant.

The other thing was appallingly clear.

Secondly; It was no wonder the huntsman had taken such an interest in his family. Of all the houses that his father might have chosen in Cedar Banks, he had settled on the old camp kitchen building; Dekker's own private lair.

Hugh had moved his wife and son right onto the goddamned killing floor.

49

Squinting and keeping his eyes trained on the lake, Nick Wren clutched the wheel of the boat so tightly that he wondered if his gloves had frozen to it.

They had been going at a good clip for a while, and even though he had the GPS screen to show him his location, it kept losing signal in the storm and at this point he was not entirely confident in its accuracy.

Snowflakes rushed toward him, smashing against the windshield of the boat and rendering it a blurry, slushy mess. Despite what Nick knew about the lake, there had been frozen spots along the way, but those bits were thin because the fishing boat pushed right through. Even so, it had been one hell of a trip. Mentally and physically taxing.

The door that led down into the cabin swung open and his son popped halfway up through the opening. He could barely hear him over the grind of the boat's two outboard motors.

"Can't you go faster, Dad?"

Nick glanced at his son for a moment but then fixed his eyes back on the black water before him illuminated by the boat's halogen lights.

"Dammit, Tommy, I'm going as fast as I dare. Faster than I should."

The boy nodded.

"How long?"

He looked down at his navigation screen.

"Ten minutes out," he replied.

When Tommy made to join him on the deck, Nick pointed a stern finger in his direction and shouted, "Stay below deck, son! Even when we get there, you stay until I say otherwise."

"But Dad—"

"Do as I say, Tommy, or when this is over, I'm grounding you for the whole next goddamn summer!"

"All right, fine," his son, said. "I just got a real bad feeling is all, Dad."

"Thomas . . ."

The cabin door slid closed as his son reluctantly complied and Nick returned all his attention to navigating the boat.

It had been just over thirty minutes since they shoved off back in Eastlake and getting the boat this far had been no picnic. It was night, it was storming, it was icy, and as full of dread as all those things made him feel, there was something more. There was a dark notion eating at him about what would be waiting for them when they finally tied up to the dock at Ada's house.

I know, son, Nick thought, glancing to the cabin of the boat. *I've got the same bad feeling.*

50

Well, shit.

The Ford grumbled along the narrow road that was covered in ice and snow.

At least he'd had the good sense to strap chains onto the tires before he left Kemp Metalworks after pretty much getting the high hat from Mister Kemp himself. Of course, he hadn't gone straight home, Lord no. As angry as he was with Ada about the whole mess, he might have gone and killed her. Hugh Belton knew this about himself, and since that wasn't what he had a mind to do just yet, he had stopped off at the Deerstalker, a roadside tavern between work and home, and had him a few pops just to cool off.

Not much of a drinker, he had certainly been enjoying it of late. The booze and the beer made him all the things his family did not—significant, powerful even. And wasn't that how a man ought to feel?

"Ain't no man and no damned woman ever gonna cut me out, goddammit," he mumbled to himself as he sat in the truck.

He had said the same thing back at the bar, over and over, sitting there alone, sipping his whiskey. It was just a thought, but sometimes thoughts had a way of creeping out of his head and out past his lips. Anyway, it wasn't long before the fat, greasy Dago-looking barkeep shut the place down on account of the storm and scattered all the drunks to the wind.

And Hugh had been banished with them.

It was probably for the best, though. Even he had to admit that.

The white road before him rolled from side to side, weaving this way and that, and he turned the wheel, correcting. Overcorrecting, if he was to be honest. He'd had a bit too much and he wasn't fully in control.

But he soon would be.

That cheating whore and that feckless little upstart. They had taken over his castle and it was time to put an end to it. Time for the king to reign once again. He had ceded control. A grievous error to be sure, but one that could be righted.

By God, he would make it right. By God and all His terrible angels, he would see it made right.

Tonight.

Something caught Hugh's eye and as he glanced aside, he pressed the brake and the Ford went fishtailing on the ice. Letting off it, he glided to a stop in the middle of the road.

A truck sat in the ditch, the ass end of it sticking up, the taillights red and glowing.

An old Chevy short bed. The old caretaker's truck.

Hugh watched it for a few minutes but never saw hide nor hair of anyone alive. Maybe the old man was in there, unconscious and cold, getting colder. If so, he'd never last the night.

So much the better.

Hugh hadn't liked that old coot from the start. The way he hung around with Noah. It wasn't right, wasn't natural.

Let the old bastard die in the cold.

He eased down onto the accelerator. The chains slipped and slipped and then finally grabbed at the ice.

After a slide and a juddering start, the Ford was again creeping along the mountain road with Hugh Belton at the helm, grinning with dark anticipation.

51

On his way across the grounds, Noah passed Clay's house, which sat like a dark stone at the edge of a field of white. The lights that burned within were still few and faint, and from this he took heart that the old man was still watching over his mother, awaiting his return. The snow fell slow and steady now, tossed about on a gentle breeze. At a distance, his own house looked still and quiet—a short, broad silhouette against the black waters of Ashwood Lake. He slogged toward the front porch and climbed the steps.

Brushing off his coat as he stepped in, Noah wondered at the intense chill inside of the house. He knelt down to remove his boots, but stopped, glimpsing his mother sitting across the room in the easy chair, still dressed in her nightgown. In her fingers, she held a cigarette that lazily smoked, filling the room with a nicotine haze. So pleased was he to see her that he paid no heed to the unusual sight of the cigarette or the feeling that washed over him, raising gooseflesh on his skin. He stood erect and smiled.

"Mumma, you're awake!" he shouted and started toward her but the toe of his boot slipped on something. He looked down to see the buckled body of Clay Winston and the wide puddle of dark red that had gathered around it.

"Welcome home, boy," he heard his mother say.

She placed the cigarette between her lips and exhaled a plume of foul smoke. This was followed by a bellow of terrible laughter. From the venomous tone, he knew at once that it was not his mother who had spoken.

Noah drew back, but froze. Clay lay on the floor, not moving or breathing. A lump caught in Noah's throat and the edge of a sob escaped his lips as a whimper. His only friend in this place had been cut down and his mother invaded, now turned against him. How powerful the huntsman must be to have done that, and how broken his mother to allow it. He gripped the cold doorknob in his hand, ready to run. But to where?

Noah shook with a fear that steadily transformed into anger and disgust. He thought of the bone braid in his bag on the floor—his secret, yet impotent weapon.

"What do you want?" Noah spat, his lip curling in anger.

Dekker shook Ada's head and as Noah looked on, it was as though he could see past the figure of his mother to the thing that had wormed its way inside her like a sickness. The sweet face of his mother faded and in its place he saw the gnarled, unshaven features and haunting black cavities of the huntsman's eyes.

"Just come to collect my last pound of flesh and hold up my end of the bargain."

Noah's scoffed. "The bargain."

Dekker took another long drag off the cigarette. "That's right. Got me a few good screwings out of it. In return, I slice your old man open from balls to brains. So that you and your momma can get free and go live . . . *happily-ever-after*."

Something turned cold in Noah's gut and he thought he might vomit. His gaze was pulled down to Clay, dead upon the floor.

"Happily-ever-after," he whispered, then looked back up at Dekker. "But that was never gonna happen, was it?"

"Nope." The smoke curled out from the edges of the huntsman's smile.

Noah's instinct told him to flee, to tear out of that house like his feet were on fire and go wherever, to hide in the woods if he had to. But he was now faced with the same dismal conclusion that his mother must have come to time and again with his father. There was nowhere to go that this thing would not find him. And he sure as hell wasn't leaving without her.

Noah stood in his living room, his shoulders slumped. His plan was going to fail. It had *already* failed. The huntsman's total possession of his mother meant there was nothing that Clara Amburg or the other restless dead could do to help him. Clyde Dekker had left the in-between place and was now here in the physical world, well beyond their reach.

As the foundation of his hopes crumbled beneath him, Noah heard a faint sound outside. One that seemed to grow closer every second. The groan of an engine approaching. His mind leaped to the possibility of Deputy Wren, but almost as soon as the thought had formed, he dismissed it. It hadn't been long enough for the deputy to make it all the way from Eastlake and certainly not in this weather.

Through the kitchen window, headlights flashed from the road and swept across the living room walls as the vehicle turned into the driveway. Noah glanced through the pass-through into the kitchen and thought he saw his father's red pickup coming to a stop in the driveway.

"Dad . . ."

Dekker ground his cigarette out on the arm of the chair and flicked it to the floor.

"Looks like the show's 'bout to start," he said with a grin, then stood, the knife grasped in his hand.

Noah thought perhaps his father's arrival would be his deliverance, though it would be trading one devil for another. Still, the desire to escape this place right now was so powerful that Noah was willing to put his faith in his father to do the right thing. They would have to come back for his mother. Come back with someone who knew about driving spirits from the bodies of the living; a preacher maybe, like Pastor Gorman. Noah bolted toward the kitchen, but Dekker was halfway across the room already.

The huntsman was quicker and stronger in Ada's body than Noah would have imagined, and he grabbed him by the hood of his coat, pulling him backward. Noah fought against him, though, and in all the grasping and throwing of arms and kicking of his legs, Dekker nicked the top of Noah's right ear off with the knife. The little bit of flesh fell to the floor and Noah's hand went to his head, pressing against the wound and the blood that poured forth. The huntsman grabbed him again and tossed him back into the living room where he tumbled and came to rest at the threshold of the hallway.

"That ought to settle you down," he snarled at Noah. "Sit tight, boy. Your time's a'comin'."

52

Hugh poured himself out of the cab of his truck and slammed the door behind him. The mountain night was deep, crowded with thick flakes of snow plummeting from the darkness above. He stared at his house, his castle, and the drone of power he now felt—the power they would soon know—filled his ears. He shuffled forward in the mounting snow, now almost up to his knees, and fumbled on his keyring for the one that would open the house.

The bitch had almost certainly locked him out.

There was a sound, though. One that did not belong. He cocked his head to listen for it.

A buzzing, high-pitched and distant.

He cast about the area searching for the source, then glimpsed strobing lights out on the lake. Flashing blue and white, like tiny stars, growing ever closer to Cedar Banks.

"What the hell?"

It took him a moment to put it together, to understand what he was seeing.

Police flashers. The kind used by the cops that patrolled the lake.

He grimaced. *Nick Wren. It's goddamned Deputy Nicholas Wren.*

He glanced up at the house. It was quiet inside and darker than usual. The curtains were pulled and dim light leaked out from around the edges.

Mood lighting, he thought, a sour taste filling his mouth.

Hugh doubled over and vomited into the snow. It was a technicolor mess that stank of whiskey and cheap draft beer.

Glancing back out at the lake and the speeding police boat headed his way, he spat the last chunks and wiped his mouth with the sleeve of his coat.

"Expecting company, Missus Belton?" he grumbled into the wind and dashed off to the woods near the edge of the lake.

He crouched there and waited until the steady buzz of the boat motor throttled down to a low, watery chortle. Nick was in the shallows now, slowing down, approaching the tiny dock that jutted out into the water at the back of Hugh's property. As it edged closer, Nick killed the flashers and trained a spotlight on the dock. A second later, he cut the engine and came around to the side, rope in hand, as the boat drifted toward the pylons.

The wood gave a plaintive crack when the patrol boat slammed into it and bounced away. Not before Nick got the end of one rope around it, though, and started pulling the boat toward the dock, securing the other end on the boat's cleats. After this, the deputy disappeared into the cabin below, then returned a moment later with a flashlight in hand.

Nick stepped from the boat onto the dock, almost slipping, and shined the beam of his light over the house, studying it as he approached.

A gentleman caller, Hugh thought. *Boy, is Ada in for a goddamned change of plans tonight.*

Hugh's tongue flicked out of his mouth and ran along

his lips like he was tasting something delicious. Blood would soon be spilled and his wrath delivered.

Black Billy burned with hunger in its sheath strapped to his leg.

He waited—waited until Nick stepped off the dock into the snow.

The deputy's flashlight beam scanned across the breadth of the snow piled high, then lingered at the edge of the house, on the trail of footprints Hugh had tracked from the driveway to the edge of the woods. Deputy Wren stiffened, sensing trouble, and his other hand went to the grip of the weapon on his side.

But Hugh was already charging through the dark and the snow like a murderous bear and was upon him in an instant. The deputy's gun went off with a solitary pop that was swallowed by the roar of the icy wind.

But by then it was too little, too late.

Tommy peered through the boat's tiny portal, his breath fogging the glass as his father trod down the snow-covered dock toward the house. After tying up the boat, he had ducked in and told Tommy to stay put while he checked out the house.

"If something goes wrong . . . if it even *looks wrong,* you stay put. Understand?"

It was only then that the gravity of the situation settled on Tommy. It bore down on him with all the weight of every schoolyard bully he'd ever known. This was a rescue mission; simple get-in-and-get-out kind of stuff. At least, that's how he had imagined it.

But as his father climbed the few steps to the deck of the boat, with those words of warning lingering in the air, he felt the reality of it pressing upon him.

"Dad!"

His father paused, looked back. "Yeah?"

Tommy wanted to say something, should have known what to say in that moment, but he didn't.

"Be careful," was all he could manage.

His father smiled at that, then fixed him with an unblinking stare. "You stay put, son. The cavalry's on the way."

Before leaving home, his father had called every lawman and firefighter and EMS technician he knew within fifty miles of Cedar Banks and had fed them all a ration of bullshit; whatever they needed to hear and might get them off their asses in this storm.

There was an old lady in diabetic shock, a massive chemical fire, a multiple murder-in-progress . . . all of it happening at number 5 Cedar Bay Drive in Whitetail. Anything that might work.

With his dad off the boat, Tommy was suddenly aware of how vulnerable and alone he was. He looked on as the bright beam from his dad's flashlight bounced around, fixing on the house in the distance and then the expanse of empty yard leading away from the dock.

Before his father could barely plant a leg into the snow, a dark and enormous shape came out from the woods. A thick arm shot out, clotheslining him and knocking the Stetson from his father's brow as he dropped into the snow. Then the muted crack of a gunshot.

"Shit!" Tommy whispered, fogging the glass again.

By the time he had it wiped clear, the big man was holding his father's limp body by the collar of his uniform and pummeling him with savage blows.

Tommy bit down on his lip and resisted the urge to vacate the safety of the boat.

After a few more punches, the big man—who Tommy was now sure was Noah's father—tossed his father to the ground, where he disappeared into the gathering snow.

Mister Belton looked back at the boat a moment and Tommy's heart went straight down into his stomach. If he came out to the boat, there was no hiding from him. He would be trapped. And God knows what the brutish bastard would do to him then.

But Mister Belton did not come. He turned and strode through the snow toward the house, apparently unaware of Tommy's presence.

He waited until Noah's father was gone before he even considered leaving the shelter of the boat's cabin. Tommy wanted to help his father, to see if he was all right, but all he could picture was Hugh Belton stalking back toward him from the darkness as he stood over his father's dead body, knowing that he would be joining him in the hereafter as soon as the monster got his claws on him.

I gotta do something, he chastised himself.

Sit and wait for the cavalry. That's what he was supposed to do. But how long would that be? Maybe they would get there faster if they knew of the danger they were all in. Tommy scrambled up the steps to the controls, unhooked the microphone from the CB radio and squawked the button a couple times before holding it down.

"Hello?"

After a moment of silence, a woman's voice came through.

"Dispatch here. That you, Nicholas?"

Relief washed over him, brief but powerful. It was cut short by a knife wind that rose up from the lake and plunged through him there on the rocking boat.

"No, its . . . I'm Nick's son. There's been—"

"Thomas?"

He didn't know who this woman was who called him by his proper name, nor did he care.

"Yeah, it's me. I came with Dad to Cedar Banks. Dad's been . . . I'm not sure. Mister Belton came out of nowhere. Beat him down. It looked pretty bad. I don't even know if he's still breathing."

The radio went to static then and Tommy heard only traces of the woman's voice again, emerging from the fuzz.

" . . . officer down . . . stay calm . . . help soon . . . "

Satisfied the message had gotten through, Tommy hung the mic up and went back down below deck, took up his position at the portal again and watched the snow at the end of the dock, hoping and praying to see his father emerge from it.

53

Hugh opened the kitchen door, knocking the snow from his boots against the threshold, and saw Ada standing there in the kitchen.

As he stepped in and slammed the door, he brushed the white flakes from his black-and-red checkered coat and tossed his stocking cap to the floor, leaving his hair madly askew. It was then he noticed his wife's nightgown stained dark red in places. Her hands and forearms were also smeared with dried crimson and flecks of it were mingled among the freckles of her face.

"Damn, woman, you look like you been butchering a hog. Did I miss supper? What're we having?"

His wife regarded him with a cold, steely glare for a moment, then tilted her head to the side and grinned in a manner that he couldn't quite name and had never seen from her before.

"Naw, you didn't miss it, hoss."

"What've you been up to, you lowly—" Hugh began.

Living with someone for so many years, one becomes accustomed to their nuances; the small things about them that are wholly unique but that likely couldn't be named specifically. Though he had only glimpsed her behavior for a few seconds, she seemed an entirely different person to him, even down to the cadence and tone of her speech. There was no time to think more of it, though. She was rushing at him, a kitchen knife in her grasp and her arm outstretched as she brought it up with a haymaker punch, arcing toward his throat, the sharp blade whistling through the air.

The crazy bitch was trying to kill him, and that was certainly something unusual.

Hugh raised his left forearm up to block. She closed on him and her swing was stopped cold. He had hoped the impact of their arms meeting would jar the knife from her grip but it did not, so with his right hand he pushed against her chest and sent her reeling backwards. Black Billy was itching, burning hot against his leg now and as she regained her footing, he had time to free the club and bring it up at the ready. Hugh stood there, knees bent, his muscles taut and infused with adrenaline. He hadn't intended to put Ada in the grave tonight, but if this was how she wanted it, then he was only too happy to oblige.

Didn't think the bitch had it in her.

His wife deftly reversed her grip on the knife and came at him again.

Noah didn't stay very long on the floor to see who would win the contest between his father and Dekker. As Dekker rushed back into the fray, Noah scrambled to his feet and bolted into his room, the soles of his boots still wet and slipping on the floor. He flicked the light switch in his room and saw the Louisville Slugger leaning up against his bed. The parka he wore was ripped and hanging awkwardly across his shoulders from where the huntsman had grabbed and thrown him and Noah took a moment to pull it off and toss it to the floor. His ear was still bleeding, though it had begun to slow as the cool air coagulated it into the foundations of scar tissue. From the next room, he heard grunts and growls of anguish as the two of them fought. He grabbed up the bat and stepped out into the hallway.

The two stood between the kitchen and living room,

grappling with each other. Dekker had the knife blade inches from his father's throat and from the look on his face, Noah could tell that the freakish strength being displayed by his mother had Hugh on the ropes. Noah moved cautiously around to where the television stood, though neither of the two seemed to pay him any mind. As Dekker, much shorter in his mother's body than Hugh, continued to drive the knife down toward him, his father raised a knee and jammed it into the stomach of the other. Dekker leaned in and the grip that he had on Hugh's club-wielding hand loosened enough for his father to escape.

Now free, he swatted at the arm holding the blade. Dekker's weapon arm went limp and out to the side, the knife slipping away and sailing through the air to come clattering to rest in the kitchen sink. Now, with nothing to stop him from advancing on Dekker but whatever brute strength the entity could summon, his father caught Dekker across the jaw with the shaft of the club and leaned into him, walking him back into the living room and pummeling the huntsman with Black Billy wherever he saw an opening. It was a blessing and a curse, though, because Dekker now had both hands free to grab and claw at his father and his raised arms deflected any attack that might have struck his head and stupefied him long enough for Hugh to land a damning blow.

After a few more body shots with the club, Noah thought perhaps his father had gotten the better of his opponent, but with the quickness of a serpent, Dekker shot both arms out and grabbed hold of his father's wrists, pulling them down crossways as he doubled over and dragged the taller man down with him. Again there was that look of bewilderment on his father's face as the body of this tiny woman, who he had thrashed time and again, held his thick arms and pulled them toward the floor. Then, with Dekker's chin tucked into his chest, he shot up and threw his head back, catching Hugh beneath the jaw with the crown of Ada's head. Surprised and now a bit dazed, his father staggered backwards and the huntsman spun him around into the living room, his arms sliding up and snatching the club from his father's grasp.

Dekker tossed it quickly into his other hand and then swung low to catch Hugh on the side of his knee. The big man buckled and went down to the floor.

Dekker shoved his father backwards and Hugh toppled over the body of Clay Winston, rolling the old man's corpse onto his stomach. Noah's father slipped on the pooled blood and cane to rest on his backside.

"Now," Dekker seethed, standing above him, "how's about a taste of that medicine you're so fond of giving out?"

With Black Billy gripped in his hand, he jabbed Noah's father in the chest, taking the breath from him, and began raining down blows indiscriminately. Some found his father's flesh but many went wild and caught nothing but air.

As Noah looked on, the form of the huntsman faded away and his mother became visible once again. As the punishing strokes of Black Billy fell, it was her voice that growled—not Dekker's. Incredibly, in the avenging rage against the one who had beaten her and Noah so often, she had wrested control from the huntsman.

"You—"

Thwack!

"Son of a—"

Thwack!

"bitch!"

Thwack!

"How's it feel?"

Thwack!

"How's it fucking feel now, asshole?"

Noah cried out.

"Mumma!"

She halted her assault and looked up, a stunned and vacant look in her eyes. She let go of the collar of her husband's coat and stood, stepping back and looking down at the bloodied, beaten wreck of a man before her. She looked over at her son, and in that instant, he saw the unmistakable eyes of his mother, buoyed by the familiar tone and lilt of her voice.

"Noah?" she said, confused and exasperated.

He was about to run to her and embrace her but before he could even take the first step, the sight of his mother shuddered and flickered and was replaced by the giant, scowling form of the huntsman once again.

He turned his black gaze to the right, as if addressing something beside him and said, "Back inside, you uppity cunt."

Dekker glanced over at Noah, who stood there with the Slugger dangling loosely in his grasp. He smirked and gave the boy a wink, then turned his gaze back upon Hugh.

Noah's father was on his knees, barely upright. His face was bloodied and bruised from the battle, one side so swollen that his eye could hardly open. He knelt there, swaying and moaning.

"You," Dekker hissed. "Tonight, I'm gonna cut you up and feed you to your boy."

A devil's grin spread across his face.

"Raw."

Noah's father looked up but could not manage any kind of retort even if he had cared to.

"After I take my piece, of course," Dekker added. "Cook's privilege, ya know."

Noah looked on in disbelief, a storm of emotions whirling in his heart. In that moment, all of his father's past cruelties came to him like a barrage of images and sensations, every one of them anchored with the feeling of hopelessness he had so long known. He could wade in now, take the huntsman by surprise and end it all with a few swings of the baseball bat.

Maybe. If he was lucky.

In truth, though, he had no desire to save his father from what would be Dekker's final killing stroke. None.

But the man was his father after all, even after all he had done, and perhaps that was worth something even now. On the other hand, Noah would not sacrifice his mother for the benefit of his father. Nor would he do so just to escape Crow Neck and all the evil things that called the place home. The hard truth, Noah realized, was that he wanted neither of these awful creatures to prevail and he was unable to make a choice between them. He only wanted his mother and a simple life away from all of this violence and torment.

Dekker bent and raised the club above his head and though Noah was partly compelled to do something, he stood there and watched instead.

With Black Billy grasped tightly in his hand, held aloft to strike, he glanced up at Noah to offer a final, taunting look before he took Hugh Belton from this world. But he paused, and his expression went slack, the dark cavities of his eyes seeming to look not at Noah but beyond him.

"What in the hell?" he whispered.

His father's endurance finally gave out and, with a groan, he thudded to the floor alongside Clay Winston. For a moment, Noah was confused by the shift in Dekker's attention and tightened his grip on the Slugger, brought it up to bear, but the huntsman hardly seemed to notice. He followed Dekker's gaze and turned to look behind him.

He gasped at what he saw.

Outside of the front window were the faces of the dead, crowded shoulder to shoulder as they stood, watching. All of their lifeless eyes were locked on the huntsman and it was clear that he recognized every one of them. Centered among their ranks was the glowing apparition of Clara Amburg in her blue dress. She was flanked by many others. Some Noah recognized from the crawlspace but others he did not, although he knew them all to be victims who had fallen under the huntsman's blade. In the crowd of the dead, he glimpsed the familiar face of Clay Winston with his young, golden-haired boys beside him.

Glancing around the room still cast in the dim glow of the Christmas lights, he saw pale, ghostly visages peering in from every window. The gathering faces of the slain were everywhere. For a moment, Noah thought perhaps they had come to welcome him. That they had come to count him among them.

But their collective gaze had not fallen upon him. With retribution etched into their pale and narrowed eyes, the dead looked long at the huntsman and lingered just outside of the house, waiting.

Hugh Belton ached all over from the vicious beating he had just been handed by his wife, despite her runty stature. He blamed it on a rush of adrenaline. The kind of thing that drove people to pick up a car when their child was trapped beneath it. He had heard about things like that, he was sure. It didn't help that he was also still a bit drunk from his time at the roadhouse. He lay there now on the floor, his face swollen and hot as if burning from within and one side of it awash in blood, though some of it had once belonged to the old man lying next to him. He wondered what it was the old property manager had done that could have motivated Ada to kill him. Unless, of course, something had snapped in his wife and she had simply gone utterly mad. The more he considered it, the more likely it seemed. He craned his neck to see Ada standing above him, a bewildered look on her face as she stared at something beyond Hugh's sight. The familiar club was held tight in her fist. It had been a long while indeed since a woman had grasped that weapon and used it. The last had been his mother and it was him she had used it on. Now wielded by his wife, Hugh reckoned he would soon die by it.

He was spent, and so he lay his head back down against the cool floor. As he did so, he noticed something poking out of the pocket of the old man's coat.

It looked like the butt of a pistol.

With his wife's attention still trained on something else, Hugh leaned over and plunged his hand into the dead man's pocket. It was a gun all right; an old, heavy one from the feel of it. He did not know if the pistol was loaded or not and there was no way to tell. Presumably, the old man wouldn't be toting around an unloaded gun, but then he had known of people doing far dumber things than that. There was no time to check to be sure. He would just have to take the chance.

His finger slid into the trigger guard and rested against it. With his thumb, he cocked back the hammer as he pulled the gun free of the coat. Summoning all the fortitude that he had left and ignoring the throbbing pain wracking his body from his head down to his knees, he sat up as quick as he could.

"You ain't gonna be the end of me," he growled at her.

As Ada turned her head toward him, he leveled the pistol at her and pulled the trigger.

There was no time to do anything to stop his father. Noah had been looking around at the apparitions of the dead that surrounded the house when he saw movement out of the corner of his eye, from where his father lay next to the old man's body, moaning and writhing in a pool of blood gone cold and sticky. He heard him speak those words of wrath with his arm outstretched and a pistol gripped in his hand. Noah had just begun to wonder where the gun had come from when the flash and smoke erupted from the barrel with a report that slapped against the walls of the house. The huntsman jerked backward, then lurched forward, but did not fall.

Then Noah was on the move. He had the Slugger up and was rounding to the other side of the couch where his father knelt, smiling at what he had just done. It was instinct on Noah's part—the instinct to protect his mother, even if it wasn't entirely his mother any longer.

His hope was that he could get his mother to someone who could help her. A priest or a Rabbi or even a damned witch-doctor if that's what it took. He wouldn't let anyone take her from him. Not Dekker and certainly not Hugh Belton.

His father turned to regard his son, more than a little surprise glowing in his eyes. Without a word, Noah swung and the bat crashed into the side of his father's head. Hugh's one good eye closed as his head snapped away, and the rest of his body followed, going prone, the gun slipping from his grasp and pinwheeling across the floor.

It stopped at the feet of Dekker, who bent down and picked it up.

Noah's father had fired the gun, and while he was certain he had aimed for the chest, the shot hadn't been true. The bullet had caught the huntsman in the left shoulder instead. A bloom of red spread out from the wound and that arm hung limp at his side. Apart from that, Clyde Dekker looked to be doing just fine. Noah's blood turned cold, and he dropped the bat to the floor as his shoulders and arms went slack with defeat.

Dekker cocked the hammer back and brought the gun up to aim at Noah. Out of the back window, Noah could see the lingering forms of the murdered and knew he would be joining them soon. That was fine with him. At least it was an end to all of this.

"Looks like your time's come, kid."

"Go ahead," Noah said, his voice breaking. "Please. I don't want to be here anymore."

"That right?"

He nodded.

"As you wish," he heard the huntsman say, then the click as the hammer descended and a shudder went through Noah's body.

The huntsman's smile eroded and he brought the pistol closer, held it askance for a look and saw the round had not fired and was still lying there dormant in the cylinder.

"Goddammit," he cursed and then clicked the hammer back again, rotating the cylinder to line up the next bullet.

When he brought the pistol back up, he saw the boy had opened his eyes wide, standing there and not believing he wasn't already deader than four o'clock.

That's good, the huntsman thought. *It's better for the boy to see it coming.*

It was Clyde Dekker's belief that any animal, facing the gun that was about to put it down, could see more clearly in that last second than in their entire life before. And in that final moment, as the bullet blasted forth, every creature experienced a stark terror at the impending approach of death that was unrivaled by anything that had ever come before. To witness it was an exhilarating rush.

He slipped his finger back onto the trigger and stiffened the muscles, almost pulled it back. That's when something came rushing out of the darkness at him. Not from some corner of the house, not from outside, but from within himself.

Once, when he walked these woods as a living man, he witnessed the fury of a mother bear protecting her cubs. He had barely escaped that encounter with his life, but the memory of the animal's rage paled in comparison to this. Ada Belton came screaming and clawing at him from within and tore the huntsman from his hold over her.

Noah watched as Dekker's gun arm lowered and an embattled look washed over him. Then, before his eyes, he disappeared, flickering away intermittently, and as he did so, the face of his mother was visible again. Noah saw only her. She had bested the huntsman and regained control of her body and mind. Seeing her prevail, Noah's knees buckled and he collapsed to the floor. There, on his knees before his mother, he stared up at her.

Her eyes fell upon him and she managed a smile—a mother's soft and comforting smile, despite the red scars that cut across her face. It conveyed a myriad of things to him, and when she next spoke, it was in her own voice.

"Don't give up like that, son," she said to him. "Don't ever let me catch you giving up like that again."

His eyes filled with hot tears.

"Mumma . . . "

She knelt and closed him in an embrace.

"I'm here, Noah. But I don't know for how long."

"Fight him, Mumma. Please, please fight him."

Ada sat on the floor and leaned back against the couch. She breathed hard and shook her head, though her warmth never faltered.

"I ain't got it in me, son. He's taken everything I had left," she said, her voice gentle and tired, yet firm. "Everything except for you, and I won't let him take that. No way, no how."

"Mumma, please . . . "

"It's all right, baby boy," she said, and smiled at her son. "It's all right now. I love you."

She grimaced a moment, still struggling inside with the huntsman, then brought the pistol close to her body and pressed the barrel hard against her chest.

"No, wait . . . " Noah cried and crawled toward her.

"Look away, son," she whispered to him. "Look away.."

The pistol fired and the thick smoke and smell of gunpowder filled the air as Noah scrambled toward his mother, who slumped over, lifeless. The bullet that had been intended for Noah had pierced Ada's chest and lay trapped somewhere in the dense, fibrous muscle of a heart that was now still and silent and would be forever.

54

Kneeling there with his mother going cold in his arms, Noah had never known such hollowness, never before imagined such a penetrating absence. He held her and wept over her and was broken with grief. It was only after being lost in it that he noticed the dark shape of the huntsman standing close by. Though he still feared Dekker, there was simply no room in him for it, and no energy left to cower and scurry away from the murderous spirit.

Noah looked up at Clyde Dekker but did not see the scowling phantom he expected. The huntsman's color had gone gray and the apparition shuddered, seeming less substantial than ever before. The thing that was Clyde Dekker had been feeding on his mother's life force, but she had passed on now and the stinking man's sustenance had passed with her. Now, when Noah stared into the empty blackness of Dekker's eyes, what he saw was not defiance, but defeat.

He might have smiled at this victory were it not for the cost.

The dead were inside now, gathering around. Noah glimpsed them through tear-filled eyes. There were so many and even though they had no physical presence, Noah sensed them all. They pressed inward, pale hands reaching through the throng, grasping—aching to take the huntsman.

A furious noise arose as they shouted at Dekker, some speaking the names of those they left behind, some lamenting the life they might have known if not for him, others reminding him that he was now as dead as they were and that he always had been. With every touch of one of his victims, Dekker withered to smoky shadow.

Too many, too many, Noah thought as they closed in.

His phobia was taking hold. His breaths became short and his limbs shook. He clung desperately to his mother.

The familiar girth of her arm, her body, and shoulders. But she could not soothe him any longer, and so he found himself reeling, his heart hammering in his chest so badly he just knew it would explode at any moment.

Then, pushing through the mass of spirits came Clay Winston. It was a younger version of the man, though, who smiled more easily and did not seem so peculiar. A man who no longer had that burdened, haunted look in his eyes. Beside the old man were his boys. They made their way toward Noah and knelt beside him. Clay put a ghostly hand on Noah's arm and nodded.

"It's okay now, Noah. They're taking him away. Everything will be just fine."

Noah looked on as the huntsman was slowly torn apart, the pieces of him becoming tiny drifts of black smoke that broke from the whole and were sucked downward into a dark chasm beneath them that Noah could sense was there. One after another, they came for him, and each took something from the cruel beast that had taken everything from them. The huntsman's face was frozen in an open-mouthed scream.

Noah shoved a hand into his jacket pocket and closed his fingers around the bone braid there. He thought of the murdered Abner's words in the darkness, of the blue lady's vision.

It's got to go with him . . . all the way to Hell.

He couldn't bring himself to stare down into that chasm in the floor. There was too much of the netherworld in it, too much despair. Noah balled the bone talisman in his fist and cast it toward the ravening pit.

Then he pressed his face against his mother's unmoving breast and wept in sharp, heaving sobs.

All the while, the old man's hand was on his arm and his calming voice was in Noah's head.

"It's okay, Noah. Rest easy now. It'll pass."

The gray at the edges of his vision crept in, crowding out the world, until the gray was all he saw.

And then Noah saw nothing at all.

55

Tommy had been at his perch in front of the boat's portal when he heard the shots from inside the house. Two quick pops, spaced minutes apart, that rang through the night. He'd been to the gun range with his father often enough to recognize the sound of a small caliber pistol's report, and hearing it now set him on edge.

He paced back and forth, weighing his options, though from where he stood, he didn't have many. If his father could be roused, then he needed to rouse him and get him back onto the boat so they could leave.

But what if Dad's dead?

Tommy banished it from his mind. His dad couldn't be. He just couldn't be.

Dead or alive, still there was Noah and his mother . . . they couldn't just leave them. They had come here to help, and God only knew what was going on inside that house—who was being shot and who was doing the shooting. It was nothing short of a nightmare.

Tommy decided that one thing was for certain. He wasn't going to solve anything by hiding below deck on the boat while his father lay out there in the snow and gunshots were ringing out from inside the house where his best friend lived.

"Hell with it," he said and rushed up onto the deck, leaped from the boat and went racing down the dock.

He found his father on his back, his face a swollen red mess with busted skin below his eye and blood that had coagulated and frozen to his flesh in the winter night. Tommy dropped to his knees, fearing the worst, but when he placed his hand in front of his father's parted lips, he could feel the flow of slow, warm breath.

Tears of relief welled in his eyes. He laid his head alongside his father's and spoke into his ear.

"Dad, you gotta get up. Dad, please!"

But his father didn't budge, didn't respond at all. Not even after Tommy took to shaking him and gently slapping his cheeks.

He looked up at the house, dim and still in the storm. It had gone quiet. No more gunshots. Even so, the notion of walking in there filled him with fear.

But what choice did he have? There was nowhere else to go.

He plunged his hands into the snow and, after some fumbling, found the grip of his father's gun. He yanked it free of the holster, brushed away the snow and ice, and held it aloft, feeling for the safety and sliding it into the off position.

Tommy screwed up his courage and went lumbering through the white up to Noah's house.

He ascended the steps onto the front porch, the pistol shaking in his grasp. He'd shot it plenty of times at the range but in that moment it must have weighed fifty pounds. Maybe he shouldn't have come up here alone. Maybe he should have waited.

But it was too late for any of that.

Before he knew it, his hand was on the knob and he was pushing the front door open.

56

Noah woke hunched over, his head hovering above the hole in his mother's chest, her blood soaking the side of his face. Tears had dried in salty trails down his cheeks and the house was cold—his mother even colder. Noah did not recall blacking out, though he did remember the kindness of Clay and his boys who came to comfort him. He also remembered being overwhelmed by the dead that had gathered in the room to rip apart the ghost of Clyde Dekker and escort him to Hell. He remembered the chaos and cacophony of that moment.

Now, though, all of them were gone.

The soft, rainbow glow of his mother's Christmas lights, so peaceful and evocative of a joyful season, seemed odd as they illuminated the room in which such evil things had just occurred. Christmas lights in the house where his mother and friend now lay dead.

Noah gently slid his mother to the floor, her limbs so lifeless and yielding that some deeply primitive part of him recoiled. Outside, the snow continued to fall but the storm was over, and now he was more alone in the world than he had ever imagined possible.

A stirring from the opposite end of the couch reminded Noah that his father still lived, and that he was not entirely alone.

The realization was not a blessing, though. It only filled Noah with dread and anger. That his father should live while his mother lay dead on the floor was a horror, and he was incensed by it.

Whatever happened in the aftermath of this night, his father was his only surviving family, and the police would no doubt release him into his custody. They would use words like "stability" and "continuity" as a reason for this, thinking all the while they were making the most compassionate choice for him.

Compassion.

He scoffed at the notion.

How long before Hugh killed him in some random fit of rage?

It wasn't a question of *if*, but of *when*. Noah's mother had known it, had seen it coming. Why else would she have bartered with that devil Clyde Dekker?

Noah peeked around the couch. His father was slowly regaining consciousness, though not yet enough to move under his own power.

Don't you let him hurt you, baby boy, he heard the voice of his mother in his mind. *Don't you let him do that no more. You do what you have to do to make sure of that.*

Noah glanced over at his mother's body and Clay's pistol on the floor beside her. A dark thought formed in his mind.

After all, minutes ago, the man had tried to kill Noah's mother with that very weapon. Tried and failed, yes, but that didn't change anything. Not really.

Nodding to himself at his decision, he stepped around her body, knelt and carefully picked up the gun.

Noah stared down at the groaning heap of his father, slowly drifting back to consciousness. Noah's hands quaked. His palms were sweating. The wind rattled the house and something thudded on the porch, but he paid it no mind.

Noah wanted to pull that trigger as badly as he had ever wanted to do anything in his entire life—to right all the wrongs. If any asshole father deserved his comeuppance, surely it was this one.

But there was another voice that called his name, beckoning him away from the edge of a dark decision.

His father's only useful eye cracked open and regarded him sleepily.

Could he do it? Could he put that bullet in his father's skull?

In truth, his father deserved worse. Much worse. He deserved the torment and fear with which he had filled the lives of his family. That's what he really deserved.

"Noah?" the voice called again.

He turned this time and had to blink at what he saw. Tommy was standing in the open doorway, the night at his back. His friend's shoulders were covered with a layer of snow and his skin was red with cold. His arms were stretched out, a black pistol in his grasp.

"Tommy?"

The boy breathed hard into the air as he beheld the gruesome scene inside the house. "Wh—what happened?"

Tommy lowered the gun, stuffed it into his coat pocket as his eyes fell on the pistol in Noah's hand.

"What are you doing, Noah?"

Before Noah could answer him, his legs were swept from beneath him and he heard his father groan. He landed on his back, the wind knocked from him. His grip went limp and the pistol fell away.

Next to him, his father was getting up and, in a flash, his big hands were wrapped around his son's neck.

"You shitsucking snipe," Hugh spat at him. "You fucking little Judas."

The rage in Hugh's eyes was far beyond any that Noah had ever seen in the man, and stars filled the edge of Noah's vision as he struggled for breaths that would not come.

When the Slugger connected with his father's jaw, there was a crack and a spray of spit and teeth as the man went sideways off of him. Tommy, standing there with the bat choked low in his hands, didn't wait for Hugh Belton to right himself. He drew back and swung again, this time connecting squarely with the side of his head, and Noah's father crumpled on the floor in front of the couch.

Noah got to his feet and gawked at his friend, shocked and exasperated. Tommy's eyes were locked on Noah's father. The man wasn't moving but Tommy still gripped the bat in his shaking fists.

Tommy had gotten there just in time, he supposed. A few minutes later and either Hugh or Noah would have been lying dead on the floor. Maybe both of them.

Noah wouldn't have shed a tear, but looking now at his friend and thinking of the simplicity of his life before Cedar Banks, he realized putting that bullet in his father wouldn't solve a thing. It would only leave Noah broken and haunted.

"Noah, if he gets up again—" Tommy began.

"I know."

He searched about, his mind racing and desperate,

until his glance settled on the dark chasm of the hallway and the looming darkness of the worship room.

"Will you help me?"

Tommy lowered the bat. "Help you what?"

Noah stared down at his father, so weakened and beaten. Hugh Belton deserved torment, and Noah knew just where he might find some.

"Help me get his legs," Noah said.

A heavy fog lifted from Hugh's mind, and as it withdrew, sensation returned. Along with it came the many aches and pains that throbbed all over his body. He was sliding, it seemed. Sliding on ice.

Was he on the lake? Had it frozen over?

He opened and shut his eye a time or two, trying to clear his vision and gain some focus. Wooden walls, the smell of gunpowder, the faint glow behind him of those goddamned Christmas lights that his wife had hung in defiance of him. Straining, he saw his son and the Wren boy, each with one of Hugh's legs, dragging him along the cold floor. He wanted to reach out, to throttle the little pricks, but his hands were beneath him under the small of his back and bound together with rope.

With his lazy return to consciousness, he tried to remember what had happened. He had killed Ada, hadn't he? God help him but the horrible shrew had left him no choice.

He mumbled something about defending himself, and called to his son, demanding his release, but the fiery pain in his head returned and the world tilted, then disappeared into a hungry fog.

When he awoke again, he was struck immediately by the

chilling cold. In what meager light there was from an opening in the chamber, he could see his breath, like smoke in the darkness. He turned his head. Noah was there, down on one knee and leaning over him, his head cocked as he glared at him, stone-faced.

"Son?"

Noah did not reply, but reached a hand toward him, laid something heavy on his chest and then scooted away from the opening. When Hugh saw the boy swing the small door closed and heard the click of a padlock on the outside, he understood.

The little monster had locked him in that crawlspace.

He fumbled with the object Noah had placed in there with him. It was the pistol. The same one he had used to shoot Ada. Except now, the cylinder hung open and empty. Hugh hollered at his son to open the door or all Hell would break loose when—sooner or later—he busted out of the dark hole. As if in answer, he then heard pounding from the other side of the door, repetitious and rhythmic, the clack of a hammer on the heads of sixteen-penny nails, and the groan of wood being pierced, bound into place.

That boy's gonna wall me up and let me die in here.

After another moment, the pounding stopped and Hugh heard the footfalls of Noah and Tommy Wren's boots on the floor of the worship room as they withdrew, abandoning him to the freezing darkness. The space was so tight and Hugh a man of such large stature that it felt like a metal tomb in which he could barely move.

"Noah, you let me out of here right now, you hear?" he shouted. "Right goddamn now, boy."

Silence.

"Noah!"

Then, as Hugh lay there inside the wall and tried to imagine a way out of his predicament, there was a presence with him in the tiny box—like the vague awareness of a predatory animal close to him. Perhaps many animals. There was a sound that he did not know, as if something enormous was wriggling inside the walls.

He scoffed. He was just getting spooked. Nothing more.

Slowing his breaths, he calmed. It would be fine. He just needed to talk his way through it.

Then something shifted in the black and sounds and sensations came to him that he could not explain. He was not alone in this place. There were things in the dark that moved and whispered. Things that clawed at him, reeking of death and old bones.

They pawed at him, whispering their pains, and Hugh Belton cried out with a terror he'd never known in his life.

In that hole, that chamber of darkness, he screamed and screamed.

Tommy went around back of the house to see to his father and Noah stepped out onto the front porch. He couldn't be in that house anymore. It was a place of death now, just as it always had been. The panicked cries of his father rang out from inside. They went on and on, shattering the lonely quiet of the winter's night, and Noah could not help but smile.

He sat on the porch and watched the snow fall. Just as the police trucks with the big tires and the Rockbridge lake patrol came rushing into Cedar Banks, Tommy came with his father around the side of the house. The deputy was freezing cold and wobbly, leaning on his son for support.

Noah could not have told how long he had been sitting there. In fact, he could say nothing at all. He only stared out into the night and shook his head in refusal when they wanted to take him inside to get warm and treat his wounded ear. Sometime later, Deputy Wren came to him and draped a thin, silvery blanket about his shoulders.

He looked long past Noah into the house where a half dozen Rockbridge County police milled about, taking photographs and scribbling notes. Deputy Wren kneeled before him, the look in his eyes one of tenderness and compassion. It was a look that Noah had never once seen from his own father.

The deputy did not bombard him with questions. In fact, he warned away anyone who looked like they might. He did not offer platitudes that would only dwarf the enormity of the loss that Noah was experiencing. He only sat with him and held him close.

The flashing lights of red and blue bounced and glittered off the snowy landscape and might have been a curiously beautiful sight to behold, but Noah's gaze was unwavering. His eyes searched the darkness beyond, hoping for a glimpse of something familiar that was no longer of this world.

He was looking for his mother's ghost, and knew he always would.

EPILOGUE

"I am dying. But within me is a pledge of that affection which thou didst feel for me, Morella. And when my spirit departs shall the child live."

—Edgar Allan Poe, *Morella*

March

NOAH STANDS AT a gravestone—one of many in the cemetery outside of the small church with walls of grey limestone hand-hewn almost a century before. It is Sunday and today is his fifteenth birthday. There will be a party for him later, with pizza and ice cream and all the fixings. He has even invited a few girls to attend. He's not sure if they will, but he is hopeful.

The grave still looks fresh compared to the others, though with the change of season, sprouts of grass and clover have begun to emerge in the oblong area of dirt. It is the final resting place of his mother, though he knows that only her body lies here. The woman herself is elsewhere. Noah Belton understands this better than most. He has come here before church on his birthday not to mourn her, but for another burial—his own.

He has come to tell his mother that he has cast aside his family name, relegating it to the past and the part of him that lies there in the ground with her. Today is a new day, and henceforth his life will be a new one. He has come to tell her that he will now be known as Noah Donavan Wren. He has taken her maiden name for his middle and his new last name comes from the man who—officially, as of last week—has adopted him as his own. In the few months that Noah has lived under Deputy Nicholas Wren's roof, he has found the man to be more a father to him than his own ever was. He knows that his mother would be happy at this news and that she would not begrudge him the willful act of shedding the name of his birth father.

Much has changed since the events of the past winter, though those memories are not as deeply buried as he would prefer them to be. On the rare occasion when he is asked by someone to offer some insight into what it was like to have Hugh Belton for a father, the only thing he can say is that the man was far better suited to raising pit vipers than children.

After he imparts the news, he lays a bunch of spring flowers at the base of the headstone—bluebells and crocuses, daffodils and iris, their many tones of ivory and violet, blue and yellow and peach lending a cheerful note to the drab stone. Noah visits here often, and there is much about his new life he has already told his mother. He's told her about moving with the Wrens out of the trailer at Cady's Run into a house here in Mountvale, a small town in the hills of the Shenandoah Valley. He wears his wild, red hair longer now, so different from the tight crew cut mandated by his father for many years.

Standing there, his mind wanders to the dark events of that winter night when his world was torn asunder—to things he has never spoken of to her, though he feels certain she knows.

Such as how the police found his father's fingerprints on the gun that killed her and how a jury found him guilty of the crime. For Noah, it matters none that Hugh did not fire that fatal shot.

In a way, his father had most certainly murdered her. He had done it first by wedding her and then by taking them to that place.

Crow Neck.

By whatever name, it is a place that sits in the shadow of a haunted mountain. A place unfit for any but the dead to inhabit. Still, every few weeks since Hugh was sentenced to life in prison, Noah has received a letter from him. He does not open or read them. He is content to be shut of the man forever.

Regarding the night of his mother's death, the police quickly came to their own conclusions about the details of what had occurred, and—at Nick Wren's urging—Noah had done a lot of nodding and keeping his mouth shut. There was so much he wanted to tell about what really happened that night, but Nick explained the truth to him time and again.

No one would believe such a story.

As for his friend, Clay, after a great deal of explanation and bending of truth, Noah was able to convince the Sheriff's Department to clear Clay Winston's name, telling the officers that the bones of his missing children they found in his house had been recovered by the old man only days before. It was just plain luck that he came upon their remains somewhere on Cross Mountain, though the old man never had the chance to say where. Noah explained how even through all the years gone by, Clay had never stopped looking for his boys. That he had walked the mountain always, searching. In the end, they were all buried together in Clay's family plot in Whitetail.

He never mentioned the mountain's secret cave of bones in his account, nor did he ever mention the name of Clyde Dekker.

The church bells ring out now, and Noah tells his mother he must go. His new family waits inside for him. As he walks from the grave, a stiff mountain wind rises up and blows through the valley, tossing Noah's mop of curls, and in morning sunlight it is as if he wears a crown of red flame. The breeze exposes his ear with the missing bit of flesh at the top of it, and he brushes his hair back down as the wind calms. It is another reason that he wears his hair longer now—so that he doesn't always have to look upon the injury in the mirror, or lie to others to explain it.

Noah bears many scars from that night, but the missing piece of his ear is the only one he wears on the outside.

As he walks toward the church, the bells still singing out, he considers that inside is a place where people of faith go to be forgiven and to find it within themselves to forgive others. The Gospel tells him that God is patient and loving and forgives all things of those who ask it.

Occasionally, though, in the lonely stillness of the day

or night, Noah can sense his mother nearby. In those moments of forlorn longing, he is reminded how he will never again feel her touch or embrace, and will never again look upon her radiant smile. It is then that the long shadows of the huntsman and of Hugh Belton fall upon him once again, and a bitter anger stirs a wintry coldness in his heart.

Noah reckons that—for him—there are some things beyond forgiveness. No matter how hallowed their burial or how much soil of a life comes to cover them, there are some losses too great and some wounds too deep. There are pangs that never lose their sting. These things lie beneath the surface, unseen but not forgotten, always threatening to rise.

"One need not be a chamber—to be haunted
One need not be a house—
The Brain has Corridors—surpassing
Material Place"

—Emily Dickenson

THE END?

Not if you want to dive into more of Crystal Lake Publishing's Tales from the Darkest Depths!

Check out our amazing website and online store
or download our latest catalog here.
https://geni.us/CLPCatalog

We always have great new projects and content on the website to dive into, as well as a newsletter, behind the scenes options, social media platforms, our own dark fiction shared-world series and our very own webstore. Our webstore even has categories specifically for KU books, non-fiction, anthologies, and of course more novels and novellas.

ACKNOWLEDGEMENTS

I have the greatest appreciation for the many who have helped me over the years, in some way or another, to finally drag this story out into the light of day: Leann Harris, Max Booth III, Brandon Harris, and Richard Thomas come chiefly to mind. I thank my wife and daughter, Sharon and Abigail, for their unyielding love, support, and indulgence. Excelsior!

ADDITIONAL INFORMATION

We all know someone who is now or has been the victim of abuse. Sometimes that someone is us and we've not been able to face it.

For that reason, I would like to offer some U.S.-based resources for those dealing with abuse, whether right now or in its various forms and stages of past psychological trauma. Reaching out can be the hardest step to take, but I implore you to take it. There are so many people willing and ready to help.

National Center on Domestic and Sexual Violence
Domestic Abuse Hotline: 1-800-799-SAFE

Sexual Abuse Hotline: 1-800-656-HOPE

National Child Abuse Hotline/Childhelp:
1-800-4-A-CHILD

National Suicide Prevention Hotline:
1-800-273-TALK

National Center on Domestic Violence, Trauma &
Mental Health: 312-726-7020 x2011

ABOUT THE AUTHOR

D. Alexander Ward is an author and anthologist of horror and dark fiction. In addition to *POUND OF FLESH*, he is the author of numerous short stories and the novels *BLOOD SAVAGES* and *BENEATH ASH & BONE*.

As an anthologist, he has edited and co-edited the Bram Stoker Award-nominated anthologies *LOST HIGHWAYS: Dark Fictions From the Road* and *GUTTED: Beautiful Horror Stories* as well as *THE SEVEN DEADLIEST*, *SHADOWS OVER MAIN STREET* Volumes 1-3, and *STRANGE ECHOES*.

He is an Active Member of the Horror Writers Association and very involved in the small press publishing world of horror and dark fiction, where he is Editor-in-Chief of his own press, Bleeding Edge Books.

Along with his beloved wife and daughter and the haints in the woods, he lives near the farm where he grew up in what used to be rural Virginia, where his love for the people, passions, and folklore of the South was nurtured. There, he spends his nights penning, collecting, and publishing tales of the dark, strange, and fantastic.

Twitter: @DAlexWard
Instagram: @DAlexWardVA
Facebook: facebook.com/dalexward
www.dalexanderward.com
www.bleedingedgepub.com

Readers . . .

Thank you for reading *Pound of Flesh*. We hope you enjoyed this novel.

If you have a moment, please review *Pound of Flesh* at the store where you bought it.

Help other readers by telling them why you enjoyed this book. No need to write an in-depth discussion. Even a single sentence will be greatly appreciated. Reviews go a long way to helping a book sell, and is great for an author's career. It'll also help us to continue publishing quality books. You can also share a photo of yourself holding this book with the hashtag #IGotMyCLPBook!

Thank you again for taking the time to journey with Crystal Lake Publishing.

Visit our Linktree page for a list of our social media platforms. https://linktr.ee/CrystalLakePublishing

Our Mission Statement:

Since its founding in August 2012, Crystal Lake Publishing has quickly become one of the world's leading publishers of Dark Fiction and Horror books in print, eBook, and audio formats.

While we strive to present only the highest quality fiction and entertainment, we also endeavour to support authors along their writing journey. We offer our time and experience in non-fiction projects, as well as author mentoring and services, at competitive prices.

With several Bram Stoker Award wins and many other wins and nominations (including the HWA's Specialty Press Award), Crystal Lake Publishing puts integrity, honor, and respect at the forefront of our publishing operations.

We strive for each book and outreach program we spearhead to not only entertain and touch or comment on issues that affect our readers, but also to strengthen and support the Dark Fiction field and its authors.

Not only do we find and publish authors we believe are destined for greatness, but we strive to work with men and woman who endeavour to be decent human beings who care more for others than themselves, while still being hard working, driven, and passionate artists and storytellers.

Crystal Lake Publishing is and will always be a beacon of what passion and dedication, combined with overwhelming teamwork and respect, can accomplish. We endeavour to know each and every one of our readers, while building personal relationships with our authors, reviewers, bloggers, podcasters, bookstores, and libraries.

We will be as trustworthy, forthright, and transparent as any business can be, while also keeping most of the headaches away from our authors, since it's our job to solve the problems so they can stay in a creative mind. Which of course also means paying our authors.

We do not just publish books, we present to you worlds within your world, doors within your mind, from talented authors who sacrifice so much for a moment of your time.

There are some amazing small presses out there, and through collaboration and open forums we will continue to support other presses in the goal of helping authors and showing the world what quality small presses are capable of accomplishing. No one wins when a small press goes down, so we will always be there to support hardworking, legitimate presses and their authors. We don't see Crystal Lake as the best press out there, but we will always strive to be the best, strive to be the most interactive and grateful, and even blessed press around. No matter what happens over time, we will also take our mission very seriously while appreciating where we are and enjoying the journey.

What do we offer our authors that they can't do for themselves through self-publishing?

We are big supporters of self-publishing (especially hybrid publishing), if done with care, patience, and planning. However, not every author has the time or inclination to do market research, advertise, and set up book launch strategies. Although a lot of authors are successful in doing it all, strong small presses will always be there for the authors who just want to do what they do best: write.

What we offer is experience, industry knowledge, contacts and trust built up over years. And due to our strong brand and trusting fanbase, every Crystal Lake Publishing book comes with weight of respect. In time our fans begin to trust our judgment and will try a new author purely based on our support of said author.

With each launch we strive to fine-tune our approach, learn from our mistakes, and increase our reach. We continue to assure our authors that we're here for them and that we'll carry the weight of the launch and dealing with third parties while they focus on their strengths—be it writing, interviews, blogs, signings, etc.

We also offer several mentoring packages to authors that include knowledge and skills they can use in both traditional and self-publishing endeavours.

We look forward to launching many new careers.

This is what we believe in. What we stand for. This will be our legacy.

Welcome to Crystal Lake Publishing— Tales from the Darkest Depths.